Steven W. English was born and raised in New Jersey. He currently resides in Portland, Maine where he is doing what he truly loves, writing and listening to 80's music.

CLASS OF 85 is his first book.

CLASS OF '85

STEVEN W. ENGLISH

For my friends and family

Because they have been patiently waiting for this

All these thoughts have been circling my brain lately. Everything doesn't seem real. It doesn't seem unreal either. It feels kind of surreal. Any minute now I'm expecting the clocks to start melting or a burning giraffe to go running by.

At least we're back in Jersey. Although not back in Barronsville, even though I begged mom to live back there. No, we are in Whitfield, N.J., 60 miles north. So that means that I yet again have to start my life over. This will be my third high school. All these thoughts about my life and my future. I'm going to be starting my senior year lost.

There was an article in yesterday's newspaper talking about the best ways to relax your mind. The one that I liked the most was the one that said to get them out, you should write them down. I figured, "What the hell. It's worth a shot". So I'm going to start a diary. I don't know how well it's going to help, but if it even helps a little, it will be worth it.

Ok Parker...Let's do this

THIS IS NOT GOING TO BE EASY

Saturday September 1, 1984

We've just moved into our house this morning. It's me, my mom, my younger brother Taylor and my little sister Alexa. It's not much, just a small 2 bedroom. My mother, brother and sister share one bedroom and I get the other. Mom says "A 16 year old needs his own space." I don't mind at all. After spending the summer crammed into a small hotel room, anything resembling privacy is welcomed. It's also better than Florida.

Don't get me wrong. I love my grandparents, but the place was so boring. The school sucked. The other students sucked. All I wanted was to get the hell out of there. I didn't even want to be there in the first place, but Mom had no choice. After Dad left, just before Christmas last year, to go find himself, Mom took us and we moved from our house in Barronsville, where we'd been for 10 years to Florida to stay with my grandparents until Mom got back on her feet. I hated saying goodbye to all my friends.

We stayed in Florida until the school year ended and have been in a hotel until today, while mom found us a place to live. She was lucky enough to get a job quickly. She works in the warehouse of one of those express mail companies.

Even though there was no privacy in that tiny hotel room, the four of us still had a great time. Mom took us to the drive-in to see "Ghostbusters", "Gremlins" and "Indiana Jones". There was also this big bowling alley across the street from the hotel that mom would take us to at least once a week.

She has been doing all she can to cheer us up. My father hasn't called, sent letters, sent any child support, nothing. He's completely forgotten about us. So mom has had to be both mother and father and she's doing a great job.

OK, back to my room. I've decorated it the best I can. Music posters all around. Cyndi, Stevie, Tina, Madonna, Benatar. I love female singers, can't you tell? Music is one of my other ways of coping with all this. I just pop in a cassette and I'm feeling a little better.

School starts in a few days. I have no friends, no life, no car. I so hate taking the school bus. This is going to be so rough.

SUNDAY SEPTEMBER 2, 1984

"I have a car!!!!!!"

I was playing video games with Taylor when mom came home from work. She called me outside to help her with something. I was in no mood, but I got up anyway. When I stepped outside I saw it, the "67" Mustang. I loved that car. It was my dad's.

I remember the day he brought it home. I was only 5, but I remember it so clearly. It was a very sunny and warm April day when dad came home from work and honked the horn. Mom and I ran out to see what was going on. Mom was carrying my baby brother, who was only a couple of months old at the time. I ran out first. My dad was standing on the side of this beautiful light blue car. I ran right up to my dad.

"What do you think?" he said to my mom. She had this perplexed look on her face.

"It's nice," she said quietly.

Even at that age, I knew that she didn't approve, but I didn't care and neither did my dad. He'd wanted a Mustang for years. He just ignored her and asked me if I wanted to go for a ride. I was so excited. I ran over to the passenger side and got in. My tiny self sliding onto that white leather seat. The seat was hot and I jumped a little, but I quickly got used to it. The whole car smelled of hot leather. I love that smell.

Dad got in and started the car. As we backed out, he turned on the radio. He was flipping thru the stations, searching for WHN. He would always forget what the exact station number was, so he just flipped until he heard country music. The only type of music he liked. When he found it, some song by Loretta Lynn was playing.

With the music all set, we headed out and drove around town. It felt so good being there with my dad, even when "Take me home, country roads" came on. Don't get me wrong, I love the song. The thing is, so does my dad. Whenever it came on, he would sing along...loudly, way off key, making up his own lyrics when he didn't know the words. Let's just say he wouldn't make it as a contestant on Star Search.

He's singing along, but all I'm thinking about is the car, taking in all the details and watching all the people look as we passed by. The looks could have been for my dad's "singing", but I was just thinking that they were for the car.

Over the years, my dad and I would take many trips in that car. Whenever he was going somewhere, I would always want to tag along. He knew I loved that car.

Just after my 13th birthday, he asked me to go for a ride with him. We headed out on one of our drives. Along the way, he asked me about the car. He hadn't asked me about the car since our first drive 8 years earlier.

Just like that first day, I told him that I thought it was the best car I had ever seen. That's when he told me that when I started my senior year of high school the car would be mine. I was so excited. Every day I would think about that car. I would sometimes go and sit in the driver's seat, pretending to be driving, dreaming of the day that the car would be mine. Then in December of last year, those dreams came crashing down.

I had heard my parents fighting over the years, but as 1983 wore on, their fights got louder and more frequent. By December it was becoming unbearable. I was getting so good at sensing it coming that I would take Taylor and Alexa outside so that they didn't have to hear it.

About a week before Christmas I came home and they were fighting. They didn't hear me come in. I was just going to sneak by them and head to my room, but then I heard my mom say "What about Josh?"

When they've fought, they've never mentioned us kids. They were yelling about me. I didn't know what about, so I stayed on the side and listened in. They were breaking up, I knew it.

"You can't take it! You promised it to Josh," Mom said.

"It's mine! I'll do with it what I want!" Dad snapped back.

"You fucking piece of shit! Don't do that to him."

"Leave me alone! It's my car!"

"What, you going to give it to your skanky little whore?"

Over the summer of '83 my family started hanging out with a new family that had just moved in down the block. Jerry and Joan Embree and their 3 children. Candace (21), Charlene (20) and Charles (10). My mom had gone to school with Joan. At first it seemed nice, but then after a while I started finding the family to be kind of obnoxious, so I stopped going over there. So did my mom and siblings. Not my dad though. He would go over there all the time, eventually spending more time with them than with us. He also seemed to be getting very friendly with Charlene.

"If you want me to stay here for Christmas, you will shut your mouth! If not, I'll leave right now!" dad screamed.

That's when I knew their marriage was officially over. Dad was leaving, but didn't want to ruin Christmas. For the sake of us kids, mom didn't want him to leave until after Christmas, so she stopped yelling. All she could say was...

"Think of Josh."

"I'm taking the car," he said.

That's when I came out of the shadows. They were both looking at me. I just stared at both of them, tears running down my face. I turned and ran up to my room, lying down on my bed. Mom came up a few minutes later, knocking on my door. I didn't answer. She came in, sat down on my bed, running her hand thru my hair, telling me everything would be alright. I didn't turn around. I just laid there softly crying.

Dad didn't make it to Christmas. They fought a few days later. I had been in my room all day listening to music. Dad came home from work. I heard his pick-up truck coming down the street. He uses it for work. I heard him come in the door.

SLAM!!!!!

"Where the fuck is my car?!!?" he yelled at my mother.

I ran to the window and noticed it wasn't in the driveway. He always keeps it in the driveway, to show it off. Thank God Taylor and Alexa were sleeping over their friend's houses.

"I sold it!" mom answered.

"You what?! You Bitch! That was my car!"

"It was OUR car. The car was in both our names."

"Who did you sell it to?"

"None of your business."

I crept down the stairs and watched as they fought.

"You had no right..."

"If Josh can't have it, neither can you," Mom said, cutting him off.

Their fighting got louder. Mom went and grabbed an envelope. It was dad's half of the money for the car. I just sat on the stairs crying.

Dad took the envelope and said that he couldn't stay in the house any longer. I heard this and sprinted up to my bedroom. I didn't want them to know that I heard them. Dad came up the stairs and went into his room. He was packing a suitcase. Then he went back downstairs and into the garage.

I heard the garage door open and then I saw him throwing things into the back of the pick-up truck. He already had most of his things packed up and in the garage, ready for his post-Christmas departure. Just as he finished, mom came out of the house and asked him if he was at least going to say goodbye to me. He looked up at my window, saw me looking back at him and did nothing but get into his truck and drive off.

Mom came inside and cleaned things up. Dad had thrown and broken a few things in his anger. She then came to my room, knocking on the door and coming in. Even though I had my headphones on, pretending I didn't hear anything, she knew better. There was no fooling "psychic mom". She hugged me and apologized for selling the car. I was so upset, knowing the car was gone...But now here I was staring at it. "So I have this little dilemma. I have this car here, but I have nobody to drive it. Have any ideas?" mom said.

I just ran up, moving my hand down the side.

"Where did you find it?" I asked.

"Wanna know a secret? I never sold it. I just tricked your father into thinking I did... she said whispering.

...I borrowed the money from your grandparents and put it into storage. Eileen helped drive it over for me today," she continued.

Mom went and said goodbye to Eileen, who lives a few houses away, while I went and sat in the driver's seat. It felt so good. Mom came up to the window.

"He promised you that car when you started your senior year. There was no way I was going to let him take it...So you still want it?" she asked.

I was smiling so wide. All I could do was nod my head. Mom got in and we went for a drive.

MONDAY SEPTEMBER 3, 1984

This morning mom took me out to the store to buy stuff for the car. Because it's Labor Day, the motor vehicle place is closed, so we are going to do all of that stuff tomorrow. I so wanted to just drive around in the car, but it has to wait. I spent part of the day just sitting in the driver's seat. It felt so good having the car back. It feels like a dream. I can't believe that it's back and it's mine.

TUESDAY SEPTEMBER 4, 1984

Busy day. Running around everywhere. The first stop was Madison Elementary school to get Taylor and Alexa registered for classes. Taylor for 6th grade and Alexa for 1st grade. I just waited in the car.

When they were done, it was over to Whitfield High to get me registered. It took a while to get a class schedule in place. This was because I have a love of foreign languages. I was able to get the Spanish IV class, but unfortunately the French IV and German IV classes were both the same period, so I had to choose. I hated having to choose, but I went with French IV. I did ask about getting a German IV book and workbook, just so that I can sort of keep up. They had ones to give me.

After school it was time to get the Mustang all registered in my name, new license plates and converting my Florida license to a Jersey one. The young'uns were hungry, so we had to stop at the diner for food right after. Jersey diner food is so great. Pork roll, egg and cheese on a hard roll for me please.

It felt so good having everything set and ready. I spent the whole rest of the day working on the car, getting it ready for tomorrow.

WEDNESDAY SEPTEMBER 5, 1984

Whitfield High School. Home of the Whitfield High Woodpeckers. Yes woodpeckers. Their school mascot is a woodpecker. This is my prison for the next year.

Heads turned when I pulled into the senior parking lot. I washed, waxed and polished the car yesterday. I found an empty spot, got out and stood there looking at the school, which is directly across the street. As I stood there, I didn't notice this girl standing next to me. She was also looking at the school. We both breathed a negative sigh at the same time, causing us both to turn and laugh. She complimented me on my car and then introduced herself.

"Stephanie Perrino," she said, extending her hand.

"Joshua Parker," I said, shaking her hand.

"Nice to meet you Joshua."

We started walking together towards the school, making small talk. As we were walking, I would look over at this girl who was actually talking to me. Light brown hair, feathered back slightly, brown eyes, cute smile.

I was so excited that I had made a friend so fast, that I wasn't paying attention to where I was going. As we were almost at the entrance, I accidentally bumped into this cheerleader. She had been practicing some cheer and had backed up into my path. She was with a bunch of other girls. I'm guessing that they're cheerleaders too. None of them were in uniform.

Well, the cheerleader who entered my path was holding a bottle of diet coke, so when I bumped into her some of it spilled out almost hitting her. I quickly apologized, but to no avail.

"Unh, watch it geek!! This sweater costs more than everything you have on," she snapped.

"I said I was sorry," I said, answering her back.

She just turned to her friends. "Is he like still there?"

Stephanie grabbed my hand.

"C'mon. It's no use. Wearing an ugly expensive sweater turns you into an uncaring bitch."

We ran inside laughing, before the cheerleader could respond. Stephanie and I were still laughing about it when we got to my homeroom. She walked me there because I was new and she felt that I could easily get lost using the school map the office gave me. We stood there outside my homeroom talking and comparing schedules. We have Gym and French together. I'm so glad that she's going to be in two of my classes. As we were talking, she glanced up at the clock in the hallway, telling me she had to head out. Her homeroom is all the way on the other side of the school.

"I'll see you in Gym," she said.

"Thank you for your help," I said smiling.

"No problem. I'm out," she said, waving goodbye.

I walked into homeroom and took a seat all the way over by the windows. I was one of the first ones there, so I just sat and watched everybody coming in. Nothing too exciting, just the usual assortment of Jersey teens. Girls with big hair, some with colorful clothes. Boys with wavy hair or the spiky hair look, like Corey Hart. Some even with their sunglasses on. It was just the usual sea of Levi's, denim jackets, sweats and assorted t-shirts with rock band logos or sports team jerseys.

Then in comes this girl, sort of like everybody else, but you can tell she's not like the others. Her black hair is slightly done up and her clothes are more fashionable. You can tell that she takes a little more time to get ready and thinks about what she wears very carefully.

She takes the seat right across from mine and introduces herself. I never thought in a million years that a girl like this would say hello to me.

"Evelyn Ramirez," she says with a wide friendly smile.

She instantly knew that I was new to the school. She makes sure to get to know everybody. I came to find out that she is very popular, but not in the traditional sense. She has many friends and is liked by many in the school, but she is not stuck up and doesn't travel with the popular cliques. Many of the cheerleaders hate her.

Another thing I found out is that she is the school gossip, well, more like the school info booth. She can tell you about many students in the school, stuff like what clubs they belong to, who they are dating or dated, random stuff like that. She's the one people go to to find out about things happening in the school. She has many friends, knows what's going on and pieces all the info together.

I told her that, yes, in fact, I was new to the school and then I introduced myself. She welcomed me to Whitfield High and started telling me things about the school. I was listening to everything she was saying, taken in by her friendliness.

As she was speaking, I glanced slightly at the door. Standing just outside the door was that big haired, blond bitch cheerleader. She was talking to someone, but I couldn't see who. Evelyn noticed me looking towards the door and turned to look.

"Michelle Danielson. Head cheerleader. Mother and father have bucks and she's not afraid to let everybody know it. For your own good, just stay away from that," she said

"Too late," I said, telling her what happened earlier.

"Don't let it bother you. She's just a bitch," Evelyn said.

"So I've been told," I said, laughing.

Michelle left and I saw who she was talking to. He entered the room and I couldn't take my eyes off of him. About 5' 10" tall, brown hair, brown eyes, athletic build, beautiful smile. He was wearing a Van Halen t-shirt, leather jacket and tight jeans. I can't believe how I stare at him. I know he's a guy and so am I, but I can't help it. I've been thinking about guys since I was 13. My dad used to say all fags (that's what he called them, among other things) are mental retards and are going to burn in Hell. He always told gay jokes and talked about how glad he was that his sons weren't gay. Great to hear when you are 15 and confused. I've tried to think about girls. I really have. I mean, I like hanging out with girls, but I can't think of them romantically or sexually. But sexual thoughts of guys are always there and I get turned on by these thoughts. It's just the way it is. I keep these thoughts to myself. I don't want anybody to know, not my family and especially none of the guys here at school. They'd probably beat me up if they even think I'm gay, so this secret stays with me.

"Randy Sawyer. Star varsity Quarterback. He's been dating Michelle since June," Evelyn says, breaking me out of my trance.

Randy takes the seat right in front of me. He turns and says hello to Evelyn, who introduces him to me. We shake hands and then he turns forward as Evelyn and I talk about our schedules.

As she goes down my schedule, she tells me little things about each of my teachers. I'm laughing at some of the comments. Evelyn and I have Gym, History and French together. When she mentions this I do a slight laugh.

"What's so funny?" she asks.

"Well you're the second person I've met today and I have Gym and French with both of you," I answer.

Curious, she asks me who else I met. I tell her about meeting Stephanie.

"You met Stephanie P?" she says, getting all excited.

She goes on to inform me that Stephanie is her best friend. I told her how Stephanie helped me with the "incident" this morning. Evelyn laughed.

"When do you have Gym and French?" Randy asks, turning around.

"Gym period 3 and French period 7," I answer.

"Well now you know 3 people."

"Creepy," Evelyn says, grabbing Randy's schedule.

After homeroom, Evelyn walks me to my first period class, English with Mrs. Bartone. Along the way, many students come up to Evelyn either saying hello or giving her gossip. I thank Evelyn and leave her to her gossip.

I walk into English class and grab a seat by the windows. My favorite place to sit. Mrs. Bartone stands at the door, greeting students as they enter. I'm feeling so good, just sitting there looking out the window, knowing that I've already made some new friends. I turned back towards the door and saw that cheerleader Michelle enter with 2 other girls. She just gives me this look, then turns and whispers something to the other girls, causing them all to laugh. I turned my head away, pretending not to see them.

It seems that one of the girls saw me driving in this morning, so her and Michelle came up to my desk. I just looked at them. Michelle spoke up.

"Excuse me…so tell me something, like how did a geek like you get such a cool looking car? Is it your mommy's or your daddy's?"

I looked at her, rolled my eyes and turned away. Michelle and the other girl just started laughing and returned to their seats.

All through English class I had to make sure not to look anywhere near Michelle or her 2 bitch friends. If I did, they would just look back and laugh. I was glad for that bell ringing, signaling the end of class.

On to second period, Science with Mr. Jennings. I entered class. It was a typical science room. There were long rectangular tables for 2 in the front and matching lab stations in the back.

When I entered, Mr. Jennings asked me to stand on the side with the others. He likes to assign seats. So I stood and waited with the others. Just as the bell rang, he closed the door and took attendance, assigning seats as he went along. He got to my name and I took my seat. The person sitting next to me would be my lab partner for the rest of the school year. I hoped to get somebody good. Mr. Jennings went thru the class roster and nobody sat next to me. It suited me fine. I could handle doing things by myself.

A few minutes later though, in comes this jock in his Varsity Football jacket. Mr. Jennings is not happy with the tardiness. He obviously knows this guy.

"Ah, Mr. Olsen. Nice of you to join us. I see we're going to be coming to class late again, just like last year. (Mr. Jennings teaches 11th and 12th grade science) Let's not make this a habit. Take a seat over there next to Mr. Parker," He says, pointing to me.

I see him approach. The name on his jacket says "Derek". I extend my hand to say hello. He reaches the desk, takes one look at me and then turns to Mr. Jennings and asks to have his seat changed. So much for being friends with this one.

"Take your seat Mr. Olsen," Mr. Jennings says, not even turning back from the blackboard.

Derek takes his seat. He doesn't say a word to me the whole class.

I could not wait to get out of Science and head to Gym. Two terrible classes in a row. I knew with period 3, I would be seeing some friendly faces. As I entered the gym, there they were. Stephanie and Evelyn wave as they see me and I head right over. Evelyn is the first to ask me how everything is going.

"Ok I guess," I answer, and then I turn and see Derek enter. "Ick" is all I can think of to say.

"Derek or Garrett?" Evelyn asks.

Derek entered the gym with this other jock. A chunky, obnoxious looking slob. I saw him pushing some freshmen around this morning.

"Derek," I answer, telling them what happened in science class.

"Oh and Michelle is in my English class... (just as I say this, Michelle enters the gym arm and arm with Randy)...and my gym class...Great."

I just shook my head and watched as Michelle and Randy went and joined Garrett and Derek.

"Of course they're all friends," I continued, still shaking my head.

"Yup. Derek and Randy have been best friends since elementary school," Evelyn says.

"And you've managed to get two of them to hate you already," Stephanie says laughing.

"Hey, the day's not over yet," I laughed back.

"Oh my god. I can't believe we're all together in the same class. It's the first time since 6th grade" came this voice from behind me.

I turn around and see this girl approach. She has long straight brown hair, big glasses, she's rail thin and wearing plain looking clothes. She has her arm around a boy who looks like the male equivalent of her, except with shorter hair.

They both came up, hugging Evelyn and Stephanie. They were then introduced to me. The girl is Megan Lewis. Her boyfriend is Stuart Nelson. They are both part of the brainiac group here at school. Both are very book smart, but a little ditzy on the life smarts. They have been dating for 2 years now, have almost all the same classes and belong to the same clubs.

"Practically joined at the hip," Evelyn whispers to me.

Evelyn introduces them to me and 2 more friends are added. Half a year in Florida - nobody. Half a day here - 4 friends.

Because it was the first day, we didn't have to get dressed. We were all just standing around, waiting for Ms. Annasandy to come and assign seats. The gym is divided into 3 sections, but our class is the only one using the gym this period, so the sliding doors are open.

Ms. Annasandy comes out of the locker room. She blows her whistle to get everybody's attention and assigns seats in alphabetical order. By some stroke of luck, all of my new friends are around me. Stuart is to my right. Megan is sitting in front of him. Stephanie is behind me and Evelyn is behind her. As an added bonus, Randy is seated to my left. I think I'm really going to like this class.

Period 4 is my free period. Underclassmen must either take an extra class or have a study hall, but seniors are free to do what they want, sort of. Many seniors don't have a free period. Many leave school early to go to jobs. Only those with 8th period classes or after school clubs have free time.

The school is very liberal when it comes to seniors and their free period. We're not allowed to leave school or roam the halls, but we're not confined to a classroom either. Students can opt to spend the time in the library, the auditorium, the computer room, the weight room or out on the bleachers.

I decided to go out to the bleachers today. I took a seat all the way on the top and in the corner. There is nothing going on below and there is nobody on the bleachers. I am alone and for now it feels good. I just used the time to clear my head, look over my English Lit book and study the first science lab project.

The time on the bleachers felt so good. I left there and headed to my 5th period Spanish class. Due to a large school population this year, fifth period is split into 3 sections. Each section is 20 minutes long. Every student has class for two of these sections and lunch for the third. I have Spanish with Mrs. Tavares the first 2 parts and lunch the 3rd.

This stupid school map has me all confused and I got a little lost. I'm rushing around, panicking that I'll be late. The final bell rang just as I entered the classroom. No problem, right? Wrong.

In my Spanish class are Michelle, Garrett and Derek and the only seat left is behind Garrett and across from Derek. I don't want to sit there, but I have no choice. Walking to the desk, that bitch decided to make a snotty comment. So I turned my head back towards her as I'm walking. As I do, I don't notice that Garrett has stuck his foot out. I went falling to the floor.

"Have a nice trip?" Garrett says. He's not funny or original, but my trip to the floor got a laugh out of everybody. Forty tortuous minutes later, I'm finally out of there.

I'm so glad that lunch is next. After that mess, I needed to clear my head. I'm not a fan of school lunches. In elementary school it was fun, looking at the menu for the week. The Monday to Thursday sections always changed, but you could always count on Friday being pizza day. A rectangular piece of pizza that was supposed to be Sicilian style, but was nowhere near. Being from Jersey, you know good pizza and that wasn't it, but to a third grader it was amazing. Ever since middle school though, I prefer to bring my own lunch.

I turned the corner and headed to the cafeteria. I could hear the noise already, even with the doors closed. Opening the doors I was confronted with what could best be described as the loudness, chaos and cliques of hundreds of students. All it took was 2 steps inside for me to go "oh hell no".

I turned around and got out of there. Don't need any of that. Thank you very much. Back to the bleachers I went. They were a little more crowded than during my free period, but still better than cafeteria hell.

On to period 6, History class with Mr. Stanton. He's one of those ex-jocks turned history teacher/coach. He coaches Varsity football and Varsity wrestling. Garrett came in and they had a jock bonding moment. Barf-o-Rama. He then took a seat all the way on the other side of the room. Thank God I chose a seat by the door for this class. Evelyn came in and took the seat across from mine. I filled her in on all the drama of Spanish class.

Evelyn and I left History class and started walking towards our 7th period class, French IV with Mrs. Rosario. On the way we ran into Stephanie, who was coming from her English class. I'm so glad to have made friends with them today. It helps to have someone to talk to about all this drama.

We entered and took seats next to each other over by the windows. Evelyn is across from me on my left and Stephanie is seated in front of her. I looked towards the door and saw Michelle and Randy hugging. He came in and once again took the seat in front of me. This is going to be my favorite class of the day. I just know it.

At the end of French class, Stephanie and Evelyn asked me to join them at the mall. They both forgot that I have Math class 8th period. Another casualty of wanting to take 2 languages. Most seniors have this period off. This is usually when they head home or off to their jobs. If I wanted both languages I would have to take Math last period.

"Come after class. I'm sure we'll be there for a while," Evelyn says.

I told them I would and then I was off to Math class with Mr. Tovar. Math class was boring, boring, boring, just like Florida. Nobody said hello. Everybody seemed to ignore me. All I did was look at the clock, waiting for the bell to ring so I could join Stephanie and Evelyn. At 2:06 that bell rang and I was out of there. The senior parking lot was virtually empty, so it was very easy to pull out and leave. Out I went to the mall.

Ah, the main bastion of capitalism for the Jersey teen, the mall. Garden Creek Mall is about 5 miles or so from the school. It's your typical Jersey mall. Two floors of fun and excitement. Complete with the assorted anchor stores, (Macy's, Penney's, Sears, Bamberger's) plus many smaller shops, (Jeans Joint, Merry-Go-Round, Chess King, Benneton, O.P.)

I got to the mall and started searching for them. It was like trying to find a needle in a haystack. I passed the arcade. As much as I wanted to go in and see what games they had, I knew it would have to wait. I needed to find Stephanie and Evelyn.

My search continued and then I passed Total Eclipse Records, the largest record store in the mall. I had to go in. As I entered I saw a sign on the window that said they were looking for p.m. and weekend help. So I went and asked for an application. The manager, Mr. Totino handed me one and asked me to fill it out on the counter. As I was filling it out, this woman came in with a question about Cyndi Lauper. Mr. Totino couldn't answer it, so I stepped up and helped. They both thanked me. Two more times as I was filling out the application I stepped up to help. When I was finished, I handed him the application, but he didn't even look at it. He turned, looked at me and said "You're hired."

I couldn't believe it. It would only be for a few days a week, but I would be working in a record store. Oh and I also get a 20% discount on stuff in the store. That was such an awesome thing to hear. I start Friday night. I can't wait.

I thanked Mr. Totino and then headed out to continue searching for Evelyn and Stephanie. I found them a few minutes later heading into Jeans Joint. I ran over and told them the great news. The three of us spent a few hours at the mall just hanging out.

THURSDAY SEPTEMBER 6, 1984

Day 2

Another fun day with Steph, ("We're friends now. You can stop calling me by my full name") and Evelyn.

HOMEROOM - Even with his friends not liking me, Randy's still friendly with me. He said "Hi" to me as he sat down. Evelyn spent the whole period filling me in on some more gossip.

ENGLISH - Michelle is back in her stuck up world, so she's stopped bothering me. Thank God.

SCIENCE - Derek is still not saying anything to me. He's eventually going to have to say something, seeing as we have to work together on many of the science assignments.

GYM - Today was our first day of having to change for Gym. We aren't assigned lockers. We have to bring in a lock and take our stuff out when the period's over.

I chose one a little ways away, hoping it wouldn't be a crowded area. The locker room is large enough and there weren't really that many guys there, maybe only about 15 of us.

Nobody was choosing this area and then I watched as Derek and Randy turned the corner. They picked the same row, just a little ways down from me, followed by a few others. It took all my willpower to not turn and watch him change.

The willpower wasn't totally strong. I did turn a couple of times, catching quick glances of Randy in his underwear. One time he almost caught me. I have got to be more careful.

FRENCH - Definitely my favorite class of the day. It feels so peaceful and relaxing being around Steph, Evelyn and Randy.

FRIDAY SEPTEMBER 7, 1984

There was a big Randy and Michelle fight today, right before French class. They were arguing right in the hallway. Well she was doing most of the yelling. He just stood there taking it all. She was screaming about him not spending enough time with her or not paying enough attention to her. I have no idea what he sees in her. They seem to be total opposites.

Tonight was my first shift at Total Eclipse. I was so nervous, but as the shift went on, I calmed down. It was so much fun. Mr. Totino has a whole bunch of cassettes for us to play. He let me choose what to play. So it was Tina Turner, The Pointer Sisters, Cyndi Lauper and the Thompson Twins.

SATURDAY SEPTEMBER 8, 1984

10-5 at the record store today. We were a little busier than yesterday. Steph came in to say hello. She only stayed for a few minutes. She was at the mall to fill out some job applications. I asked Mr. Totino if he needed anybody. It would be so cool to work with Steph, but he was already filled up. I wished her luck and she was on her way.

SUNDAY SEPTEMBER 9, 1984

Megan stopped in today. She asked if I wanted to join her and Stuart tonight. On Sunday nights they invite a few friends over and play Trivial Pursuit.

"We need some new blood," she said laughing.

I left work and headed home to eat dinner, shower and change before heading over to Megan's apartment. She lives in a 2 bedroom apartment with her dad. Her mom passed away when Megan was 5. Mr. Lewis was on his way out as I arrived. Megan quickly introduced us.

I was then introduced to everybody there. They were all members of the brainiac groups at school. I was paired with Tommy Decatur. Tommy is this skinny blond haired guy. He's a junior at Whitfield High. He also works at Total Eclipse, although we haven't had any shifts together.

We didn't win, but I think we held our own, considering we were up against some of the smartest people in school. It was a fun night.

MONDAY SEPTEMBER 10, 1984

Derek was yet again complaining about sitting next to me. What he needs to do is concentrate on the paperwork for the lab project, which he didn't even look at. So I had to do most of the work. He spent most of the time talking with the girl at the next lab table over.

TUESDAY SEPTEMBER 11, 1984

Another Randy/Michelle fight today after Gym. This time he didn't even stay around to listen to her. He just walked away.

Our 1st French Quiz was today. Piece of cake. 25 questions. I had it finished in less than 15 minutes.

WEDNESDAY SEPTEMBER 12, 1984

Mrs. Rosario didn't have our quizzes graded yet. We were talking about it after class. Evelyn and Steph didn't feel that they did that great on the quiz. When I said that I thought it was real easy, they asked me to join them when they get together to study. So after school I joined them at Steph's house.

The three of us were all gathered on Steph's bed to study. As I looked around the room, I could see that Steph is still holding on to her childhood. Her room is full of stuffed animals and there are some dolls sitting on shelves.

Her walls, which are pink, all have pictures and posters of these hot male actors and singers. Many of them clipped out of magazines that I would love to buy, but wouldn't dare risk it. Seeing as we just had a quiz, there wasn't much French work to study, so we spent most of the time just talking.

I left there to go home and eat dinner. After I finished, I headed back to Steph's. The three of us were going to watch a movie. Tonight's video tape feature: "Risky Business" with Tom Cruise.

Tom Cruise dancing in his underwear. Forget Randy, I'll take Tom. Just kidding, Randy is hotter.

THURSDAY SEPTEMBER 13, 1984

Gym class might as well be called jogging class, because that seems to be what we'll be doing most of the year. I spend most of the time jogging with Steph and Evelyn.

Today, Steph brought in this mini cassette player. We jogged around listening to this new singer called "Madonna". One of the songs, "Burning up" seems to fit real well with all this running around. Four times around the track in this September heat is no fun, but the music makes it so much better.

FRIDAY SEPTEMBER 14, 1984

Steph and I have become friends outside of school too. I'm sitting here at McDonald's with her, killing time until the first school dance of the year begins. She's just gone up to get some more fries, seeing as she said she wasn't hungry, yet proceeded to eat all of mine.

"Did you see the scouts in the stands?" she says upon returning to the table.

She's referring to the football scouts in the stands at the Whitfield Varsity football game we just came from. I nod my head yes, trying carefully to open the ketchup packets. I do not want to get ketchup on the new jeans mom just bought me.

"Good thing they came at half time," I tell her.

Randy was playing horribly the first half. He was arguing with Michelle just before the game. I think that threw off his concentration. Someone must have told him about the scouts in the stands, because for the second half he threw 3 touchdowns to help Whitfield win the game.

Steph then changes the subject and brings up tonight's dance. I'm not a big school activities person, especially dances, but because Evelyn is the DJ, I said I would go. She's been the assistant DJ the past 3 years. This year she gets to be in charge. She's going to be the DJ for all the school dances this year. This is one of her passions. She loves doing it. She eventually wants to be a record producer and someday own her own recording studio and record label.

We left McDonald's and headed over. The dance is in the school gym. We get there and it's packed, wall to wall students. This is sort of a welcome back upper classmen, hello incoming freshmen dance.

Making our way through the crowd, we head to the DJ booth. The sounds of Patty Smyth and Scandal filling the gym. Many hands go up, forming guns as everyone goes "bang bang" just like Patty does in the video.

We got to Evelyn just as the song ended. We said our hellos to Evelyn and then headed back to dance.

Steph and I were dancing to a slow song when this guy comes up and asks to dance with her. She didn't seem to mind, so I left and headed to the bleachers. I sat there and watched everyone. Randy was dancing with Michelle. They seem happier now. I'm guessing because he won the game.

SATURDAY SEPTEMBER 15, 1984

Had to work the dinner shift today, so I spent part of the afternoon with Steph. She had a lot of errands to run, but we were able to meet up at Whitfield Subs for lunch. The place was packed. We had to park at the shopping plaza across the street and walk over. The line was out the door. We didn't mind. The place makes some of the best subs in the state and they're very fast, so the line moved quickly. There was obviously no place to sit, so we went and had lunch on the hood of the Mustang.

SUNDAY SEPTEMBER 16, 1984

More trivia tonight with Megan, Stuart, Tommy and the brains. The instant I walked in the door Tommy saw me and wanted to be on my team. Another loss, but still lots of fun.

MONDAY SEPTEMBER 17, 1984

Today in Gym class, Evelyn, Steph and I were talking about school clubs. They were wondering why I hadn't joined any. Like I said before, I am not a big high school activities person. Steph is in the Math club and the French club. Evelyn is on the Student Council.

Megan overheard us talking and mentioned that there was an opening for a photographer on the yearbook staff. She is president of the yearbook committee. Her and Stuart are in so many clubs, many of them academic, brainiac clubs. I love photography, so I said yes.

The first meeting was tonight. It's only a small group, but everyone was friendly and they welcomed me aboard. Megan gave me the camera the school provides, but I just looked at it and laughed. I told her I would use my mom's. It's so much better.

I'm allotted up to 3 rolls a week, unless there are major events happening. One roll has to be used at the football games. The newspaper photographer, Tanya Bednick, usually takes the football pics and provides a few for the yearbook. This year though, I will be stepping in and getting many for the yearbook. Fine with me. Many chances to photograph Randy.

TUESDAY SEPTEMBER 18, 1984

Another Randy/Michelle fight. This one I got caught in the middle of. They were fighting right in front of the English class door. Mrs. Bartone wasn't there yet. As I approached, I saw a lot of people standing around. Nobody wanted to go by them. I wasn't waiting. I walked right up and squeezed between them. As I did, Michelle snapped at me...

"Uhm, excuse me, geek."

Randy told her not to snap at me. Michelle just shook her head and stormed into class. Randy walked away. She kept giving me dirty looks the whole class.

WEDNESDAY SEPTEMBER 19, 1984

"It's ok if you are. We don't mind. We're not going to tell anybody."

I couldn't believe Evelyn said that. How was I supposed to study?

The three of us were sitting on Steph's bed studying. We've decided to get together at least once a week to study our French homework and help each other out. We'll get together more if there is a major project due. Today was going to be all about the first major French test.

This was our second study time together. The last one was so much fun. Today though, just as we started, I heard the two of them whispering back and forth.

"Ask him."

"No, you ask him."

"You're more of his friend."

"No."

I would occasionally look up, knowing they were talking about me. Eventually Evelyn gave in and asked.

"Josh, Steph wants to… (Whap!)

She stopped because Steph hit her with a pillow. This only stopped her for a second.

…know… (Whap!)

...if you... (Whap whap!)

...are gay." (Whap!)

I couldn't believe that they could tell. The question freaked me out, but I quickly said "No." I felt good that I said it with force. I wanted it to end there, but Evelyn has to go and say "It's ok..."

I've so wanted to tell somebody, but could I trust them? "I'm not" was what came from my lips. They let it go.

Fifteen minutes later I'm sitting there wondering if I should say something. My eyes go all over the room. All the guys on the wall seem to be staring at me.

"You know you are."

"You've been checking us out."

"Just tell them."

"I've only known them for a few weeks. I can't," I silently answer them, but my mouth didn't get the message from my brain.

"Ok, maybe I am" comes pouring out.

My hand goes right to my mouth, as if to stop anything else from coming out. I'm sitting there waiting for them to call me a fag and kick me out of the room.

"I knew it! I've seen the way you look at Randy," Evelyn says laughing

I hit her with a pillow. We had a little pillow fight and were all laughing.

"Promise me you won't say anything," I asked them.

They promised.

THURSDAY SEPTEMBER 20, 1984

Even though they promised, I was still a nervous wreck. I didn't sleep at all last night. All I kept thinking was "what if they slip and accidentally tell the wrong person?" My mind was going crazy. My mouth kept saying...

"Everything will be alright."

I pulled into the parking lot, expecting the worst. Nothing. Steph and Evelyn acted as if nothing had changed. Although Evelyn did smile and do a light laugh if she saw me looking at Randy. By French class I was breathing normally. Our study group is going to be the perfect place to relax and get these feelings out.

FRIDAY SEPTEMBER 21, 1984

Randy was really frazzled today when he walked into French class. He seemed ok most of the day, so I'm guessing it was another fight with Michelle. He was definitely not in the right frame of mind for our first major French test.

He seemed stressed the whole period. Steph and I finished the test quickly. No problem. Evelyn took all period, but she finished it. Randy was fidgeting the whole period. He seemed lost. At one point I glanced over his shoulder and saw that most of the test was blank. He just couldn't concentrate.

Class ended and he dropped it on Mrs. Rosario's desk and bolted out the door, pushing some people out of the way to do it.

SATURDAY SEPTEMBER 22, 1984

Went to the football game today with Steph. Randy was playing horribly. We were down 28-3 at the half. Randy had thrown 4 interceptions. When the team came out for the second half, Randy was nowhere to be seen. They brought out David Bernado, the backup quarterback for the second half. I hope Randy's ok.

SUNDAY SEPTEMBER 23, 1984

Worked all day. Evelyn stopped in, asking me if I could believe how bad Randy was playing. I told her that it was probably another fight with Michelle. She thinks it's something more.

Tommy came in at noon. Our first time working together. We spent the whole time between customers, throwing top 40 music questions at each other. He thinks he knows more than me. No chance.

MONDAY SEPTEMBER 24, 1984

Randy was very nervous when he walked into French today. Steph, Evelyn and I all said hello to him, but he didn't respond.

Today was the day we got the tests back. Steph and I both got a 97. Evelyn was so excited about her 85. She was so sure that she failed.

Randy wouldn't show anybody his. He kept it folded up, looking upset. He would open it every once in a while and look at it. I'm guessing he was hoping that the grade would magically change. I glanced over and saw it. He got a 45.

At the end of class he stopped Evelyn and asked to talk to her in private. Steph and I headed out. I called Steph tonight. I wanted to know if she found out what Randy wanted to talk to Evelyn about. She didn't know. She was waiting to hear back from Evelyn.

TUESDAY SEPTEMBER 25, 1984

Found out from Evelyn in homeroom what Randy wanted. She said he asked her to tutor him. It seems that he can't fail French or any other subject for that matter. He must maintain a "C" average in all his classes or he's off the football team. This is one of Principal Angelino's big things. No free rides for athletes, no matter how good. With this 45, he's just barely scraping a "C".

"So are you going to tutor him?" I asked.

She told him that she was busy with her DJ stuff and her other jobs and that she didn't really feel that she was doing much better, even with the 85. She told him that he should ask either Steph or me. He asked Steph, who agreed, but she told him that she has study time with me and Evelyn. He told her that he didn't mind and asked if it was ok to join us. Steph said yes, so now he's going to be studying with us. It's great that he's going to be there, but it also means that the door is now shut on gay talk, at least whenever he's around.

WEDNESDAY SEPTEMBER 26, 1984

Randy was there for the study group tonight. All 4 of us crammed on Steph's bed. That lasted about 10 minutes, when Steph decided that it would probably be better to move the study group to the dining room table.

At first, Randy seemed a little nervous, but as each of us took turns helping him out, he seemed to calm down.

THURSDAY SEPTEMBER 27, 1984

Evelyn stopped over tonight. We had just finished dinner. Tomorrow is our first major History test and she was real nervous and asked if I could help her study. Of course I said yes. We sat on the couch and I taught her some easy study techniques. When she left she felt really confident about everything.

FRIDAY SEPTEMBER 28, 1984

Randy is back to his usual upbeat self, asking when the next study group is. After History class, Evelyn hugged me, telling me how my techniques helped.

SATURDAY SEPTEMBER 29, 1984

"My treat," Evelyn said.

She was calling to invite me to go bowling with her and Steph. I was not going to turn that down. Out to Whitfield Lanes. Being Saturday night, the place was packed, but with over 100 lanes it wasn't a problem. Evelyn is a phenomenal bowler. She left me and Steph in the dust. A totally awesome night.

SUNDAY SEPTEMBER 30, 1984

Had the day off from work. Good thing. It was Taylor's first soccer game today. My little brother is a soccer jock. He loves playing it. If a game is on TV he always wants to watch it. It doesn't matter who's playing.

I stood on the sidelines taking photos, cheering him on. Mom sat in the bleachers, wearing her big cowboy hat, yelling louder than all the other mothers. Taylor scored 2 goals, helping his team win 4-1. Great job little brother.

MONDAY OCTOBER 1, 1984

Evelyn was nervous, but a fun type of nervous. We were getting our history tests back today. She really wanted to know how she did. Mr. Stanton didn't hand them back until the very end of the period. He handed me mine (98) and I headed out to the hallway to wait for Evelyn.

"97! 97! 97!"

She was jumping up and down, so excited at how well she did.

"You are helping me study from now on," she said, hugging me.

TUESDAY OCTOBER 2, 1984

Nothing much today. When I got home from school, I changed and was heading out the door when mom stopped me.

"Big surprise tomorrow," she said.

That's all she said, before heading back into the kitchen. I was running late for work so I couldn't ask her what she meant. When I got home from work she was already asleep. I guess I will find out tomorrow.

WEDNESDAY OCTOBER 3, 1984

Woke up and headed downstairs to see this "surprise". Mom was in the kitchen making breakfast.

"Wow. Scrambled eggs, bacon and toast. This is a surprise," I said sarcastically as she placed the plate in front of me.

"Shut up. You will see the surprise when you get home," she said.

Ok it was a great surprise.

I walked in the door. Mom was standing in the living room, smiling. Nothing seemed different.

"Well?" I said.

She grabbed the remote control and turned on the TV.

MTV

My eyes got so wide. We got cable. Since we moved in I've been asking if we could get cable.

Thank God. I want my MTV. I need my MTV. I gotta have my MTV. Friday Night Videos is nice, but I need more than an hour and a half of music videos a week.

In 1982 we were one of the first houses to get cable. When we moved to Florida, grandma and grandpa didn't have it. They thought it was a waste of money. It was so good having it back. So just like that first day in 1982, I stayed glued to the TV, watching Martha Quinn and Mark Goodman bring me all of today's hottest videos.

THURSDAY OCTOBER 4, 1984

Mrs. Brandon stopped me in the hall, reminding me that it's my turn to take photos of this week's football game on Saturday.

Randy joined us again for the study group. He's a lot more relaxed now. Totally different than the group of people he hangs out with. He needs to break free from them. There wasn't a major French test, quiz or assignment due tomorrow, just a worksheet. Steph and Evelyn helped him with that while I spent most of the time studying up for the science test.

FRIDAY OCTOBER 5, 1984

Derek, the dumb jock that he is, didn't study for the Science test. Big shock. I kept seeing him try to look at my paper. At first I didn't let him, but as some gesture of good will I let him copy from me. Some good will, he spent all of Spanish class shooting spitballs in my hair.

SATURDAY OCTOBER 6, 1984

Today's football game was an away game against Cascade Park, which meant I had to drive 10 miles to the field. Not knowing how to get there, I got to school early and followed the school bus with the players on it. I was hoping someone would join me, but everyone was busy.

I got some great photos, even with it being so cloudy. Thank God it didn't rain. I was in just the right spot to snap this photo of Derek lifting Randy up after he threw the winning touchdown. It's always great to see Randy smiling.

After I took the shot, I was standing on the sidelines with everyone, looking for another good shot, when Michelle bumps into me. On purpose I'm sure. She got in my face and started asking me all these questions. Asking me about Steph and Randy and what's going on.

"Are they really studying?" she says.

Not only is she a stupid bitch, she's a jealous one too. I didn't really want to talk to her about it, but I told her that nothing is going on and that I'm there most of the time they study.

"You better be telling the truth," she snaps. Then she turns and sees Randy approaching and switches gears. All smiles

"Great job babe," she says, running up to him. I just shook my head and left.

SUNDAY OCTOBER 7, 1984

Taylor's soccer game was at 3 o'clock today. I had to work until 3:30. I quickly left work and headed over. There was a light rain coming down, but they were still playing. I grabbed my camera and a big umbrella and stood on the sidelines taking some pictures. Mom and Alexa watched from the car.

Taylor seemed so glad that I was there. Dad leaving was hard for him. He doesn't say much about it anymore. The first month after dad left he would cry almost every night. We shared a room together in Florida and I would sometimes hear him cry in his sleep. So I've had to step up the big brother role.

After the game he wanted to drive home with me in the Mustang.

"All that mud? Are you crazy?" I told him.

He seemed sad when I said that. He started walking away.

"I'm kidding. C'mon," I said.

He ran over and we went for a drive around town for a little bit before heading home, stopping for some ice cream before dinner.

MONDAY OCTOBER 8, 1984

COLUMBUS DAY

We're off from school, so Mr. Totino asked me to open the store today by myself. Even though I'm only 16, he trusts me. I'm his best employee. He's been giving me extra responsibilities since I started. I just brought in my 24 slot cassette case and I was good to go. All was ok until Derek and a few jock jerks came in. Well all jerks except one, Randy was with them.

"Can I get some help here?!" Derek yells, even though I'm standing a few feet from him.

He tells me that he needs the new Twisted Sister cassette. We had sold out earlier in the week, but had gotten some more in. They just hadn't gotten to the floor yet. After all the drama with the Science test, I was over doing him favors.

"Sorry, we're sold out," I said.

I felt really good saying it, but then Randy says…

"Damn, I really wanted to hear that tonight. Everybody seems to be sold out."

So like some stupid love struck little girl, I go and say…

"Let me check the back. Maybe he got something in today that I didn't notice."

Tommy had just come in at this time, so I told him to watch the front while I headed to the back.

I came out of the back with a box and sure enough the Twisted Sister album was there. Randy thanked me as I handed it to him. Derek snatched it from his hand.

"Let's go" he said. They went up to Tommy, paid and headed out.

TUESDAY OCTOBER 9, 1984

Another big Randy/Michelle fight, right before homeroom. She was asking him where he was yesterday. All thru homeroom he had a very angry look on his face. I was going to ask him what he thought about the Twisted Sister album, but decided against it.

WEDNESDAY OCTOBER 10, 1984

"Can you see what's wrong with mom? She's playing that song over and over and over."

Taylor was freaking out. I had just come home from hanging out at Total Eclipse with Tommy. The sounds of Dolly Parton filled the house.

"Starting over again. Where do you begin…"

As I made my way up the steps, I tried to think what could be wrong. Then just before I got to her bedroom door I figured it out. It's October 10th. Today would have been my parents' 20th wedding anniversary.

Every year my dad would plan a special day for the two of them. Mom would get all dressed up. It was the one day of the year I knew that there would be no fighting.

The door to her room was open so I peeked in. Mom was sitting there, looking at herself in the mirror. She was spinning the wedding ring around her finger, occasionally mouthing a line or two from the song. I rarely see my mom this depressed. She always comes off as a tough woman who can handle anything. She must have been keeping this all inside. I knocked on the door. The song had just ended and the record player was getting ready to start the song again.

"Ah, my #1 son," she said, wiping away tears, yet acting as if nothing was wrong.

"What's wrong?" I said, calling her bluff.

She sat there silently, so I just stared at her.

"I don't know what I'm going to do," she said.

"About what?"

"Where did I go wrong?"

I had to get tough to make my mom tough. I was hating the fact that my father was still making her feel like this. This was all his fault.

"You did nothing wrong," I said, taking her hand.

"As far as what you're going to do...

I took the wedding ring off her finger and put it in one of the small compartments of her jewelry box.

...That's what you're going to do. You may not have him, but you've got us...

She did a light laugh, wiped her eyes and hugged me. I hugged her back.

...Now can I please turn off that depressing song?" I said, laughing.

She laughed and nodded her head while I turned it off.

"Thank God!!!" Taylor yelled from downstairs.

Mom and I cracked up laughing.

THURSDAY OCTOBER 11, 1984

Just a regular day at school. Taylor was over a friend's house when I got home, so I commandeered the TV. MTV time.

FRIDAY OCTOBER 12, 1984

The Whitfield Woodpecker, our 8 page school paper comes out every Friday. They sell them for 25 cents during homeroom. I always make sure to buy one. Today I especially do. That photo I took of Randy and Derek is on the front page. Mrs. Brandon loved it and felt that it should go in both the paper and the yearbook.

I notice that Randy doesn't buy one. He's too stressed. Another fight with Michelle this morning. When I realize this, I signal the girl from the newspaper staff back. I buy a second copy.

Everybody who bought the paper is looking at the photo and looking at Randy, who is just sitting there with his head down on the desk. Every time he looks up, he sees somebody staring.

"Why is everybody looking at me?" he says, turning to Evelyn.

She shows him the photo. He grabs the paper from her and his eyes light up. This puts him in a better mood.

Evelyn grabs the paper back and tells him that I took the photo. He turns around and tells me that...

"It's great." Flashing me that killer smile that makes me melt.

I hand him my extra copy, telling him that I picked it up for him, knowing he'd want it.

"Thanks," he says.

I used this opportunity to ask him if he's ready for today's French quiz. He's a little nervous, but said he'd be ready.

"Just avoid fighting with Michelle and you'll be fine," I said

Once again, my mouth was speaking without my brain. Luckily he just laughed.

All day, people were talking about the photo. Derek wouldn't shut up about it in Science class. He didn't know it was me who took it. Randy must have told him, because in Gym, he came jogging up to me and Steph, "Great photo". That was all he said and then he kept jogging. At least he was trying to be nice.

SATURDAY OCTOBER 13, 1984

"You will dance tonight. No standing on the sidelines. No parking on the dance floor."

Evelyn scolds me as we enter Masquerade. Masquerade is this teen dance club in North Whitfield. It was once a baby clothes warehouse. Now it's *the* place where many 14-18 year old Central Jersey teens go on Friday and Saturday nights. I don't think I've ever seen so much neon lighting in one place. The place is packed.

We enter and everyone is dancing to "Cruel Summer" by Bananarama. Even though it's my favorite song, I can't enjoy it, because I'm being bumped, pushed and squashed.

"Will you relax. C'mon," Evelyn says, grabbing my hand.

She drags me onto the dance floor. Somehow she found a danceable spot. Steph has gone to get us some soda. She returns with 3 cokes. As she's handing one to me, Evelyn goes "Hold on". She then took out a bottle and poured something into my cup.

"What is that?" I ask.

"It's just my friend Jack. You'll love it," she says.

I took one sip and nearly gagged. It tasted awful. They were both laughing. I handed it back to her. She gave it to Steph, who handed me her plain coke.

"I think somebody is checking you out," Steph said into my ear.

"Who?"

She glanced to my left. I looked over my shoulder and saw this blond boy pretending not to stare. He was skinnier than me. I only weigh about 120 pounds. This boy couldn't have weighed more than 100 pounds wet. He was cute though.

Blond boy and I spent the next half hour pretending not to be looking at each other. Then he disappeared. I just continued dancing with Steph and Evelyn. "Chaka Khan. Chaka Khan."

We were having fun singing along, then the club got more crowded. As if it wasn't crowded enough. We were packed in. I told them I needed some air. I headed outside.

When I got outside, I sensed that someone was watching me. I turned around and there was blond boy.

"Hi," He said. Any higher and I'd swear he was sucking helium. I said "hi" back

"Kevin," he said, introducing himself.

"Josh," I said back, smiling.

Kevin then started looking around. "C'mon." he said, heading around the building. We walked around the side of the building, passing people hanging out, smoking or drinking. There were even a few people making out. I recognized a few of the girls from school. I followed Kevin. He led me to this area behind the club. We were alone.

"What's going on?" I said nervously. That was when he pushed me to the wall. I could feel the music from inside pulsing thru my body. The beats of "The War Song" by Culture Club thumping thru the wall. I was panicking, but then he kissed me. So I kissed him back. Then I felt his hand move down my chest. He was going where no man, hell nobody but myself had gone before. It felt good, but strange at the same time. He then grabbed my hand and placed it on his chest, moving it slowly down. In my head I was softly singing along with Boy George, "War war is stupid..." I needed to relax. It was helping. I was slowly relaxing, enjoying what was happening, then all of a sudden we heard a noise, somebody was coming.

"Damn. Oh well," he said, breaking off the kiss and letting go of my hand. I stood there watching him walk off, wondering what the hell just happened.

I made my way back inside and found Steph and told her what happened. She was heavily buzzed, obviously from Evelyn's friend Jack. She looked at me and laughed. I told her that I had to go and that I would see her later. Somehow I don't think I'll ever see Kevin again. Doesn't matter. It was good, but for some reason it also felt meaningless and cheap.

SUNDAY OCTOBER 14, 1984

Mr. Totino needed me to work an open to close today, so I couldn't get out to Taylor's game. They won again (1-0). He scored the goal.

MONDAY OCTOBER 15, 1984

Steph applied to many places in the mall last month, but no takers. So she gave up. Yesterday she filled out another application on a whim. She had an interview tonight. I hope she gets it.

TUESDAY OCTOBER 16, 1984

"SHE GOT IT!"

Steph's new job is at this accessories store called Bingle Bangle Bongle. They sell jewelry, socks, scarves and other girl type things. It's right near the food court, which is right around the corner from Total Eclipse, so we are going to be able to take our lunch breaks together and not have to rush. This is so cool.

Steph started her job tonight, so when she stopped in, I took my break and we headed to the food court.

"I saw these and thought of you," she says, reaching into the bag she was carrying and pulling out these fluorescent blue socks.

I know they came from her store, so I gave her a strange look. "They're not girl socks...we sell a lot of unisex items. You'll look great in them."

I look over at the socks, thank her and tell her that I will wear them...maybe.

WEDNESDAY OCTOBER 17, 1984

Mrs. Brandon tells me today that I need to take more shots of seniors.

"There's nowhere near enough."

So I spent all non-class time today taking random shots. I did also take some posed ones of Evelyn, Megan and Stuart. Steph thought she looked awful today and didn't want her picture taken.

THURSDAY OCTOBER 18, 1984

All through school today, Steph kept giving me these looks, mostly looking at my shoes. I'm sure it's because I haven't worn the socks yet.

Yup. That's what it was.

"Why haven't you worn the socks?" she finally says, right as we take our seats at the food court for our lunch break. Before I can even answer, she continues...

"It's ok. I found something else to go with them."

She then pulls out this belt that's the same color as the socks.

"Tomorrow you better be wearing both."

FRIDAY OCTOBER 19, 1984

"Oh don't you look cute," Evelyn says as I walk into homeroom.

I'm wearing the blue socks, white sneakers, white pants with the blue belt and a Hawaiian style shirt I got at O.P. a few weeks ago, over a white t-shirt. Evelyn knows style, so I take it as a high compliment. I couldn't wait to show Steph.

"Parker! What are you, some kind of fag?" Derek said, breaking the silence of the locker room. All eyes were on me.

"Excuse me?" I said, as macho as I could sound through my nervousness.

"Those socks and that belt. Only a fag would wear those," he answered, laughing, causing others to laugh.

"These were gifts from Stephanie," I said, still trying to sound macho. I was so nervous I sounded about as macho as Richard Simmons.

I quickly changed and headed out to the gym floor, nervous that I was starting to exhibit gay qualities that others were picking up.

"Evelyn was telling me how great you look. I can't wait to see," Steph said.

"Do you think I've been acting gayer lately?" I asked them.

"No. Why?"

I told them what Derek said

"He's just an asshole. Don't be so paranoid," Evelyn said.

After gym I changed back, debating whether or not to put on the socks and belt. For Steph, I did. She loved it, but all day, the jocks from my gym class would laugh whenever we passed in the halls. Regardless of what Steph and Evelyn think, the socks and belt are probably not going to be worn ever again.

SATURDAY OCTOBER 20, 1984

Yesterday, Mrs. Brandon came up to me, telling me how much she loves the candid shots I took of the seniors.

"Now you need to take some around town."

There was no chance for me to take any yesterday. I was too busy. Luckily I'm off today, so I spent most of the afternoon taking photos around town. City hall. Fire Station. Statues. Parks. Historic buildings.

I think I have plenty now.

SUNDAY OCTOBER 21, 1984

Another full day at work. Another missed game. They lost this one (2-0). When I got home Taylor told me that he wished I was at this game. I felt so bad.

MONDAY OCTOBER 22, 1984

It's a really chilly day today. I laughed when I walked into homeroom. I'm freezing and Evelyn is there wearing a leather mini-skirt.

"Shut up," she said as I was shaking my head.

She did look great though.

As we're sitting in History class, Mr. Stanton comes in and notices what she's wearing.

"Miss Ramirez, that outfit is inappropriate for class, please go change."

"I don't have anything else and it is not inappropriate," she snaps right back at him.

"Well I feel it is," he tells her.

"Well you are the only teacher who does," she said, standing her ground.

He threw her out of class. The stupid ex-jock. She didn't care. She just grabbed her books and left. We were laughing about it in French class.

TUESDAY OCTOBER 23, 1984

Yesterday I stayed outside during my free period. It warmed up a little as the day went on. Today it's much colder. So now I needed to find a new place to sit during lunch and my free period. Now where?

LIBRARY - Quiet, but can't eat lunch there.

COMPUTER ROOM - Noisy, no lunch.

WEIGHT ROOM - Jock central. Don't think so

CAFETERIA - Don't make me laugh.

AUDITORIUM - ?

Debating the possibilities, I've chosen the auditorium. So far I've had the place to myself. Me and 500 empty red and gold seats. There is a large stage area in the front. It's mostly used by the chorus or the band. Sometimes other clubs use it for small gatherings. Oh and of course for assemblies. We also have a Drama club here, I think. I have yet to see any performances announced.

WEDNESDAY OCTOBER 24, 1984

Today during my free period I was bored and curious, so I decided to do some exploring. The 2 sets of giant curtains were open and I could see all the way to the back. I made my way up the stage steps, stopping to look out into the auditorium. I've always wondered what it's like to stand in front of a crowd.

Making my way around the stage, I peeked behind one of the curtains. I found a rope ladder. I decided to climb it and see where it leads.

It leads to a giant platform. It appears to be a large storage space for costumes and old files. By the looks of it, nobody has been up here in a long time. From up here you can see the entire stage. It's so high up and hidden that you can sit up here and nobody can see you. There is plenty of room for me to stretch out. The lights from the auditorium are bright enough to see everything.

I climbed back down, grabbed my backpack and climbed back up. I spent my whole free period up there, not wanting to come down. I'll be back for lunch. It's so peaceful. I need to keep this to myself.

THURSDAY OCTOBER 25, 1984

PSYCHIC MOM STRIKES AGAIN

My responsibilities at work have increased. I've opened and closed the store, handled the money and checked in inventory. Mr. Totino just gave me a 50 cents an hour raise. I was so excited. I came home to tell mom and what does she say...

"That's great honey. I just got a raise too. I'll be making more money now, so you can stop slipping money into my purse."

Ever since I started working at Total Eclipse I've been putting money into her purse. I had to. She wouldn't take it when I offered it to her. She is paying for the rent on the house, the insurance on her car and my car, the groceries and all the bills. I feel that because I'm working I should contribute.

"Spend your money on yourself," is all she says.

FRIDAY OCTOBER 26, 1984

On Monday we were all given a time when we were required to go see one of the guidance counselors. So today during my free period was my time.

Mrs. Schwartz started talking to me about what I want to do about college. I have no idea what I want to do. She told me that I really need to get going on it.

"I think I want to do something with foreign languages" I tell her.

"That's great. There are many opportunities," she says, digging thru some large filing cabinets, handing me all these pamphlets for different colleges and universities. Then she went into the other room and came back with pamphlets from foreign language schools around the world.

"Look these over and see if any interest you. If they do, fill them out. If you have any questions, feel free to come and ask. Did you sign up to take the SATs?"

"Yes," I told her.

They are coming up next month.

SATURDAY OCTOBER 27, 1984

DOUBLE DOUBLE NO TROUBLE

All day at work. Placed up all the displays for the new Pat Benatar album, Tropico. It comes out next week. I cannot wait. She looks so awesome on the cover. I hope we get t-shirts with the album cover on them. I want one.

SUNDAY OCTOBER 28, 1984

Drama drama drama

"Are you going to be at this game?" Taylor asked me this morning. He had a sad look on his face. I said I would definitely be there.

Because I did Mr. Totino a favor and worked a double yesterday, I told him I needed to be out early for the game. He said it was ok.

Of course work was very busy and I couldn't get out in time. The game started at 3 and I didn't leave work until 3:30. I raced to the field. Of course there was a lot of traffic.

Mom wasn't going to be at this game. She goes to all of them, but today she had to go fill out some forms for Alexa's ballet class. So it was doubly important that I be there. I was getting angry at all the traffic.

"Green light means go people!"

I finally get there. Three games are going on. I spotted his team's bright yellow uniforms and headed over. As I get closer, I can see his team playing, but I don't see him.

"Josh!" I hear to my right. It's Mrs. Sawyer, Randy's mom. She is a teacher at Whitfield High. Randy's little brother Adam is on Taylor's team.

"Hi Mrs. Sawyer. Where's Taylor?" I ask nervously.

"He fell and hurt his wrist. They took him to County Hospital. Your mom wasn't..."

She was still speaking, but I took off. I had to get to the hospital.

"Oh my God. He's hurt and by himself. He's probably a nervous wreck," I say, speaking to nobody. Thank God the hospital is not far from the field.

"Can I help you?" says this nurse. I read her nametag. It says Sandra. I can't catch my breath.

"OK Parker, breathe," I think to myself.

"Are you alright?" Sandra says.

I just nod.

"OK, relax," she says, making motions for me to take a deep breath. I follow her motions and manage to get the words "Parker...Taylor" out. She knows who I'm talking about.

"Are you his brother?" she says. I once again nod and she points down the hall. I didn't stay to hear which room, so I just started looking in all the rooms. Then I hear Sandra yell "Room 112." I turn and see her standing there shaking her head and smiling. I smiled back and headed to Room 112.

I get to the room, he's there. He has his arm in a sling. All I could do was run up and hug him, telling him I was sorry I wasn't there. I think I was more of a wreck than him. He was just glad to see me.

"What happened?" I asked him.

"Ah, this big doofus on the other team tripped me when I was about to score. The doctor said I fractured my wrist."

As he says this, Dr. Bancuso entered, asking me if I'm Taylor's brother. I nodded my head yes and he mentions how they still haven't gotten hold of my mother. He handed me some forms to fill out, but because I'm not over 18, we have to wait for mom to come and sign them so he can be released.

The doctor left and I told Taylor that I was going to try and call mom. I didn't even make it to the door. Mom comes rushing in, pushing right past me.

"My baby. My little baby."

She's so dramatic.

MONDAY OCTOBER 29, 1984

"PLEASE PLEASE PLEASE PLEASE PLEASE"

"No" I tell her for the 10th time today.

"Why not?" she whines.

"It's another gay reference. I know people are talking. I don't need to give them more ammunition."

"You are paranoid. It's all in your head. Nobody is saying anything. Evelyn would be hearing about it if they were."

The Halloween dance is in a few days. Steph is trying to get our little group to all go as famous singers. She's going as Cyndi Lauper and has been pressuring me to go as Boy George.

"You'll look great. It will all be ok. I promise," she says, continuing with the begging.

"Ok, but you have to help me with it," I say caving.

Let's hope this all goes well.

TUESDAY OCTOBER 30, 1984

No gym class today. Third period, all seniors had to go to an assembly. Yesterday was for the freshmen and sophomores. Today, the juniors had to do it 2nd period. Seniors 3rd period.

I hate assemblies. This one was "Just Say No". Nancy Reagan's anti-drug campaign. Is that the best she can come up with? "Just say no?"

It was so long and boring. Many students weren't paying attention. I'm just glad it wasn't during my free period. I need my quiet time.

WEDNESDAY OCTOBER 31, 1984

"See, I told you not to worry," Steph says, digging into the big plate of cheese fries the waitress has just placed in front of us. The five of us are sitting at this big booth in the back of the diner. We've just come from the Halloween dance.

It was so funny when we walked in the door. It was like one big music supergroup. I, of course as Boy George. Steph looking great as Cyndi Lauper. Don't ask me how she was able to get her hair those colors. Megan came as Madonna, the Borderline video version. Stuart was Weird Al, with the curly hair and glasses. But Evelyn's costume was truly the best and she won 1st prize too. She came as, believe it or not, Prince, all in purple. She even had the ruffled shirt.

"Well there was Garrett's comment," I said, answering Steph while trying to get some fries.

"Oh please. He's a Neanderthal," Steph said.

Right as we entered the gym, Garrett was standing there with a couple of other wrestling jocks. He went...

"Are you a fag? Because only a fag would come as a fag for Halloween."

It bothered me most of the dance, but now, sitting here at the diner, surrounded by my 4 newest friends, I realize that all is ok and I'm not going to let others make me feel down. My friends care about me and that's all that matters.

THURSDAY NOVEMBER 1, 1984

Off from school today and tomorrow. New Jersey Teacher's Convention. All Jersey teachers meet down in Atlantic City for I guess…conferences? Who knows? All I know is that we get 2 days off.

Mom of course has to work, so I can't leave. Part of the day watching MTV and part of the day playing video games with Taylor.

FRIDAY NOVEMBER 2, 1984

"Happy Birthday to you….Blah Blah Blah"

I woke up to see mom, Alexa and a reluctant Taylor standing by my bed singing it to me. I have a dorky family.

Had to babysit the young'uns until mom came home. The instant she did, I was out the door.

"Be back by 6 for dinner!" mom yelled.

"Pizza!" I said, laughing, not turning around.

I headed over to Steph's. We have a big French assignment due Monday and we're going to help each other out. The instant I walked in the door…

"Happy Birthday…Blah Blah Blah"

They were singing it from the dining room. As I approached, I saw that Steph was holding a Cookie Puss cake. 17 candles on top.

"Make a wish." Steph and Evelyn said in unison

I looked over at Randy, who came in just at the end of the song. Then I turned back to the evil duo, giving them this sinister smile. They knew exactly what I was thinking. Then out went all the candles.

"Here's hoping it comes true," I think to myself, knowing full well it won't. Even if Randy were gay, oh how I wish, he could do way better than me.

"How did you know it was my birthday and that I love ice cream cake?" I asked Steph, grabbing Cookie Puss' ice cream cone nose.

"The cake was a guess. It's my favorite too. As far as your birthday, Alexa told me on Monday. She said you didn't want anybody to know or to make a big deal out of it."

Little sister has a big mouth, but I love the little munchkin. I didn't want anybody to know. It's no big deal. I'm 17 now. Whoop-de-doo.

"We only wanted to do something small," Steph said.

"Thank you," I told her, giving her a big hug. Then it was time to work on the assignment.

SATURDAY NOVEMBER 3, 1984

Steph wanted to drive us to Randy's game today. It was an away game. I didn't mind. When we got back to my house, she wanted to come in and hang out for a little bit. The instant I open the door...

"SURPRISE!!!!!"

I should have known something was up yesterday when everybody wished me a happy birthday but there were no presents.

My mom and Steph's mom got together and cooked food for everybody and decorated the living room. Balloons everywhere.

They were there, along with my brother and sister, Evelyn, Megan, Stuart, Tommy and a short time later, Randy. He couldn't stay long. He dropped off my present, grabbed some cake, wished me a happy birthday and was off. It was such a fun little surprise.

SUNDAY NOVEMBER 4, 1984

Being off from work Friday and Saturday meant an all day Sunday shift today. I didn't mind. Steph stopped in. I had to thank her once again for all the birthday stuff.

MONDAY NOVEMBER 5, 1984

We are off tomorrow for Election Day. Mr. Stanton is the only one who gave us homework. We have to write a paper on the election. I have to work tonight, so I can't watch any of the news. I don't know what I'm going to write.

Before heading into Total Eclipse, I stopped and said hello to Megan and Stuart. They were manning an election booth at the mall. They were handing out buttons and bumper stickers for Reagan and Mondale.

TUESDAY NOVEMBER 6, 1984

"JOSH!!! TELEPHONE!!!!"

Oh my God, who's calling me this early? It's only...oh hell it's 1 o'clock already? I trudged downstairs.

"It's A-live," Taylor says as I pass by. I smacked him in the head. "Mom!" he whined.

I entered the kitchen. Mom had the phone in her hand and that look on her face.

"What? He was bothering me," I said.

"You two behave," she tells me, smiling as I grab the phone from her.

"Hello?"

"What the hell are you still doing in bed?" Steph barked into the phone

"Good morning to you too," I answer.

"It's afternoon. Get your butt dressed and meet me at the mall. It's rematch time."

She's talking about air hockey. A few weeks ago we found out that we both love playing. Although I don't know why she insists on thinking she's going to win. I beat her every time, but it's still fun.

"I'll be there in about an hour," I tell her.

"I will win," she says as we enter the arcade. The air hockey tables are all the way in the back. The place is a little crowded. We make our way past the video games. They have some of my favorite ones. Centipede, Ms. Pac Man, Tapper, Donkey Kong. I also see that they've gotten some new pinball machines in. Have to play those next time.

Steph has gone ahead and commandeered one of the air hockey tables. As I got closer I noticed that Derek and Garrett are playing at the second table and Randy and Michelle are playing at the third one. The tables are all next to each other. They look up as I approach, but don't say anything. Steph and I start our game.

The whole time, I'm expecting them to say something. They don't. They were actually watching us play.

"Victorious," I say, beating Steph 7-4.

"Rematch," she says.

"Bring it on," I say, laughing.

"Shit!" she yells as I score the first point. Ten minutes later...

"Yes. Reigning champ," I yell.

As I'm putting the quarters in for another game, I hear Garrett say to my left...

"You're not that great. Play me."

"I'm playing with Steph," I tell him.

"It's ok. Kick his ass," Steph says.

We started playing. This was laughable. He plays worse than Steph. I easily defeat him 7-2. Steph clapped as that 7th point was scored.

"Look out. It's my turn," Derek said, pushing Garrett out of the way.

He scored the first two points, but then I figured out his playing style. I scored the next 4. He started getting nervous. Fifteen minutes later...

"Let's get the hell out of here," he says, slamming the paddle down, after I win 7-5.

"Wait. I want to play him," Randy says.

"Let's go. I'm tired of hanging around these geeks," Michelle says, grabbing his arm.

"I want to play. I'll beat him," he tells her.

"Fine. You play. I'm going home," she says, leaving the arcade with Derek and Garrett.

"Let's see how good you really are," he says to me.

He's good. Real good. We were going back and forth for about 30 minutes. It got to be 6-6, neither of us able to score the winning point, until...

"Yes!" I scream loudly, causing everyone in the arcade to turn and look

"Rematch!" Randy says instantly.

Once again another 30 minute game. "That's 2," I say, winning once again.

"I will win. Once more."

Just before we started round 3, Steph came up, giving me a hug.

"I've gotta go. Have fun," she said, kissing me on the cheek.

"Bye Randy."

"Bye Steph."

We stayed at the arcade until they closed, playing air hockey the whole time. It took him 3 more games, but he finally won one.

His jeep wasn't parked too far from the Mustang, so I walked out with him. We talked about little things along the way. It was so much fun, getting to spend the evening, just me and Randy.

WEDNESDAY NOVEMBER 7, 1984

Back to school

Randy came up to me in the halls today. He started talking about the air hockey match. Michelle saw us and dragged him away. We were finally able to talk in French. He really had fun and wants to do it again.

Had to spend my free period in the library today. I forgot all about the stupid election assignment due for History today. So I grabbed yesterday's and today's papers, sat down at one of the tables, read the articles and pieced something together. "Reagan won the election. Four more years. Ho-hum."

Another study night at Steph's house. It is so much fun being able to joke around with Randy without any interference.

THURSDAY NOVEMBER 8, 1984

Lots on my mind today. I'm watching all these couples here at school. Where is that somebody for me? Stuart's got Megan. Randy's got Michelle. Evelyn's dating this guy from Princeton. Steph has a date with this guy she met at work, Todd Carnaski. She introduced me to him during one of our work breaks. He's so completely not her type, but what do I know.

Even Tommy is seeing somebody, this sophomore named Beth, but nobody for me. Not like it would be easy for me, even if there was another gay boy here at school. I can't advertise.

My secret is still safe with Steph and Evelyn. I know people have been asking Evelyn about it. She won't tell, but every day it seems to be getting scarier.

FRIDAY NOVEMBER 9, 1984

I was asked to stop in to the newspaper staff meeting after school. They wanted to see some of my photos from this week. When I walked in, they were discussing why there was no paper today. I was just going to drop off the photos and head out, but Megan asked me to stay.

They were deciding whether or not the paper should come out on Mondays from now on. With the current issue being delayed, it meant extra work for them. It also means having to work on weekends to get the issues ready for Monday. This would also mean that this issue would be packed. Between both football games, the election and other school news.

I was just sitting there listening in, but then they wanted my opinion on it. I told them that I felt it was a great idea having it come out on Mondays.

SATURDAY NOVEMBER 10, 1984

VERY BUSY DAY TODAY

In the morning I joined Steph and Evelyn out at the community college. Today was S.A.T. day.

There was no time to hang out with them after, I had to go and take photos of the football game. Of course the game went into overtime, so I had to race home and get ready for work.

One of the girls called out this afternoon and it was busy. Mr. Totino needed to head out, so Tommy and I jumped on register while Mr. Totino pointed to a bunch of boxes.

"All of these boxes have to go out. Put them up all over the store before you leave." He said, rushing out the door.

When it slowed down a little, I went over to the boxes. I had no idea what was inside, although I should have known.

Inside were all the promo items for the new Madonna album "Like a Virgin". It comes out next week.

Posters, square boards, even a giant life-size Madonna cardboard cutout. I ran to the back to grab my camera. Tommy and I took turns taking photos of us posing with it.

SUNDAY NOVEMBER 11, 1984

As I headed downstairs, Taylor was watching a soccer game. He seemed to be enjoying it, but I knew he was still sad about not being able to play. Today was the final soccer game of the season. He didn't want to go watch the team play. So after dinner I asked him if he wanted to go for a ride in the Mustang. Of course he said yes.

We headed out to the mall. It was already closed, so I took him to a far area of the parking lot and let him practice driving. Mom would've had a heart attack if she found out.

"What were you thinking?"

"He's only 11."

"He has a fractured wrist."

"It's dark out."

I didn't care. I wanted him to have a fun time. He needed it. Our secret.

MONDAY NOVEMBER 12, 1984

Even though it's gotten very cold outside, we still had to jog around the track. Of course everyone switched from shorts to sweats as it got colder.

Well today they finally moved us inside, so I'm back to shorts. Six times around the gym.

TUESDAY NOVEMBER 13, 1984

Well it seems that the photos weren't the only reason they wanted me to attend that newspaper staff meeting the other day. Mrs. Brandon and Megan were testing me.

Today they asked me if I wanted to be part of the newspaper team. It seems that Tanya moved away and another staff member dipped below the "C" average. It appears that Angelino's rule applies to the newspaper too.

I of course said "yes". I won't have to do much, just submit some photos and occasionally write some articles. It sounds like fun.

WEDNESDAY NOVEMBER 14, 1984

Big French test Friday, so it was a major study day. Steph was coughing the whole time. I told her that she needs to see a doctor tomorrow or at least stay home and rest. She laughed, saying she was fine. She had her medicine, orange juice and hot tea.

THURSDAY NOVEMBER 15, 1984

Steph decided to come to school today. Although why she did, I have no idea. She looked worse than yesterday. She made it through the day, but she was getting worse. Sniffling, coughing, and sneezing. Every time I saw her, I told her she needs to go home.

"Keep your germs to yourself."

FRIDAY NOVEMBER 16, 1984

MY SECRET SPACE IS NO LONGER JUST MY SECRET

"So this is where you go," Randy said, scaring the shit out of me.

I was sitting up there concentrating on my first article for the school paper, deciding what I wanted it to be on. I've chosen a few ideas and written out some rough articles.

"How did you know I was up here?" I asked him.

"I followed you. I was calling your name, but I guess you didn't hear me. I thought it was weird when you disappeared behind the curtain. Then I saw you for just a split second climbing onto the platform."

"So what can I do for you?" I asked him, curious as to why he was following me.

"Steph's not here today?" he tells me, looking around the platform. The fact that she wasn't in gym should have been a clue for him that she wasn't here today.

"No, she has the flu. She finally stayed home. Her mom took her to the doctor's yesterday after school. I called last night. She's staying home and resting," I told him.

"I needed to ask her about the French test today…Wow, this is kinda cool up here," he said, looking over the side.

"You come up here all the time?" he continued

"Most of the time."

"Nobody bothers you?"

"Nobody until now," I said sarcastically

"Please please please, do me a favor and don't tell anybody about this place, not even Steph and Evelyn know I come up here. This is where I go to get away from those psycho friends of yours and to clear my head. I don't want to lose this," I continued.

"Can I come up here and hang out?" he asks, smiling.

How was I going to say no to that?

"Sure, but from now on...make a noise or something first. Now what do you need to know about the test?"

We spent the rest of the period studying for the test. Today was also report card day. Of course I got an "A" in every class, except History "B".

SATURDAY NOVEMBER 17, 1984

Worked the day shift today. I made sure to stop over Steph's after work to see how she's doing. She feels a little better. She was really glad I came over.

"I've been so bored," she said.

"What about Todd?" I asked her.

"We're breaking up. All he talks about is sports...and himself," she said, laughing.

I laughed back. I stayed for a few hours, keeping her company.

SUNDAY NOVEMBER 18, 1984

I visited Steph again. She's feeling a whole lot better. She'll be back to school tomorrow. Her mom was home and asked me to stay for dinner, so I said yes, remembering to call mom. I forgot to yesterday and got a lecture when I got home. She worries too much.

MONDAY NOVEMBER 19, 1984

Can you guess who was in my secret spot today when I climbed the ladder for lunch? Of course, Randy. He looked over the side and called my name as I was climbing, showing me that smile. He was sitting there looking over his French homework, well more like just starting it. I helped him out and then we started talking about various things. He wants an air hockey rematch.

It's fun having this quiet time with him. It's also a little rough too, being up there all alone with him. My feelings for him are so strong. So close and yet so far. I have to be careful.

During lunch Randy asked me to take some photos at practice today. I told him I would, so here I am at practice. It's the last practice before the big Thanksgiving Day game. The last game of the season. Everybody is out here. The football players are on one side. The band is rehearsing on the other field and the cheerleaders are over to the side. I've taken a few shots, now Randy is calling me over.

"Guys, this is Josh. He's going to be taking pictures of the practice for the school paper and the yearbook," Randy said, introducing me to the team.

Although I didn't know if any of the photos would appear in either, I went along with it. I watched as Derek pulled Randy aside. They were lightly arguing about something. I watched Derek return.

"Just stay out of the way," he barked at me, returning to practice.

I got some nice shots and then they took a break, so I went over to the band. Tommy saw me coming. He plays drums. As I approached, they stood up and started posing. I laughed and took my photos of them and then I headed over to the bitches...I mean cheerleaders.

Michelle was leading them in a routine. As I was taking some shots, Michelle started messing up. She was forgetting the steps, and she's head cheerleader. She instantly blamed it on me. I started walking away when I heard...

"It's not his fault you're incompetent."

I turned to see this redheaded cheerleader confronting Michelle.

"Shut up!" Michelle retorted.

They started arguing. I of course got it all on film. I then left them to their fighting and made my way back to the football jocks. I will have to ask Evelyn about this cheerleader. The name on her sweater said "Debbie".

TUESDAY NOVEMBER 20, 1984

"Debbie Paletto. Her and Randy dated for most of our junior year. Michelle stole him away from her. She started all these rumors about Debbie, just after last year's Junior Prom after Debbie was crowned prom queen. Most were lies and Michelle totally denied starting them. Debbie couldn't handle it. She left him.

Unlike with Michelle, Randy and Debbie rarely fought. He tried saving the relationship, but it all fell apart. The instant she was away, Michelle did all she could to move right in. It took a month, but with Derek's help, she was able to get Randy.

This year Michelle became head cheerleader, which made things worse. Debbie tries every once in a while to talk to Randy, but if Michelle catches them anywhere near each other, she loses it. I asked her once if she wanted Randy back. She told me she didn't. I think she just wants to be friends with him. Any opportunity Debbie has to get back at Michelle, big or small, she'll use it," Evelyn said.

Ooh I love her. Don't you?

WEDNESDAY NOVEMBER 21, 1984

Everybody was busy or had to work, so we couldn't get together to study last night. There were all these projects and tests due today, so I spent most of the night in my room studying and getting everything ready. We have a 4 day weekend coming up. Tomorrow is Thanksgiving, so we are off from school.

THURSDAY NOVEMBER 22, 1984

HAPPY THANKSGIVING!!

Spent the morning taking photos of the big Thanksgiving Day game. The final game of the season is always between Whitfield and our crosstown rivals Central High. We won. Randy threw 2 touchdown passes.

I left the game and headed home. Mom was cooking all day yesterday and today. When I walked in the door, she asked for my help. She was standing there looking at the dining room table.

"Help me adjust this table," she said.

We pulled the table out and she removed the insert and we pushed it back together, making the table smaller.

"There, that looks a whole lot better," she said, before returning to the kitchen.

She came out a few minutes later, getting everything set. When she had everything set and all the food on the table, we all sat down. She asked me to sit at the other end, across from her. This would be the spot my dad would have been at. All was fine and we started eating and then Alexa started crying...

"I miss daddy."

Mom went over and picked her up, taking her into the other room to talk. Taylor and I just kept eating. When they came back, Alexa was calmer. Everything was fine for the rest of the day.

FRIDAY NOVEMBER 23, 1984

Mom was off from work today, so I was able to work a double. Mr. Totino really needed me. We were slammed. Big Black Friday deals. Tommy never left the register.

SATURDAY NOVEMBER 24, 1984

Another double, although I was allowed to leave a little early. The mall hours have now extended to Holiday time. Normally the mall closes at 9 on weekdays, 10 on Friday and Saturday and 6 on Sunday. Well now the mall closes at 11 every night except Sunday, when it closes at 8.

SUNDAY NOVEMBER 25, 1984

Was supposed to work all day, but because I worked 2 doubles in a row, Mr. Totino let me leave at 5:30. This was great because Steph wanted to go to the movies. She got out of work at 5. She came over to say goodbye, but when she found out I was getting out at 5:30…

"Let's go see "Terminator," she said, all excited.

The movie started at 6 and I knew it was going to be packed, so I told her to go grab tickets, so we could go right in and hopefully they wouldn't be sold out.

"Maybe we should go up to the multiplex. It's larger and playing on 2 screens up there," she said.

Garden Creek Cinemas is this small 4 screen theater on the other side of the mall. Central Jersey Multiplex Cinemas is the big 12 screen theater about 3 miles up the road.

"No, I think it's best to stay here at the mall. Traffic is a nightmare. It will take us forever to get there," I told her.

She went to go grab tickets. She lucked out and got the last 2 tickets. The movie was so cool. Arnold Schwarzenegger as this evil cyborg from the future that comes back in time to 1984. Everybody was cheering during many of the scenes.

MONDAY NOVEMBER 26, 1984

Back to school. It wasn't so much of a restful four day weekend, but it was still a fun one. Now I'm off from work until Wednesday.

TUESDAY NOVEMBER 27, 1984

I was going to go over Steph's for study time, but mom picked up a shift for the woman who picked up her shift last Friday. This meant she was working a double, so I had to be home to babysit. She left a note saying "Make dinner". I called and ordered pizza. That's making dinner...right?

WEDNESDAY NOVEMBER 28, 1984

"Have you seen Randy?" the Bitch says, coming up to me after Gym, giving me all this attitude.

He was in homeroom and then she was waiting for him after and they had a slight argument. I hadn't seen him since then. He wasn't in gym.

I told her "no" and then headed to my secret spot. Randy hadn't been up there the past few days, but today he was there when I climbed the ladder.

"Hey. What's up?" I asked him.

"Hiding from Michelle," he said, laughing.

"Me too," I said.

THURSDAY NOVEMBER 29, 1984

Steph had another study day this week so that I could be there. French Quiz tomorrow. Randy wasn't there. I guess the Bitch needed him for something.

FRIDAY NOVEMBER 30, 1984

Ok I know I don't have much of a social life, but still...my days off?

Last week Mr. Totino asked me if I could work a few extra hours a week for the holiday season. I said yes. The schedule usually goes from Monday to Sunday and he posts it on the

Sunday before. Normally it's posted week to week. Well this schedule was for the whole month of December.

I looked at it and thought I was going to have a heart attack. I'm on 3 nights during the week, a double Saturday and an all day open to close Sunday shift. All these school projects are going to be due before the Christmas break, not to mention big tests.

"I really need you here," he says when I tell him this.

"Ok, but I'm bringing my homework to the store," I say.

"No problem," he said, smiling.

So now I will only have 2 nights to myself...NOT

Right as I walk in the door, "I'm going to be working extra hours for the next few weeks," mom says to me.

"Mr. Totino gave me extra hours at work. I'm only off 2 nights," I tell her.

"Well then I'll pick up extra hours on those days," she says.

My days off?!!?

With her working those nights, that only means one thing, babysitting duties for me.

REALLY? REALLY?

SATURDAY DECEMBER 1, 1984

Well she's picked up shifts for those 2 nights. She even said that she might pick up some overnights. They're very busy and very shorthanded.

"Don't overwork yourself," I told her.

She so wants this to be a great Christmas. The day dad left, everything was in shambles. There was no tree (they were going to pick it up that night). They hadn't finished the Christmas shopping and mom was doing her best to try and keep everything under control.

So now she's doing all she can to make it better. She wants a big tree with lots of decorations. Dad destroyed a lot of those on his last night there as he and mom fought. He occasionally liked to throw things and the glass ornaments were the most handy. She wants a big meal and lots of presents under the tree. She's determined and nothing is going to stop her.

SUNDAY DECEMBER 2, 1984

I brought my homework into work today, seeing as I had to work 10-8. Of course we were so busy that there was no free time except during my lunch break with Steph. She's going to be working a lot too. We both sat there silently working on our homework. Couldn't hang out with Steph after, mom picked up an overnight and had to be at work by 10.

MONDAY DECEMBER 3, 1984

Mom was still at work, so I had to get the young'uns ready and off to school. Alexa wanted banana French toast for breakfast. One of my grandmother's (dad's mom) recipes. She used to always make it for us when we went over and visited. She taught me how to make it 5 years ago.

Sadly, she passed away a short time after. Dad was so devastated. It was the only time I ever really saw him cry. It was so hard on grandpa. They'd been together and married for so long. Nothing in the house was allowed to be changed or removed. He kept everything the same. The sadness took its toll on his health and he passed away 6 months later.

TUESDAY DECEMBER 4, 1984

Tonight was going to be another babysitting night. At school, Steph said that she would come over. This was so cool. I stopped off at the video store and was lucky enough to get the last copy of "Sixteen Candles" they had.

Money was too tight when it came out in the theaters earlier this year and I never got a chance to see it. Steph never saw it either.

Mom left money for us to order pizza. When the pizza arrived we started the movie. Taylor and Alexa had no desire to see it, so Alexa headed off to her room to play with her dolls while Taylor went to the dining room table to work on the model car kit I bought him the other day. Watching the movie, all Steph and I could think was... "JAKE JAKE JAKE".

WEDNESDAY DECEMBER 5, 1984

Another work night. Just me and Tommy. Surprisingly it wasn't too busy. We were acting goofy, dancing around, lip-syncing to the new Billy Idol song "Catch my Fall". He messed up the lyrics halfway thru. I won the challenge. It's so great working with him.

THURSDAY DECEMBER 6, 1984

Evelyn came and visited me at work tonight. She was out at the mall, shopping. We were kind of busy and couldn't really talk, so she walked around the store, checking out the new albums, asking me to put on the new Bryan Adams album "Reckless". I hadn't heard anything from the album except the first single "Run to You" (which I like. It has a really cool video too) so I put it on for her. It's got a few other good singles on it, especially the duet with Tina Turner. I can see this album being a big hit for a while. Evelyn liked it too.

FRIDAY DECEMBER 7, 1984

During my free period I went over to the newspaper/yearbook room. It was time to submit my first article for the paper. It was a short article about the possibility of a new wing being built to increase the size of the school. It's nothing great. I must have rewritten it 50 times. Megan loved it.

SATURDAY DECEMBER 8, 1984

"REMATCH"

Mr. Totino got somebody to cover my night shift, so I didn't have to work a double. Just as I left the store, there was Randy standing there in his leather jacket. Of course I wasn't going to turn him down. We headed to the arcade.

"My turn to win this time," he said, putting the quarters in the machine.

"Oh yeah? We'll see," I said, laughing.

It took him 3 games, but he finally won one. It was a lucky shot. We were about to play another game when Little Miss Bitch came in.

"The movie starts in 20 minutes. Let's go!" she screeched, dragging him away.

I ran into Steph as I was leaving the arcade. She was on her lunch break, so I joined her.

"You better be careful. You don't want to be found out by a jock, even if that jock is Randy," she says as we sit down with our food.

Why did I tell her that I hung out with Randy again? I know what I'm doing. I know that he's straight. That doesn't mean that we can't hang out together.

SUNDAY DECEMBER 9, 1984

Megan stopped into Total Eclipse today to tell me that Mrs. Brandon loved my article and that it will be in the paper tomorrow. I was so excited.

MONDAY DECEMBER 10, 1984

Sitting in homeroom, I couldn't wait for them to come in selling the paper. Stuart came in at almost the end of homeroom. He was in charge of selling them in this part of the school today. He came in and went right to me. I handed him the quarter, but he shook his head...

"No charge. Great job man."

I quickly opened it up. There it was, right on page 3.

IS WHITFIELD READY FOR AN EXPANSION?

By Joshua Parker

All day my friends were congratulating me. It felt so great. When I got home, I cut the article out and put it into a frame, hanging it on my wall.

TUESDAY DECEMBER 11, 1984

"Are you coming over to study?" Steph asks as we leave French class.

"I can't. Mom's working tonight and I have to babysit. Why don't we study at my house this time?" I tell her. We've never studied at my house. It's always been at Steph's.

"Ok, I'll tell Evelyn and Randy," she says.

Even though football season is over, Randy still studies with us. He says he enjoys studying with us and he loves his time away from Michelle. Well he says his time away from everybody, but I know he meant from her.

As we're sitting at the dining room table, I have to get up and calm down the brother and sister every once in a while.

"Nuh-uh...Uh-huh," they whine back and forth.

"Hey! We're studying!" I yell, getting fed up.

They quiet down and Taylor goes to play video games.

"Turn that sound down," I tell him as the sound of advancing aliens fill the air.

Confident we all have our French papers ready for Monday, the study group ends. Steph and Evelyn have to go to work. Evelyn got a part time job working with Steph at Bingle Bangle Bongle for the holidays. They headed out and Randy went upstairs to use the bathroom. `

I was cleaning up the table when Randy came back down. He goes and sits next to Taylor. He grabs the other joystick and plays video games with my brother.

"Don't you have to work tonight?" I ask him.

"Nah, I'm off," he says, mesmerized with the game. His father has a friend who owns a pizza place in the mall. Randy has taken a job there for the holidays.

"I play winner," I tell them.

It got to be 10 o'clock and Randy was still here playing. It was Taylor's bedtime.

"Can I stay up a little longer?" he asks.

"No. I don't want to hear it from mom," I tell him.

"She won't know."

"Psychic mom." That's all I have to say. I waved my hand for him to go upstairs. Randy and I continued playing.

Between Taylor and me, we have about 20 different games. We were playing Combat when mom came home from work about 10:30. It's her favorite game.

"Ooh, I get winner," she says.

I introduced her to Randy. They said their hellos and mom watched us play. Randy won and he started playing Combat with my mom. He stayed until a little after 11 and then he was off, telling me how cool he thinks my mom is.

WEDNESDAY DECEMBER 12, 1984

Randy was extremely quiet in homeroom. I should have known something was up. Here she comes.

"Look, I know you don't have a girlfriend or much of a life, but I'm sick and tired of you hanging out with my boyfriend. I'm being nice enough to let him study with you and your little geek friends, but that's where it stops. You got it. If you don't, I've got some friends who can help you stop," Michelle says, coming up to my desk in English class, forceful but quiet enough for only us to hear.

Then she stands up, puts on that fake smile and acts like she just asked me a question about something. All rainbows and sunshine. BITCH!!!! Do you believe that? What an overprotective jealous bitch. Like Randy is some kind of possession of hers.

"Don't worry about it. She's more bark than bite," Steph says after I told her and Evelyn.

"If she gets anybody after you, I have friends who can take care of her," Evelyn says.

I laughed, but she's serious.

"She's just afraid of losing Randy," Steph says.

"Why?"

"Who knows? The girl is nuts."

THURSDAY DECEMBER 13, 1984

Tommy and I again at Total Eclipse. Us and a trainee. Mr. Totino has hired a few people to work temporarily for the next few weeks. So I spent most of the time showing the trainee what to do and what's expected. She's not too music smart, but seems nice.

FRIDAY DECEMBER 14, 1984

If you think that bitch threatening me was going to keep me from hanging out with Randy, you are sadly mistaken. He joined me during my babysitting duties. Taylor was so excited. Randy joined him for a video game showdown. He even stayed for dinner. Mom made chicken parmesan. All I had to do was throw it in the oven and make some pasta for a side.

When Taylor got up to set the table, I decided to tell Randy what Michelle said to me the other day. He apologized to me for that.

Mom came home early and joined us for dinner. She started making small talk with Randy. I told her how good he is at football and that he could go pro. He was embarrassed by the flattery, but he said it was true. He hasn't decided where he wants to go to yet. He's been getting many offers. He's weighing all his options.

SATURDAY DECEMBER 15, 1984

All day at work (10am-11pm). I am exhausted and we still have 10 days to go til Christmas. Mr. Totino gave me an extra half hour to do a little Christmas shopping. I've hardly done any yet.

Everywhere was so crowded. I spent 15 minutes shopping and 45 minutes in line. Dinner was a slice of pizza that I grabbed and ate while sprinting back to work.

SUNDAY DECEMBER 16, 1984

Here I am at Randy's house, on his bedroom floor. He stopped in at the end of my shift and asked if I wanted to hang out at his house. Of course I said yes, trying not to sound too enthusiastic.

After dinner we headed to his bedroom to play video games. My heart was pumping so fast. I was in Randy's bedroom. We sat down on his bed. All I could think of at first was taking him and making out on his bed. Needless to say I quickly moved to the floor.

"What the hell are you sitting down there for?" he asked.

"It's more comfortable," I told him, even though it wasn't, but in a different way it was.

MONDAY DECEMBER 17, 1984

Michelle was back in my face again today. This time she had Garrett with her. He grabbed me by the shirt. There was nobody there to help. Mrs. Bartone wasn't there yet and everybody else was in their own little worlds. He raised his fist. I turned to try and avoid the oncoming blow. It didn't come. He just backed away.

"That was a warning," he said, before leaving.

I was a bundle of nerves the whole class. In Gym, I told Evelyn and Steph what happened. Evelyn had had enough of Michelle's shit. Michelle had gotten in Steph's face last Friday.

"Excuse me for a minute," she said, leaving us and jogging up behind Michelle.

Steph and I jogged slowly and watched. Evelyn pushed Michelle, who went stumbling forward. Sabrina, one of the other cheerleaders who were jogging with Michelle, pushed Evelyn. Wrong move. That was it. Girlfight.

Sabrina didn't realize the trouble she just got herself into. She was on the ground in no time flat. Evelyn was smacking the shit out of her. It didn't last long though. Ms. Annasandy came flying over. She got there before we did. She broke them apart and sent them to the office.

I didn't see Evelyn again until French class. She said Sabrina was crying like a baby, lying through her teeth. Principal Angelino wasn't buying it and they both got 2 days in school suspension.

TUESDAY DECEMBER 18, 1984

It was another study night at my house, but it was a quick one. We all agreed to tell our bosses that we would be late today because we had all these projects due Friday. Mr. Totino was cool with it. He agreed to stay until 6. Randy, Steph, Evelyn and I all worked on the French project. Then it was off to work. I grabbed my keys and my stuff, but Randy asked if I wanted to drive in with him.

"Finding a parking space is going to be crazy. Better to have one car than 2," he said.

It's a week before Christmas. The mall is a zoo. No sense in both of us looking for a space, plus I get to ride with Randy in his jeep.

We drive in and he drops me off at the entrance.

"Ok, I'll meet you here at 11:30," he says. He's going to give me a ride home.

"Cool," I say, waving goodbye and heading in. It was freezing outside.

Work was a mob scene. We're running our big sales this week. Twenty-five percent off all Top 40 albums.

8:45 – I've restocked Madonna's "Like a Virgin" album 3 times already

11:20 – The mall closed at 11. I finished everything quickly. I don't want to leave Randy waiting. I set the alarm, pulled down the gate, locked it and am heading out.

<u>12:00</u> – I'm freezing. No sign of him. Where is he? He's probably running late cleaning things up. The stupid security guards won't let me back in.

<u>12:45</u> – I think everyone has left the mall that's going to leave. I can't believe he left me here. What am I going to do now? I can't call mom. She's probably asleep. She'll get all paranoid and then have to wake up Taylor and Alexa and drive out here. Can't have that. I guess I'll have to call a cab.

<u>1:15</u> – Still no cab. They told me they were sending one right away. Time to call them back.

<u>1:30</u> – Busy signals. That's all I've been getting from the cab company for the last 15 minutes. I guess I have to walk. Wish me luck

<u>3:45</u> – I'm home. "Yes mom, I know what time it is. Yes, I know I have school tomorrow. We all just went to the diner and lost track of time. I need to get some sleep. Good night," I said to her while heading to my bedroom. She's still mumbling something. I can hear her through the door.

WEDNESDAY DECEMBER 19, 1984

It's morning. Hmmm, now how should I handle this? Yell? Scream? Beat the crap out of him? With only 3 hours of sleep these are all good options. No, I think I will just remain silent and let him apologize. Off to school.

UNBELIEVEABLE

I get to homeroom and he's not there yet. I was sitting, waiting for my apology. He comes in and what does he do? He smiles and says "Hi".

I couldn't believe this. He turns back to the front, not saying another word.

"You look like hell," I hear Evelyn saying from my right. I didn't see her come in.

"Yeah, I only got 3 hours of sleep last night. I got stuck at the mall. SOMEONE was supposed to drive me home. There were no cabs and I had to walk."

Ding. The light finally went on in his head and he remembered.

"Oh my god. I totally forgot dude. I'm so sorry. Michelle came into the pizza place and started on me...(bullshit, bullshit, bullshit). I'll make it up to you," he says.

"Make it up to me?" I say to myself. How does he expect to do that? I just ignored him. He knows I'm pissed. Homeroom passed and I didn't say a word to him. I ignored him in Gym class too. Now I'm just sitting eating my lunch and...

"So are you ever going to speak to me again?" Randy said, climbing onto the platform.

It's only December and he seems to always be apologizing to me, either for himself or for that bitch girlfriend of his. I accepted his apology. How can I be angry at someone so adorable? But I told him that if he ever did it again I was kicking his ass. He said we had a deal. No more apologizing.

"So what are you going to be doing during Christmas break?" I asked him, hoping to get some air hockey time in.

He said he's spending the break in Connecticut at Michelle's aunt's house.

"What about your family?" I asked.

"Michelle is coming over on the 24th and we're having a big dinner and opening presents. We're heading out early on the 25th and staying in Connecticut until the 1st," he said.

He didn't sound too excited about it.

THURSDAY DECEMBER 20, 1984

Tomorrow is a huge test day. I have a major test in every class except Gym. In Gym we are doing something called the Presidential Physical Fitness Test. I have no idea what that is. It doesn't sound like fun though.

We all went over to study at Evelyn's house. Megan, Stuart and Tommy joined us. We went over to Evelyn's house because her mom is cooking for the holidays. Evelyn's house is going to be completely full. Aunts, uncles, cousins, grandparents and other family and friends are coming over. Her mom wanted us to be the taste testers for some of the food. She was so excited.

Halfway through our study time, her and 2 of Evelyn's aunts brought out all this food. It was all phenomenal. My first taste of Puerto Rican food.

FRIDAY DECEMBER 21, 1984

Oh my God, no more tests...please. My whole body is exhausted. My brain is fried. My hand hurts from writing. My head hurts from all this thinking and my body is sore from that Presidential Fitness thing.

It appears that test is some sort of torture regimen for High School students. Sit-ups, pull-ups, push-ups. After all of that, I just wanted to sit down. I think Nancy Reagan's "Just say No" would be better used here. At the end of class all I wanted to do was say "No".

SATURDAY DECEMBER 22, 1984

Here we are at the last shopping weekend before Christmas. I got to the mall super early so that I didn't have to deal with any traffic or parking. I got a spot right near the entrance.

It was non-stop craziness all day. The line at the registers was so long. The line didn't end until about 10:45, but with all 3 registers going and Tommy at one of them, the line moved quickly.

SUNDAY DECEMBER 23, 1984

Another crazy day at work. All these last minute shoppers. Halfway through the shift, one of the seasonal girls lost it. She started freaking out at all the non-stop people and walked out. Of course she picked the time that the other seasonal girl was on her lunch break. I had to quickly jump on register.

Tommy and I working together got the line down to nothing. By the time she came back from break, the line was small. It stayed steady the rest of the day. I spent the whole rest of the time, restocking shelves and helping people out.

MONDAY DECEMBER 24, 1984

Another round of all day crazy busy at work. Luckily today was an early close, 7 o'clock. Now it's an all-night crazy, getting the house cleaned and ready.

Mom's in the kitchen cooking and baking. Alexa and Taylor are upstairs cleaning their room and I'm taking a break. I just finished cleaning my room and now I'm getting ready to clean the living room.

My Uncle Matt (mom's brother) is coming down from New York City and my grandparents are driving up from Florida. They will all be here tomorrow. My grandparents will be staying for a few days, so everything has to be spotless. Ok, let's get some motivation. MTV time. I'm good to go. Time to clean...oh doorbell.

Steph is here.

"Good, just in time to help clean," I tell her.

"Oh goodie," she says, laughing.

"Your mom still have to work tomorrow?" I ask her. Steph's mom works as a nurse at Mt. Mercy Hospital.

"Yeah. She couldn't get anybody to cover, Christmas and all. So she's going to work a double. She figures if she's going to have to be there anyway, might as well collect on the double-time."

"So what are you going to do about Christmas then?" I ask her. She just shrugs her shoulders.

"You can't spend Christmas by yourself," I continue.

"What do you mean by yourself?" mom says. She overheard what I said. I explained the situation to her.

"Well that settles it then. You're coming over here. I'm not having you spend Christmas alone," mom says. Steph lightly protested, but mom wasn't having it...

"One more is not a problem. You're coming."

Steph looked at me. I just shrugged my shoulders.

"Thank you Mrs. Parker. Can I bring anything?" Steph asked.

"Uhm...yes...yourself," mom joked, heading back into the kitchen.

Steph and I laughed and then went back to finish cleaning the living room.

TUESDAY DECEMBER 25, 1984

MERRY CHRISTMAS!!!!!!

"It's Christmas Josh. Get up! Get up!"

I open my eyes to see Alexa jumping up and down on my bed. I look right at her. "What time is it?"

"I don't know. Come downstairs," she says.

I look over at the clock. 6:05 am. I should have known. Last night mom told Taylor and Alexa no earlier than 6. I can just picture them up earlier, looking at the clock, watching the minutes tick by, trying to will the time to move faster. I get up and head downstairs, wondering if mom is up.

"Wait! Not until I have my coffee," I hear mom yell from the kitchen. She's up. Mom's a wreck in the morning before she has her coffee.

Taylor and Alexa are standing there looking at all the presents under the tree. Mom said she wanted a big Christmas and she got one. We have a huge 7 foot tree. The angel on top has to bend a little so her halo doesn't touch the ceiling. I reach over and plug in the tree. The multi colored lights twinkle. I catch a look at my reflection in one of the glass balls. I look like a nightmare.

"Come here," I say to my brother and sister, who are driving me nuts with their sighing. The temptation is killing them. I have them both sit down and I hand them each a present.

"Don't open it until mom gets here," I tell them.

Ten minutes later, an eternity for my siblings, mom came into the living room. Before she could even sit down, they ripped into the first presents.

I continued playing Santa. Mom outdid herself on the presents too. Taylor and Alexa are so excited.

 By 6:30, they've torn through all the wrappings and every present is open. Mom and I take a little longer to open ours. When I was done, I let them play with their toys as I went from designated Santa to designated clean-up crew.

At 7 o'clock our first visitors arrive. Harry and Elaine Wright (aka grandma and grandpa) are here. Mom answered the door. Big hugs. Taylor and Alexa drop what they're doing to run and say hello. Also to wonder what's in the bags they're carrying.

"Josh, go get their luggage from the car," mom asks.

I give my grandparents quick hugs and head out to get the bags. They're going to be staying in my room while they're here. I'm sleeping on the couch. It's fine with me, late night MTV watching.

Of course as I come back downstairs, Grandpa has to comment about what's on the TV. MTV is on, of course.

"How can you watch this junk?" he says.

"How can you watch Lawrence Welk?" I say right back.

"Lawrence Welk, well that's music, not this garbage."

"You two," mom says laughing.

My grandfather and I have this fun bond. We like to kid around with each other. He makes fun of Boy George; I make fun of Lawrence Welk.

Grandpa shakes his head, laughing. "Old people," I say, patting him on the back. He heads into the kitchen to help my mom. Grandma is talking with Alexa, listening as she tells her everything that Santa got her. I just grab the presents they brought for me and sit down on the couch, singing along with the new Foreigner song. "I want to know what love is. I want you to show me..."

11 o'clock---Guest # 2 arrival

The whole house is quiet, except for the sounds of MTV. Mom and grandma are in the kitchen cooking. Taylor and Alexa are on the living room floor asleep. Grandpa is in my room taking a nap. Of course upon entering my room, he couldn't help but comment about my cassettes "Waste of money. I'll give you 5 cents apiece for them." Or the posters on the wall "Oh look at this one. He needs a haircut, looks just like a girl."

With everyone preoccupied, I get up to answer the door. It's Steph. She's carrying presents and a cake she made for the day.

"Merry Christmas," I say giving her a quick kiss.

"I needed to bring something. I feel bad," she says.

"It's cool," I tell her.

"Who was at the door?!" mom yells from the kitchen.

"It's Steph," I yell back.

"Merry Christmas Stephanie!" mom yells, having a conversation with my best friend through the kitchen door.

I helped Steph with her coat and brought the cake in to my mom. My grandma had this funny smile on her face. I can just imagine what she's thinking, visions of girlfriend for Josh in her head.

"Sit," I say, directing Steph to the couch as I go to the tree to search for her presents.

"So what did you get for Christmas?" she asks me.

"Well, Alexa made me this, (Alexa made me this colorful pinwheel thing). Taylor got me a sweater. I'm sure my mom picked it out. My mom got me some new jeans, a new pair of sneakers, the Stevie Nicks shirt I was searching forever for; don't ask me how she found it, oh and a note "The holder of this card is entitled to 2 tickets to the concert of his choice". Uhm, my grandparents gave me the usual grandparent things, although my grandfather slipped me some cash and told me not to spend it on cassettes, even though he knows that's exactly what I'm going to spend it on. He doesn't mind, as long as he gets to complain about it later."

"Oh here they are."

Over to the couch I go. I hand Steph her presents and she hands me mine.

Well it seems we know each other too well. We got each other the exact same things, a Madonna shirt, poster and buttons. Even the buttons are the same. We just laugh at the fun of it.

1 o'clock---next guest

The old people are all in the kitchen. The kids are upstairs in their room playing with their toys. They were being noisy so I told them to go play in their room.

"C'mon Alexa, he just wants to be alone with his girrrlllllfriend," the little smartass says. I chased them both upstairs. As I come back down the stairs, the doorbell rings. I go and answer it.

"Uncle Matt!!" I say excitedly.

My uncle is so cool. It's so great seeing him. I haven't seen him since Thanksgiving 1983. Although he does send cards and presents on birthdays and holidays and makes the occasional phone call, I hardly get to see him. But now here he is. Matt is mom's younger brother. He's 33, maybe 34. I forget. I remember dad not liking him for some reason.

"How's it going kiddo? You wanna help me out here?" he says.

He's bogged down with lots of presents and food. I grab the bags of food and invite him in.

"Nice place...Where's your mom?" he asks.

"In the kitchen with grandma and grandpa." When I say this, he makes a face.

"They're here?" he says disgustedly.

Before I can ask him what's wrong, grandpa comes out of the kitchen. He spots Uncle Matt. They just stare at each other.

"Matthew."

"Dad."

No hugs, nothing. That's all they say to each other. That and they stare and then my grandfather goes back into the kitchen. Uncle Matt shakes his head. I go to ask, but he changes the subject.

"So who is this?" he says smiling, looking at Steph. I introduce them and then head into the kitchen with the food. These bags are heavy.

When I entered the kitchen, I could sense something was up, although I didn't know what. You could feel the tension in the air. They all got quiet. I dropped the food off with mom and headed back out. Uncle Matt was on the couch watching MTV and talking with Steph.

"So how are..." I start saying.

"Shhh," he says cutting me off. "Madonna," he says, pointing at the TV. The new Madonna video "Like a Virgin" has just come on. I laugh and sit down and watch with them.

Alexa and Taylor must have finally realized Uncle Matt is here. They come running down the steps. Without saying a word or taking his eyes off the video, he gives them quick hugs and points to the presents. My uncle always gets us the coolest presents. They take off right for them. Mom then comes out of the kitchen. He holds up his finger, signaling one minute.

"Get over here," mom says laughing.

Uncle Matt laughs and gets up. They hug and kiss. Even though mom is 6 years older, they have a strong bond.

"We'll be eating around 2," mom announces to us. Steph and I mumble "Ok". We're still watching the video. Uncle Matt rejoins us on the couch. The video ends and the obnoxious blond VJ comes on. He's making some lame Christmas jokes.

"Oh man, I just can't get enough of her. The new album is so great," Uncle Matt says. Then he reaches over and tosses my present onto my lap.

"So you going to open your present or what?" he says

"Thank you." I say, laughing as I open it.

It's a rectangular box. I break the tape on the side and open it up. Inside are 7 cassettes. Of course my eyes go wide. I'm super excited. Bryan Adams, Foreigner, Duran Duran, REO Speedwagon, Eurythmics, Julian Lennon and Frankie Goes to Hollywood.

"I hope you don't have any of these. I kept checking back with your mother. She says you seem to buy cassettes all the time," he says.

"Well that explains why you've been asking me about cassettes the past 2 weeks," I say, turning to mom.

"I called the other day and bought these yesterday," he says.

"No, I don't have any of these. Thank you," I said.

Dinner Time

On big holidays we eat at 2 o'clock. You have a big meal, relax and digest and then later you go back and eat whenever you want.

So now we're all seated around the dining room table. My mom is at one end and my grandfather is at the other end. Grandma is to his left and Taylor is to his right. Uncle Matt is seated to mom's right and I am to her left. Steph is seated next to me and Alexa is next to Uncle Matt. Everyone is quiet, so mom decides to break the ice.

"So how's the job going?" she asks my uncle.

Uncle Matt works for some big international company in Manhattan.

"Great. Business is up. Just so busy busy busy...Oh, speaking of that, Josh, with your foreign language knowledge you might want to think about interning there next summer. We do a lot of foreign business. It'd be great experience for you. You can see New York, get a feel for the marketplace and if you want you can stay with me so that you don't have to commute back and forth all the time," he said.

"Over my dead body," my grandfather snaps.

"Dad," mom says to him.

"My grandson is not going to stay with you and your fruit friends," he says, pointing his fork at Uncle Matt, ignoring my mother.

"Dad!" mom says more forcefully.

"What? You want him living there? What if he turns into one of them?"

I then understood why dad didn't like Uncle Matt. Uncle Matt must be gay too. I was so embarrassed, knowing Steph was hearing all of this. Uncle Matt couldn't take anymore.

"There you go dad, being a narrow minded piece of..."

"Don't you yell at your father. We raised you right and you go and hurt us like this," my grandmother said, cutting my uncle off.

"Not in front of the children," mom said, trying to calm everyone down.

"Let it go please," she said softly, grabbing my uncle's hand.

Steph and I knew what was going on. Taylor and Alexa were just staring, wondering what all the yelling was about. Alexa looked like she was about to cry. Grandma took her hand to calm her down.

"I just lost my appetite," my grandfather grumbled, standing up. At this point, Mom lost it.

"Sit down! Nobody leaves this table. It's Christmas. So I want everybody to put their differences aside. Got it? We're all going to be the freakin Cosbys today...even if it kills us."

My grandfather sat back down. Everybody became quiet and we all finished dinner.

Dinner was cleared from the table and my mother and grandmother set up the desserts. We all returned, got what we wanted and headed in different directions. My mother, grandmother, brother and sister stayed at the table. Grandpa grabbed a couple of cookies and went upstairs to take another nap. Steph, Uncle Matt and I went back to the couch and MTV.

A few minutes later, Uncle Matt got up and put on his jacket. He grabbed my jacket and tossed it at me, signaling me to head outside. I wonder what he wants to talk about. It has to be important if he wants to go outside. Is he going to tell me he's gay? Maybe it's about the internship. We head out to his rental car, which is parked on the street in front of the house.

"Sit down. Take a load off," he says.

I jump up on the hood. He joins me.

"I really appreciate the offer..." I start to say before he cuts me off.

"That's cool, but I need to talk to you about something else."

"Oh man, he's going to talk to me about him being gay. This is going to be weird," I think to myself.

"Ok shoot," I say to him.

"The other day when I called to ask about the cassettes, your mother asked me to talk to you."

"About what?" ("Here it comes")

"Man, how do I put this? Alright, I'll come straight out and say it. Are you gay?"

"You're ga...wait what? NO! Jesus, mom asked you to ask me that?"

I got off the car and started heading back to the house.

"She's worried about you..." Uncle Matt called to me. I stopped.

"... She's seen how it's affected me and..." he said, continuing.

"She knows? How?" I said, cutting him off.

"Your mom is a smart woman. They say a mother always knows."

"Did grandma know about you?"

"God no," he says laughing. "Well if she did she wasn't saying."

"When did you tell her?"

"I didn't. One day she walked into my room and caught me making out with my friend Paul. Oh man, you should have seen the look on her face. You know how white your grandmother is. Well she turned 10 shades whiter. I thought she was gonna pass out."

"That's probably what Mom's going to do," I say, interrupting him.

"Don't underestimate your mother. She had a feeling you were gay. If it freaked her out, she probably would have confronted you by now. Trust me, your mom will understand. She may not be too happy about it at first, but you know what she always says. She loves you no matter what."

"When I came out to her 16 years ago, I was just like you are now and she told me those words. That's the kind of woman your mother is. She's the first person I told and she's the first one there to stand up for me. When your grandmother found me that day, she and your grandfather kicked me out. I had turned 18 the week before. Your parents were married and you were just a baby. Your mom said I could stay with you guys until I had enough money to move out on my own. I had some money saved and was planning to move out soon anyway, so I would only have to stay there for a little while. Your mom didn't mind. She liked having me there, somebody to help take care of you. Your dad didn't mind either. We would hang out, watch sports, have a few beers. Everything was going great...until your father found out from your grandfather why I got kicked out."

"Your mom knew the real reason and she kept diverting your grandparents from having your dad find out. He just thought I had a big argument with them and got kicked out."

"It was your birthday and there was a little party at your house. Your grandparents didn't know where I had gone and didn't care. They said they couldn't make it to your party, so it wasn't going to be a problem. Well surprise surprise, their original plans got cancelled and they showed up. Your father flipped when your grandfather told him. A homosexual around his son. He went right up to your mother and wanted me out. Your mom wasn't going to be like your grandparents and kick me out."

"They got into some wicked fights about it. He wouldn't speak to me and if he was home, I was not allowed anywhere near you. He would do all this macho stuff with you, G.I. Joes, football, baseball...you were 2."

"One weekend your father left and went to stay with his parents. He took you and said he wasn't coming back until I was gone. He was making her choose between him and me. I told her I would go, but she wouldn't have it. I didn't have as much money as I wanted, but the next night I snuck out and moved to New York City, where I've been ever since."

" I would stop over on birthdays and certain holidays, but after a while it was too much, dealing with your father and grandparents. His parents were worse than mine. So I stayed away, which was wrong for you guys. That Thanksgiving when I last saw you was rough, your father and grandfather hanging out with your dad's friends, making gay jokes. They wouldn't say anything around you guys. Your mother would have killed them."

"Your mom, like I said, has been so cool with it. She's met a few of my friends. She's listened to me bitch and cry when my relationships ended. Trust me, she'll be there for you, just like she's there for me, probably even more so. Do yourself a favor though and don't tell your grandparents. The less they know the better. Let them live in their fantasy world. Besides, they'd probably just blame me for it."

We got off the car and headed back to the house.

"Oh before I forget," he says, motioning me to sit down on the porch steps. "I have something else for you. I didn't want to leave it in the box for everyone else to see. It's a little gay."

He reaches into his pocket and pulls out a cassette. The cover says "Bronski Beat. Age of Consent". As he's handing it to me, Steph comes out of the house. Uncle Matt hides the cassette.

"It's ok. She knows," I tell him.

"She knows? And she's ok with it?" he says.

I nod my head yes

"Lucky you. I wish I had a friend who knew and understood when I was in school."

"I have 2," I say laughing.

"You little bitch," he says, laughing back, pulling the cassette back out.

"This cassette is popular now in England. It hasn't really hit here yet. They're called Bronski Beat. They're really cool. A few of their songs are gay oriented, so listen to them with the headphones on, concentrating on the lyrics. It's an awesome album."

I hug him, thanking him for the cassette and the talk.

"Anytime kiddo. You call and talk to me anytime you want. Call collect if you have to."

The door opens again. This time it's Mom.

"What are you guys doing out here in the cold?" she asks.

"Talking," Uncle Matt says to her. I see him give her a little nod.

We took this time to get back up. Uncle Matt went over to Steph, who has been standing a little ways away. He hugs her goodbye.

"Take good care of him. He's a great guy. He's going to need his friends."

He whispered this to her, but I still heard it and smiled. He then left and went inside. I walked Steph out to her car, thanking her for the presents and for coming. She wants to go down to the hospital and spend some time with her mom.

"Hopefully it won't be too hectic and she'll be able to take a break," Steph says.

I hugged her goodbye, telling her to wish her mom a Merry Christmas for me. She hugged me back and thanked my mom, who was still standing on the porch.

I waved goodbye as her car drove out. Then I walked back towards mom. She was sitting down on the porch steps. I went and sat next to her. I turned towards her and couldn't say anything. We just stared at each other, neither of us able to say a word, but we each knew what the other was thinking.

I just started crying. I felt the tears running down my face, then I saw that she was crying too. She went and hugged me.

"Shhh, it's going to be alright. I love you no matter what. I want you to remember that. You come to me for anything...anything, ok?" she said, rocking me.

I just nodded my head, hugging her tighter.

WEDNESDAY DECEMBER 26, 1984

Back to work. All these after Christmas shoppers. Plus all the pissed off people. These are the type of customers that make me hate people.

All of our cassettes are wrapped in plastic. We always have signs up saying that we will not accept returned cassettes that are out of the wrapping, except for exact exchanges, even with a receipt.

Since November, Mr. Totino has had extra ones of these signs posted everywhere. Many customers are leaving angry when I tell them they can't get their money back. Luckily Mr. Totino was here for most of the day to handle them.

THURSDAY DECEMBER 27, 1984

Mom was pissed that I had to work all day yesterday. She knew my schedule at the beginning of the month. Because my grandparents were down, she wanted me to be home. There was no way I was going to be able to get the whole end of the month off. I had to beg Mr. Totino last week to give me the 31st and 1st off. He wasn't going to be able to give me the 26th-28th off too. I had to be at work at 4 today, so I spent the whole morning and part of the afternoon with the grandparents.

FRIDAY DECEMBER 28, 1984

"Don't even think of doing anything else tomorrow before work," mom said to me yesterday before I went to work.

Mom was off from work. Today was a whole day with the family. Grandma and grandpa are leaving tomorrow, so we all needed to be there. It was a fun afternoon of lunch and some bowling with the family. My grandmother is hilarious when she bowls. She's one of those "stand there and roll the ball between her legs" bowlers. Grandpa and I spent the whole time joking around. They were then heading out to dinner, but I had to leave for work.

SATURDAY DECEMBER 29, 1984

Said goodbye to the grandparents this morning. They were leaving after lunch, but I had to work a double. Grandpa slipped me a $20 bill as he shook my hand. I just smiled and shook my head. It was so great seeing them both again, but it's also great having my bedroom back.

SUNDAY DECEMBER 30, 1984

Halfway through work I started feeling real tired.

"No no no, no getting sick."

"You don't look good," mom said the instant I got home.

"I'm fine," I told her.

"Come here," she said, feeling my head. "You feel warm."

"I bought medicine." I told her I was going to take some and lay down. I'm so tired. I'm going to stop here and take a nap. I'll write more when I wake up.

MONDAY DECEMBER 31, 1984

Didn't write more because I didn't wake up from the nap. The nap turned into full sleep. I woke up at 10 this morning. I was hoping I would be better. Mom came into my room and took my temperature (102), so I had to go to the doctor, who told me to stay home and rest.

NO! NO! NO!

Evelyn is the DJ at Masquerade tonight, well for 2 hours at least. They are having rotating DJ's. Everybody is going to be there. That's why I begged for the days off.

The doctor prescribed this medicine. I don't want to take it. I know it will knock me out. I told mom I needed some lunch first. She made me some soup and a grilled cheese sandwich. I wolfed it down and then took the medicine, hoping to wake up in time, feeling better. I want to go out tonight.

TUESDAY JANUARY 1, 1985

"HAPPY NEW YEAR."

It's midnight...and where am I? On the couch. I can't believe I'm still sick. Everybody is probably out having a great time at Masquerade, but me. I'm wrapped in a blanket, sipping hot tea, watching the ball drop on the boring old television. Mom let Taylor and Alexa sleep over friend's houses so they don't catch anything.

Steph called today to check up on me. I was asleep when she called. Mom told her what was up and she wanted to come over. Mom told her it was best not to. No need for her to possibly catch something.

Speaking of the crazy lady, Mom had gotten a ticket for this fancy ball that everybody from her job was going to tonight. She bought a new dress and everything, but wasn't going to go because of me.

"I'll be fine. Go," I said.

"It's ok. I'm staying," she said.

"You're going," I said more forcefully.

She still refused to budge on this, so I got up from the couch and threw the blanket on the floor.

"Where are you going?" she asked.

"I'm going upstairs to change. If you're not going out then I'm going out," I said.

She gave me this look. She knew I was serious.

"Stubborn!" was all she could say.

"I don't want to see you until tomorrow morning. Go have fun," I said, returning to the couch, pulling the blanket back over myself.

She left a little while ago. God I hate being sick.

WEDNESDAY JANUARY 2, 1985

I was feeling better, but Mom wanted me to stay home and rest some more, so I didn't go to school. I called Steph before she left for school. I wanted to hang out with her later. We're going to meet at the mall. I spent the day watching music videos.

Just as I was about to leave and head out to the mall, Steph called and cancelled our "date". She didn't say why. I guess I will find out tomorrow.

THURSDAY JANUARY 3, 1985

Found out why she broke off our "date". She's got a new boyfriend, Justin something. She met him at Masquerade on New Year's. Evelyn says he's "cute cute cute".

FRIDAY JANUARY 4, 1985

Came home from school and ran up the stairs to quickly change. I was meeting Tommy at the movies at 4. We were seeing "Johnny Dangerously".

I was rushing because I always like to get to the movies early. One of my pet peeves are people who want to go to the movies with me, but get there less than 15 minutes before the movie starts. I like to be there early. That way you can get your ticket, get your popcorn and get a decent seat and relax before the movie starts.

I'm all changed and rushing down the steps when Mom calls my name.

"I gotta go," I tell her.

She's got the phone in her hand and that look on her face.

"Wish your grandmother a happy birthday," she says, covering the phone.

I quickly rushed over and wished her a happy birthday. My grandmother loves to talk when she's on the phone. I enjoy talking to my grandmother. I really do, but today I had to go. It took me 15 minutes to finish. I said goodbye and raced out the door, meeting Tommy 10 minutes before the movie started.

SATURDAY JANUARY 5, 1985

Steph and I met each other during our work break. I finally got her to tell me more about Justin. In school, she's been real quiet about him.

"You'll get to meet him tonight. Let's all hang out," she said.

Well it won't be tonight. She came in at the end of my shift saying that there was a change of plans and that she had to meet Justin and some of his friends at some party.

"So when am I going to meet him?" I said.

"Soon," she said, blowing me a kiss. "We'll hang out tomorrow. I promise," she said over her shoulder before heading out.

SUNDAY JANUARY 6, 1985

So much for that promise. Once again she broke our "date" to go spend time with Justin. At first I was upset, but she seems really excited about him and I want her to be happy.

MONDAY JANUARY 7, 1985

Mom needed me to babysit tonight. I asked Steph to join me for another movie night at the house. She had to pass. Randy came over though, so movie night became video game night.

TUESDAY JANUARY 8, 1985

Another attempt at hanging out with Steph and Justin, but once again she had to cancel. I don't know, things just seem weird now. He seems kind of controlling. Always stuff with his friends but never with her friends. Evelyn hasn't even had a chance to hang out with her.

WEDNESDAY JANUARY 9, 1985

Steph broke off a date with Justin and his friends to spend some time with me. She said he seemed pissed, but she felt bad not hanging out with me. It felt so good hanging out with her. Arcade time and then some dinner. We talked about our SAT scores. I got mine back today (1350). Steph hasn't gotten hers back. Probably tomorrow.

THURSDAY JANUARY 10, 1985

Steph was all frazzled in school today. Something was up and she wasn't talking. We told her we would cancel studying tonight. Evelyn and I couldn't stay long anyway, but Steph wouldn't have it. She didn't want to cancel.

I get to her house and see that she's still a mess. Evelyn told me what's up. She's no longer with Justin. Seems after she left hanging out with me, she went over to his house and caught him with another girl. On top of that, her SAT scores came back today. She got a 1200. She felt that she did better and now she thinks her whole future is shot. Evelyn and I have tried calming her down.

Evelyn just left for work. I have to leave soon, but I am waiting until Randy gets here. I don't want her to be alone right now. Now what is she doing?

"What are you looking for?" I ask her. She's running all around, going through books and papers and not answering me. Oh thank God, Randy's here.

"She's a little upset. She just broke up with Justin and she thinks her SAT scores are too low. Just tell her she has nothing to worry about. I gotta go. I can't be late," I whisper to him. I then kissed Steph goodbye, hoping that Randy can calm her down and make things better.

FRIDAY JANUARY 11, 1985

Something happened over Steph's house yesterday. She's not any calmer today. In fact she seems worse. She's not telling me. Randy's not talking to me either. In Gym class, every time I was talking to her and Randy passed by or turned towards us, she would start to panic.

"Did something happen between you and Randy?" I ask her

"No." she says.

Randy didn't climb up to see me during break or lunch, so I couldn't ask him. She must have told Evelyn sometime during the day, because most of the day she didn't know what was up, but during French class she was acting just as weird. Randy and Steph weren't in class. Whatever is going on involves Steph and either me and or Randy. But what? Why aren't they telling me? I'll just have to talk to Steph tomorrow during our break at work.

SATURDAY JANUARY 12, 1985

"WHAT THE HELL!!?!!"

"Can't today. I'm busy," Steph says as I meet her at Bingle Bangle Bongle for our lunch break. She never says she's busy, plus there's hardly anybody in the store.

"I'll see you after work," I say angrily, before heading back to work. I spent the rest of the day at work wondering what was going on.

"She left early. Said she had to go. Left 15 minutes ago," her boss said as I arrived at the end of my shift.

I got home and started calling her. Still no word back from her. I've left tons of messages on her machine. She won't return my calls.

SUNDAY JANUARY 13, 1985

Had to work an open to close. Steph was off from work. After work, I tried calling her again, leaving more messages. Getting no response, I decided to give Evelyn and Randy a try. No answer from them either. More messages. Come tomorrow, this will be settled. The first one of the three I see will not get away until I know what's going on.

MONDAY JANUARY 14, 1985

NOW WHICH ONE WILL IT BE

Right as I got out of my car, I saw Randy. He was heading into school, but he was with Michelle. He sees me coming and quickly runs inside.

"You won't be able to run away from me in Homeroom," I think as I enter the school.

"Not here yet," I notice as I enter and take my seat...ah, here comes Evelyn.

"What's going on?" I say, looking straight at her.

"Don't worry, everything is fine. You just need to talk to Steph," she says.

"What about Randy?" I ask.

"Talk to Steph."

GYM CLASS

I'm sitting on the gym floor. The cold gym floor. All I'm thinking is "Don't we have any heat in this place?" I'm waiting for Steph. I watch her come out of the girl's locker room. She doesn't head to her seat. I watch her go over to Randy. This was good. I can talk to them both at the same time. I got up and headed over. Randy sees me coming and takes off for his seat.

"What the hell?"

I turned to Steph, ready to yell, when what does she do? She smiles and starts acting as if nothing happened the past few days. She goes to hug me and I lightly push her away.

"What the hell is going on?" I angrily ask her.

"I'm sorry. I've just been so upset over the break-up and then the SATs and then I got my period," she says.

I can sense that she's lying, but there's no way I can get it out of her without causing problems.

TUESDAY JANUARY 15, 1985

So things have sort of returned to normal with Steph and Evelyn but not really with Randy. He seems to have returned to the way he was when I first met him, occasionally saying "hi", but other than that, ignoring me. And not a very caring "hi" at that.

WEDNESDAY JANUARY 16, 1985

Another sort of normal day at school. I tried talking to Randy today, but he didn't really say much, just mumbling. Maybe once we're all together at the study group, things can get better.

"I just can't believe them."

It was Evelyn, Steph and I at her house. No Randy. Then there was a knock on the door, so I was glad he was there, but it wasn't him. It was Tommy.

"What's up?" I asked him.

"I invited him. He's having trouble in French," Steph said.

Tommy is in French III, so I took some time to help him out. Everything seems ok, then out of the blue, Steph goes...

"So when are we going to play air hockey."

"I love air hockey," Tommy says.

"Josh is really good. Nobody can really beat him. You might want to try sometime," Steph says.

"I'm free now," he says, all excited.

I'm sitting there listening to this. They sounded so fake. What the hell are they up to? She was shoving me out the door and using Tommy to do it.

Tommy was grabbing his jacket. My eyes were going all over, staring at all of them. I was angry. I grabbed my jacket and headed out the door. Tommy followed.

"So should we…" he started saying right as we got outside.

I stared at him, slowly shaking my head. He stopped mid-sentence as I turned and walked away. He watched as I got in my car and drove away. I can't believe them.

THURSDAY JANUARY 17, 1985

I was in no mood for any of them today and they all knew it.

"How was your hockey game?" Steph said as I was getting out of my car.

I ignored her and kept walking. When I walked into Homeroom, I saw Evelyn and Randy talking. They both looked up and saw me. I turned and walked out. I just didn't want to deal with any of them.

"I'm sorry," Tommy says as I'm walking to Gym.

I didn't want to deal with him, so I just walked past him. He caught up to me.

"Look, Steph asked me to do it," he said.

"Why?" I asked him.

"I don't know."

"Well that doesn't make it right," I said, once again walking away from him. This time he didn't follow.

Gym was going to be harder for me to ignore them. I spent the warm-up exercise time talking to Megan and Stuart.

"What's wrong?" Steph would occasionally ask, but I ignored her. Megan knew something was wrong, but chose not to ask.

"Stop acting like this. Tell me what's wrong," Steph says, catching up and jogging with me.

"Oh you want to know what's wrong? I'll tell you what's wrong," I think to myself. It was time for the drama queen to come out.

"I'm sick of all the bullshit. Everything seems fine and then all of a sudden nobody wants to talk to me. Then you go and act as if nothing happened...and what the hell was that weird thing sending me away to play air hockey with Tommy? If I'm such a problem for you to have around, then I'll just stay away. I thought we were friends."

She didn't say anything, so I stopped and sat down on the bleachers.

"Just stay away from me," I said.

She went back to jogging. I just laid down on the bleachers, pretending I had a stomach cramp. I left Gym and went to my secret spot. I didn't want to see any of them today.

HAPPY BIRTHDAY LITTLE BROTHER

When I got home from school, I helped Mom get some things ready. Taylor's birthday is today, but his party is this Saturday. The plan was to give him a cake and presents today, so that he didn't suspect the surprise party Mom had planned. Well, Mom told Alexa about the party and the little munchkin blabbed, so it's not a surprise anymore. Taylor still doesn't know about the corniness Mom has planned. I can't believe I'm going to help her.

He loved his cake and presents. Time to go rest in my room and calm down from all the drama of this afternoon. Sheena Easton, take me away.

"Josh!!!" Mom screams from downstairs, breaking the sounds of Sheena's "Sugar Walls".

"What?!" I say, getting up and opening my door. I see Steph coming up the steps. I rolled my eyes, turned around and went back into my room.

"Cut out all the drama," she says.

"You cut out all the drama," I tell her.

She goes and sits down on my bed. I'm pacing around my room.

"I'm sorry about everything. Randy's in some weird mood about you. I don't know why. I think it has to do with Michelle. I just wanted him to come over, but he wouldn't if you were there, so I made up the air hockey thing to get you to go... (I was shaking my head)...It was a stupid thing to do and I'll never do it again. You come first," she says. Then she comes up and hugs me. "Forgive me?" she asks, breaking apart and looking at me.

I forgave her and we hugged again. As we were hugging, Mom knocked on the side of the door. We broke apart.

"Steph, what are you doing Saturday?" Mom asked, all bubbly and perky. She had a script in her hand.

"Just say no. Just say no," I kept repeating to Steph, laughing.

"You shut up," Mom said to me.

"I'm free," Steph told her.

"How would you like to help Josh and I with what I have planned for Taylor's party?"

"Sure."

Mom was so happy. She handed Steph the script and then headed back downstairs. As Steph was reading the script, I just had to ask her. "So, do you have a crush on Randy?"

"Shut up. You're just as bad," she said, laughing.

"I am not."

FRIDAY JANUARY 18, 1985

Had to head straight to the mall after school. I was working tonight, but mom gave me a list of things she needed me to pick up for Taylor's party tomorrow. It was pretty much just a lot of cheesy decorations. So I had to shop. I also took the time to get him a card and another present.

SATURDAY JANUARY 19, 1985

Steph and I are back to normal. We're sitting here enjoying Taylor's second birthday cake of the week. We just finished the corniness. It went over well.

My brother is a big Star Wars fan. So that meant that the party had to be Star Wars themed. Steph came over and helped Mom and I decorate the whole living room in a Star Wars motif. The cake was a giant light saber for crying out loud. Way over the top.

Then came the skit. Mom came out as Obie Wan, calling Taylor up to play "Taylor Skywalker", Luke's younger brother. I was Han Solo and Steph was Princess Leia. While Steph and I were having our scene with Taylor, Mom went and changed into Darth Vader and had a light saber fight with Taylor, totally dorky, but Taylor and everybody else loved it.

SUNDAY JANUARY 20, 1985

Another all day shift at work. Mr. Totino had to leave early, so I had to close up. No problem. Things have started slowing down already. Tommy and I hung out and closed together.

MONDAY JANUARY 21, 1985

Now that Steph and I are back on good terms, it was time to try and get back on good terms with Randy. There was no reason for him to act like a jerk to me because of the Bitch. I made an attempt in Homeroom. I was there early and watched him come in.

"Hi Randy," I said as he took his seat.

He mumbled something, ignoring me again. So I lightly smacked him on the back of the head.

"What the hell's your problem?" he says, turning around.

"You are," I said jokingly. "Why aren't you talking to me anymore?" I asked as he turned forward.

"I've been busy and Michelle's getting testy...

Evelyn entered at this time

...So did you hear about the party at Sabrina's?" he says to her, ignoring me and changing the subject.

"Don't change the subject," I snapped at him

He still ignored me, shaking his head and rolling his eyes. Before Evelyn could answer his question, I turned to her...

"I know you know what's going on. Tell me."

I could tell she wanted to, but couldn't bring herself to do it. Let's see how the study group goes tonight.

Study group was only Steph, Evelyn and I. No Randy. The whole time I kept looking at the door, hoping he would knock. We didn't have much time to study. We all had to work tonight. We're all meeting again tomorrow. Big French project due at the end of the week.

TUESDAY JANUARY 22, 1985

At first it was just Steph, Evelyn and I again at the study group. Evelyn kept looking my way. She wanted to tell me what was going on, but she wouldn't with Steph there. There was a knock on the door. Steph went to answer it, so it was now my chance.

"OK, no Steph or Randy around. What's going on?" I say to Evelyn.

She still seemed nervous about wanting to tell me. She kept looking towards the door. She's finally about to when Randy comes in and they start walking our way. He sees me and starts to leave.

"What the hell?" I think to myself.

Steph is talking to him. I wish I could hear what they're saying. Well, I guess he's staying. Here they come.

He's been here for 30 minutes. I can't take this anymore. He's acting like he doesn't want to be here. Steph is starting to get uncomfortable.

I LEFT

"I'm out of here," I said, standing up. I grabbed my jacket and headed to the door. Steph ran after me, catching up to me just as I got to the door.

"Please stay," she said.

"I'll study on my own."

"I want you to stay."

"No," I said, shaking my head.

"Why?"

"Look, there's some little secret you guys have and I don't feel wanted. So you can just study without me. Have fun," I said loud enough for all of them to hear.

WEDNESDAY JANUARY 23, 1985

Steph tried to talk to me today about yesterday's study group.

"I want you to study with us," she said.

"I love you and we can still be friends, but regardless, I'm going to study on my own," I answered.

"Please."

"Tell me what the big secret is..."

She stood there silent. She was lightly biting her lower lip. Nothing.

"...I'll study on my own," I say, shaking my head and walking away.

With all this drama I needed arcade time. So when I got home from school...

"Yo little brother, wanna go to the arcade?"

"Yeah," he says, jumping up from the couch to get ready.

We got to the arcade and he wanted to play video games, but I wanted to play some air hockey first.

"Victory," I say, winning the game.

"Where are you going?" I ask him.

He doesn't answer. He was heading to the front of the arcade. Then I saw where he was going. Randy just came in with his little brother. All I was thinking was if Randy treats Taylor the way he's been treating me, I'd kick his ass.

I approached and saw that they were getting along the way they always have.

"You want to play some games?" Adam says to Taylor. Taylor turns to me. I know what he wants.

"Where's your birthday money?" I ask.

"I spent it. I'll pay you back," he says.

There's no way he'll have the money to pay me back for a while, but I didn't care. I hand him a $5 bill and tell him to get change and give me half.

He leaves with Adam, which leaves me there alone with Randy. He just keeps looking around. He wouldn't look at me. We watch Taylor and Adam returning.

"You want to play air hockey?" I say to Randy, trying to break the tension.

"Uhm…nah…I gotta go," he says.

He didn't have to go. He had a roll of quarters in his hand.

"I'll be back," he says to Adam and then he's gone. Now I had all new anger for the games. I never played so well.

FUCK HIM!

THURSDAY JANUARY 24, 1985

Steph and Randy had a study time today. Evelyn had to work, so it was just the two of them. I managed to get the project finished on my own.

FRIDAY JANUARY 25, 1985

Report card day #2. Once again all A's and one B. Of course the B is in History.

Taylor's grades slipped this marking period. No F's, but one D and a few C's. So he's being punished. No video games until mom makes sure that all his homework is done and mom quizzes him to make sure he's studied for tests.

SATURDAY JANUARY 26, 1985

Steph called out from work today, so we didn't get to have our lunch break. It wouldn't have mattered anyway, I was by myself at the store for most of the morning. Mr. Totino had to go run errands and the girl he hired to be on-call didn't show up. I got Tommy to come in a little early and we handled everything.

SUNDAY JANUARY 27, 1985

After work I grabbed Taylor to go for a ride in the Mustang before dinner, making sure that all his homework was done. It was. We were heading out, when mom yelled from the kitchen.

"No letting him drive...and no ice cream before dinner."

Taylor and I looked at each other. Neither of us said anything to her about those days.

"Psychic mom," we said at the same time.

MONDAY JANUARY 28, 1985

In school today, Tommy asked if I could pick up his shift tonight, something about tickets for a concert in Philly. I think he said "Foreigner." He was babbling so fast and I was running late for class. I wanted to say yes, but mom was working a double today, so she wouldn't be home til about midnight.

TUESDAY JANUARY 29, 1985

"That boy owes me big time," Mr. Totino said, as I walked into work.

Tommy must have done a lot of begging and pleading to Mr. Totino yesterday, because he stayed and closed so that Tommy could go to that concert.

"Be careful when you leave. It's supposed to start getting bad out there," he said before he left.

The weatherman is saying that we could be getting a big snowstorm tonight and tomorrow. The potential of up to a foot of snow starting sometime tonight. When I left the mall there was already about 2 inches on the ground and it was coming down heavy.

WEDNESDAY JANUARY 30, 1985

When I woke up, the first thing I did was look out the window. There was a lot of snow out there and it was still coming down. Mom left the house early to give herself extra time to get to work.

When I got downstairs, Taylor and Alexa were in front of the radio in the kitchen, waiting to hear the school closings. So far Whitfield schools were not closed. I went to the living room window and saw that the street hadn't been plowed yet. I was highly doubting we would have to go in.

"The following school districts are closed today..." I heard the DJ saying.

Taylor and Alexa cheered so loudly when they heard Whitfield, so that meant we were all home for the day.

After breakfast we all went outside to play in the snow. Taylor was making a snow fort and Alexa was making a little snowman while I cleaned all the snow off the Mustang.

I should have known Taylor was up to something, building a snow fort. He decided to hit me with a snowball from behind his fort. He expected me to throw a snowball back. Nope. I charged the fort and chased after him. Eventually picking him up and throwing him onto his fort. We were all laughing. The three of us were having so much fun. When it got too cold, we headed inside and I made us all some hot chocolate.

THURSDAY JANUARY 31, 1985

The town was able to get most of the streets plowed, so school was open today. They didn't do such a good job on sanding the side streets though. They were an icy mess. The 'stang was sliding all over the place. The senior parking lot was worse. It was a giant sheet of ice. I chose to park a little ways away from everyone, near the snowbanks.

When I left school, I checked to see if someone slid into it. If there was a dent anywhere on the car I would be so pissed. There wasn't. Thank God.

FRIDAY FEBRUARY 1, 1985

Steph and Randy had another solo tutoring session last night. They seem to be studying a lot more lately, now that I'm not around.

SATURDAY FEBRUARY 2, 1985

Movie night with Evelyn tonight. She wanted to see this film called "Passage to India." None of her other friends wanted to see it and she didn't want to see it alone. I didn't really want to see it either, but for Evelyn I said yes.

The movie wasn't really that bad. A little long in spots, but not too bad. I saw that it was written by E.M Forster. He also wrote a book called "Maurice" that is about a gay relationship. Surprisingly, we have it in the school library, but there's no way I'm going to risk checking it out of the library.

SUNDAY FEBRUARY 3, 1985

I'm off from work today and everybody was busy, so I decided to grab my camera and go for a drive and see how things looked around the state all snow covered.

I got on the highway heading west and took a random exit. There are a lot of little towns in Jersey. Lots of farmland too. We are "The Garden State" after all.

I wasn't worried about getting lost. I had a full tank of gas and I figured if I kept driving, I would eventually see signs for either the Parkway or the Turnpike or some other highway I know. And I did, 5 hours later.

It was great though. I made a pit stop for lunch, did some walking around and shopping in some small towns I never knew existed and took plenty of pictures. A fun, sunny day out of the house.

MONDAY FEBRUARY 4, 1985

An unflattering photo of the cheerleaders appeared in today's school paper. I didn't take it, but boy oh boy did I get shit for it. Michelle was right in my face. I told her I didn't take it. There was no name under the photo. My name is usually under it when it's one of mine. I also showed her that there was nothing from me in the paper. This was a small issue and they didn't need anything from me.

Five minutes of trying to explain all of this to her, while she continued bitching. Why do I bother?

"Find out who took it," she tells me as she's walking away, like I'm going to listen.

I asked Megan about it in Gym.

"Yeah, Stuart took it. You like it?" she said.

I told her that I loved it, but I told them to watch out because the cheerleaders are really pissed. They laughed it off. The cheerleaders don't scare them.

TUESDAY FEBRUARY 5, 1985

More snow talk from the weatherman. Possibly another day off tomorrow. It was supposed to start tonight, but there was nothing on the ground and the sky was just a little cloudy when I left work.

WEDNESDAY FEBRUARY 6, 1985

The snowstorm didn't start until early this morning, so the brother and sister were upset when the DJ said that there were no school closings. We all went to school wondering if there was going to be an early close.

Principal Angelino came on after the morning announcements to say that school would be closing after 4th period, but the storm was getting worse as the morning went on. During Gym he was back on, announcing that school would be closing after 3rd period. They were closing the high school first and then the middle school and elementary schools after.

We were all excited leaving. Evelyn and I left together. She loves snow. She ran out to the large lawn in front of school and made a snowball, throwing it at me. I ran over and threw one at her.

As I was throwing it, I didn't see Steph leaving the school. She saw us and snuck up and threw one at me, hitting me in the head. No fair 2 on 1.

I saw Tommy leaving and called him over. 2 on 2. Megan and Stuart ran over and joined us. 3 on 3.

We were having a fun time running around, throwing snowballs. Steph saw Randy leaving the school. She called him over. He was going to, but then the Bitch was right there.

"Don't even think about it. C'mon." she said, grabbing his arm

I made a snowball and threw it right at him. It hit him right in the back. He turned around. I was looking right at him, giving him a "Yeah I threw it. Whatcha gonna do?" look. He bent down to make a snowball. Michelle gave him a look. He threw the snow down and left with her. I shook my head and went back to playing around with everyone. Such a great time.

THURSDAY FEBRUARY 7, 1985

Steph and I had our first lunch break in a long time.

"I miss you at the house," she said.

"It's for the best...so...tell me what's going on with you and Randy. You seem to be studying a lot more lately," I said. They studied together again last night and a little before work today. She said he wants to study tomorrow too.

"I know. It's not my idea. Not that I'm complaining. I don't know though. He's always nervous when he comes over, like he wants to ask me something, but seems afraid to ask."

"Do you think he wants to go out with you?"

"I don't know."

If that's what it is, it would be so great. He'd be away from Michelle and maybe after he sees that I'm not a threat, he'll talk to me again. Here's hoping that whatever it is resolves itself soon.

FRIDAY FEBRUARY 8, 1985

"Name the 7 top 40 songs off of Michael Jackson's Thriller album" Tommy says as I walk into Total Eclipse after my lunch break.

"The Girl is Mine, Billie Jean, Beat it, Wanna Be Starting Something, Human Nature, PYT, Thriller," I rattle off in seconds. Too easy. Not gonna beat me. He has yet to get me in top 40 trivia. We're laughing about it when I look up.

"Oh shit," I say to him

"What's wrong?" he says.

I nod towards the entrance. Here comes the Bitch. She's by herself. That usually means that I'm going to hear a whole lot of shit.

I'm standing behind the counter with Tommy, watching her walk quietly around the store. "What the hell is she waiting for?" I think to myself. OK here she comes. She places the cassettes on the counter (nothing). I'm ringing them up (nothing). She pays (nothing).

"Thank you," she says quietly and leaves.

"What the hell was that?!?" I say, turning to Tommy.

Even he was in shock. Everything is getting a little too weird around here for me lately.

SATURDAY FEBRUARY 9, 1985

Only a lunch shift today. Mr. Totino has started slowly cutting hours. I don't mind. I have some money saved. I just hope he doesn't cut my hours too much.

SUNDAY FEBRUARY 10, 1985

Uncle Matt called today to give me all the info on applying for the internship. They will be taking applications starting later this week. He's going to express mail the application to me tomorrow. They will be taking applications the whole month and then they will look over them and narrow all of them down to 12 potential interns.

The 12 will have to go into the City for face to face interviews sometime in April. They will make their decisions on the 3 people that will get the internships sometime in May.

"Tell them all about yourself and your love of foreign languages. Oh and don't forget to tell them that you happen to have the most fabulous uncle who works for them," he said.

My uncle is such a trip.

MONDAY FEBRUARY 11, 1985

"Another one?" I said to Steph as we're walking to French class. Another jock had come up and said hello to her. This was the third time today. It seems to have been happening a lot lately. Most of these guys have ignored her all year, now they're being friendly. I'm guessing it has to do with all the time she's been spending with Randy.

TUESDAY FEBRUARY 12, 1985

Big French test coming Friday. I miss studying with Steph and Evelyn. Every day seems to bleed into one. It's not as much fun anymore. That's it. I'm going over there.

"I knew you'd be back," Steph says, answering the door, giving me a big hug. Evelyn is here. Randy isn't.

"Have you seen all the jocks talking to her?" Evelyn says, referring to Steph's new "friends".

"Are they still coming up to you?" I ask Steph. She nods her head yes.

"Are you going to go out with any of them?" I ask, curious.

"No...well I might consider it," she says.

As she says this, Randy enters. He just walked in the door, didn't even knock. Are they that friendly now? He sees me but doesn't leave. He goes and sits on the same side of the table as Steph, sitting real close.

As we're studying, he's acting awkward and silent, but there's no way I'm leaving. If he has a problem with it, he can leave. I still don't know what I did wrong.

"Let's hang out after school," Steph says to me as I say goodbye.

"Sure," I tell her. We haven't really hung out in a while.

WEDNESDAY FEBRUARY 13, 1985

"Just come, I need someone to keep me company," Evelyn says.

I had just come from school and joined Steph and Evelyn at the mall. I hadn't even been walking around for 5 minutes when she asked me. Another dance is coming up. My most despised holiday too.

Two-Two Disasters in one. The Valentine's Day dance.

Of course she is the DJ again. I do not want to go and watch a bunch of happy couples dancing together when I have nobody, but once again I cave and reluctantly agree to go.

"Maybe you'll get lucky," she says, causing us all to break out laughing.

Steph and I head into the arcade. Evelyn passes of course. Shopping needs to be done. I make my way over to the pinball machines, but Steph pointed to the air hockey tables.

"You want an air hockey challenge?" I say, laughing.

We start playing and she's doing a lot better than she normally does, not winning, but better.

"How did you get better?" I asked.

"I've been practicing," she says

"With who?"

She gives me this devilish smile. It seems that they've been doing more than just studying.

"What's going on between you two?"

"Nothing," she says, still smiling.

We continued playing and joking around. She would occasionally try to get me to slip up.

"I thought we were going to study," I hear coming from behind me. I turn and see Randy. He seems very nervous and jumpy. He passes by me and heads to Steph.

"We can study later. C'mon and play with us," Steph says.

"No thanks," he says grumpily.

Then he turns to leave, purposely bumping into me as he passes me, giving me this weird upset look as he does. I watch as he storms out of the arcade. Steph had no idea what that was all about. Someone needs to talk to him.

THURSDAY FEBRUARY 14, 1985

Randy has been a mess all day today. He seems so tense. He even snapped at Steph. Michelle started in on him just before French class. Normally he either stands there or he tries to calm her down or walks away. Today he yelled at her. She was taken aback. She started to say something, but he was right in her face. She stayed silent. He looked at her for a few seconds and then stormed off. He needs to chill out.

VALENTINE'S DAY DANCE

More like Valentine's Day Massacre

I arrived with Steph and we spent the first hour or so dancing, sometimes dragging Evelyn away from the DJ booth to dance for a minute or two.

Steph was wearing this great looking hat, kinda like the one Ralph Macchio wore in the movie "Teachers". We were taking turns wearing it. Well I kept taking it off her head and putting it on mine. It looked better on me.

Some guy asked to dance with her, so I went over to the bleachers. I sat watching Steph and then scanned the crowd. All the happy couples. I decided to head outside for a few minutes and get some air. As I left, I watched Steph say goodbye to the guy and head over to Evelyn.

Twenty minutes later I headed back in. Right as I walked into the gym, some dumb jock came up to me.

"You're friends with Stephanie Perrino, right?" he says.

"Yeah," I say, looking at this jock, wondering what he wants.

"Here, give this to her," he says, handing me an envelope.

I watch as he goes back to his girlfriend. I look around the gym, searching for Steph.

"Where the hell is that girl?"

Tired of looking, I head over to the DJ booth.

"Where's Steph?" I ask Evelyn.

"Don't know. Why?" she says.

I tell her about the dumb jock giving me the note.

"Which jock?" she asks.

"I don't know. They all look alike."

Who's it from?"

"Doesn't say."

All it is is a plain white envelope with her name on it. I can tell that there's some kind of note inside. Evelyn asks me to open it. When I say no, she tries grabbing it from me.

"No. It could be private," I tell her.

Reluctantly I give in and tell her I'll open it. We were looking silly standing there fighting over an envelope.

"What's it say?" she asks, as I'm opening it.

"Meet me under the far end football bleachers. I have to talk to you about something really important," I say, reading the note.

"That's it?"

"That's it. No name. No nothing. What do you think it is?"

Evelyn proceeds to tell me a story about this ritual the jocks have about trying to get a girl under the bleachers for a quick one. They always dump the girl right after. With all the attention the jocks have been giving Steph lately, Evelyn feels that the jocks have chosen her. "They play with the girl's feelings and throw her away," She says.

"Get out of here," I say, not believing her.

"It's true."

"I may be a little buzzed from the vodka you've been giving me, but I'm not that drunk."

"Trust me, it's true," she says, looking me right in the eye.

"Really?"

"Really."

"What are we going to do? We can't let Steph get hurt," I say.

She told me to go find Steph and tell her, just in case they send another note, so off I go. I have no idea where she is. Maybe I should find Randy and ask him to help. Even though he's been in a bad mood and doesn't really speak to me, maybe he could at least talk to this jock. "Where is she?"

I've been walking around this school for over 10 minutes now. I've checked the halls, maybe she's outside.

"I didn't know you smoked," I say, running into Megan, who's outside smoking with a few other girls. She just gives me a look.

"Have you seen Steph or Randy?" I ask her.

"I haven't seen Steph for a while. I saw Randy heading towards the bleachers about 25 minutes ago."

"The bleachers? You sure?"

"Yeah. Why?"

"No reason. Thanks," I say, walking away from her and heading towards the bleachers.

What the hell? Stupid ass jock. Well that explains all the extra time he's been spending over there lately. Pretending to be her friend, needing extra help, just to get into her pants... God, I can use some more of that vodka right now. He better not be here.

"What are you doing here?" Randy says, startled at the sight of me.

"I'm not going to let you hurt Steph."

"Hurt Steph? What are you talking about?"

"The note," I say, holding it up for him to see. "Evelyn told me about the little ritual you jocks have. You just want to use her and throw her away."

"What?!...Have you been drinking?"

I stare at him. He continues.

"Look, that's not why I asked her back here."

Does he think I'm stupid? "Then why did you?"

"I don't want to talk to you about it. I need to talk to her. You shouldn't have read the note. Is she coming?"

He kept pacing back and forth. His breathing was heavy.

"She doesn't know about the note and I'm not telling her until you let me know what this is all about. Now why did you ask her back here?" I asked more forcefully.

He doesn't answer me. He keeps his head down and paces faster. I wanted an answer.

"Look, she's my friend and I don't want to see her get hurt."

"You don't understand... he said. Tears were starting to fill his eyes. Was he crying?

...I can't talk to you about it," he continued.

I was tired of this game.

"Why not?" I yelled at him.

"Look, I know you're gay," he yelled back at me.

"What? I'm not gay," I said, barely able to get the words out.

"Steph told me last month...by accident."

Well that explains all the drama. I can't believe her. I'm still trying to process the shock, when Randy goes...

"She also told me you like me."

"Unbelievable. How could she do this to me?" I think to myself.

I look at Randy. I don't know what to say. I don't know what to think...No; I'm not losing this battle. I've taken too much crap from them hiding this little secret from me.

"So, what, you wanted her to come back here so you could tell her to keep me away while you study?"

I was expecting him to yell, but he didn't. He still had that sad look on his face.

"No, I see the way she is around you, being your friend, keeping your secret and helping you through it...

He turned away from me, then continued.

...and I wanted to talk to her because...because I think I might be."

"Might be what?" I say.

"You know what," he says, turning back to me.

I looked him right in the eyes and shook my head. It all makes sense now. A fake note, an unbelievable story, Steph conveniently missing, Randy's gay.

"Ha-ha, ok, fun joke, laugh at the queer boy's expense. Great acting job. Did Evelyn and Steph put you up to this or did you all come up with it together?"

"I'm not kidding," he says, continuing the game.

"Yeah, sure. I gotta go. Wait til I get my hands on them," I say, starting to head out.

Randy grabs my arm.

"You can't say anything!"

"Look, you can stop the act. I fell for your trick. I..."

He just kissed me. Oh my god. He's telling the truth. Now I can't breathe. I kiss him back. Here's what I've wanted for months, all of a sudden happening. He's kissing me back. He likes me. He...

"What's the matter?" I ask. He looks scared.

"I have to go," he says, panicking.

I follow him.

"Don't follow me!" he says. Then he grabs my arms and looks me straight in the eyes. His grip is tight. He's hurting me.

"Promise me you won't tell anybody. Nobody."

"I won't tell anybody."

"Promise me!" he yells, gripping me tighter.

"OW! I promise. I promise."

He lets go, leaves the bleachers and starts heading across the track and field. "Maybe I should go after him." I make a move to leave the bleachers. All of a sudden...

"Yeah! Go Sawyer!"

It's Derek. He's on the bleachers on the other side, talking with Debbie. I watch Randy take off. I see Derek and Debbie looking in this direction. I can't move.

"Please don't let them come back here. Please don't let them come back here," I keep repeating.

They keep looking over, probably trying to figure out who's under the bleachers. Five minutes later, they head inside. Once I know the coast is clear, I head home. I can't go back in there.

What the hell just happened? Was I dreaming? I don't know. It felt real. Where does this put everything now? I can't tell anybody, not even Steph and Evelyn, I promised. It wouldn't be right. I don't want my secret out and I know he definitely doesn't want his out. Randy's gay. Oh my god. And he kissed me.

FRIDAY FEBRUARY 15, 1985

THE RUMORS ARE ALREADY FLYING

"Did you talk to Steph at the dance? Did she go under the bleachers?" Evelyn asked me right as I walked into homeroom.

It seems that Debbie has been telling everybody how she and Derek saw Randy making out with somebody under the bleachers. That dumb jock must have told somebody about the note, because everybody thinks it's Steph.

"I don't know. I couldn't find her," was my answer to Evelyn. I'm just keeping my big mouth shut.

Guess who was in my face during English class.

"You just better tell that bitch Perrino that she's dead. Nobody messes around with my man," Michelle screams at me.

"I don't think it was Steph," I tell her. She ignores me and goes back to her seat. I end up having to tell Derek the same thing in Science class.

As I entered the locker room, I heard Derek and Randy talking.

"I told you I was alone," Randy says.

"You weren't alone. I saw two shadows making out under there. One was you. Who was the other one? Was it Perrino? C'mon you can tell me," Derek says.

"Ok I wasn't alone, but it wasn't Perrino."

"Who were you with?"

Just as Derek said that, I came into view. Randy did a quick glance at me, but quickly turned back to Derek.

"I don't want to say right now," Randy says, tying his sneakers and heading out. Derek followed, still asking Randy to tell him who it was. I just hung my head and finished changing.

As I'm sitting on the gym floor, I watch Steph and Evelyn leave the girl's locker room. Steph's been crying. I can see it in her face. I ran over to her.

"Are you ok?" I asked as she hugged me.

"Michelle just tried to start some shit," Evelyn tells me.

"I didn't go under the bleachers. I left the dance early," Steph says as I hold her hand and walk her to her spot on the gym floor.

"How are you doing?" Megan asks Steph. Steph shrugs her shoulders.

"You headed to the bleachers. You didn't see anything?" Megan says, turning to me. Evelyn looks right at me.

"I changed my mind and went home," I tell them.

Randy leaves talking to Garrett and Derek and takes his seat, not even looking at me. Evelyn makes a move towards him.

"Back off Evelyn. Just leave me alone," he snaps, not even turning around. She returns to her seat. Everybody keeps their distance the whole class.

The whole day is a mess. Randy and the bleachers is the only thing everyone is talking about. Randy must have said something right to Michelle, because they aren't fighting anymore. French class was going to be interesting.

As I turn the corner to French class, I see Steph standing outside the class. She looks pissed. There's Randy. Ah, that's who she's waiting for. She took him into the empty class across the hall from the French room. I decided to wait outside the door.

"What's going on? You go and make out with someone under the bleachers and because you sent me a note, everyone thinks it's me. They think I'm trying to cover it up," she says to him.

"I'm sorry. I've been telling everybody it wasn't you. What more do you want from me?"

"How about maybe telling everybody who you were with? Let her get all the shit. She went back there. She deserves to deal with Michelle and everyone else."

"I can't."

"Why not?"

"I just can't, that's all."

"Fine. Then just stay away from me. Stay out of my life."

Randy leaves the classroom. He sees me standing there. Our eyes meet, but he still says nothing. He walks into French class. I waited for Steph

"Are you OK?" I say to her as she leaves the class.

"Why won't he say who he was with?" she asks me.

"I don't know," I say as I hug her.

We headed into French class. I was so frazzled at this time. I was in no mood for the French test. It actually took me all period to finish it. I just couldn't concentrate. I'm sure I did horribly. Steph and Randy seemed to have the same problem.

SATURDAY FEBRUARY 16, 1985

When I got home from school yesterday, all I did was listen to music. I needed to calm down. It helped a little. Today I am working a double, so hopefully work will take my mind off all of this.

Being able to choose the music I want to listen to at work helps so much. The drama of yesterday didn't enter my thoughts...until the p.m. shift, when Tommy came in and kept asking about it.

"Who do you think was under there with Randy?"

Eventually I had to tell him to shut up.

SUNDAY FEBRUARY 17, 1985

Another Sunday off. I didn't want to sit around the house, so I grabbed Taylor and we headed out to the movies. He hasn't been out to the movies in a while, so I let him pick. He wanted to see this movie starring Timothy Hutton called "Turk 182".

"Why yes he is 13, sir."

We had to lie. The movie was PG13. Taylor can pass for 13, so he believed us. It was a cool movie.

MONDAY FEBRUARY 18, 1985

PRESIDENT'S DAY

Another day off from school. Worked the day shift. Lots of jocks and cheerleaders came in today. The cheerleaders would all come up and say something insulting about Steph.

TUESDAY FEBRUARY 19, 1985

I haven't really said anything to Randy since Valentine's day. He doesn't look at me or say anything to me. I figured I would give him a little time before saying anything.

Today I decided to try and talk to him. He was at his locker when I approached. At first he pretended I wasn't there.

"Why are you ignoring me?" I said, speaking up.

"Look, I don't want to discuss this right now," he answered, slamming his locker and walking away.

WEDNESDAY FEBRUARY 20, 1985

Mrs. Rosario was standing at the door when Steph, Evelyn and I approached. She pulled me aside. She had my test in her hand.

"Is everything ok?" she asked, showing me my grade. "75" (a "D")

I told her that I was really stressed out that day. She asked me if I wanted to retake the test. I said yes. She handed me another test. I didn't realize before, but there was a desk outside in the hall. She motioned me to sit down, while she went back inside the classroom, closing the door.

I took a deep breath and started the test. My mind was clearer today and I finished the test quickly. Mrs. Rosario knew things were fine when I walked into the classroom 15 minutes later. Randy didn't get another chance. "65" Ouch. Oh well.

THURSDAY FEBRUARY 21, 1985

After the grumpiness the other day, I decided to wait a couple of days before trying to talk to Randy again. This time I approached him as he was heading into school. I was by the entrance and I saw him coming. The Bitch wasn't around. He saw me standing there looking at him, but he didn't stop. He just brushed right by me. I went and caught up to him just before he got to his locker. He knew I was following him. He turns around and goes...

"I never want to talk to you about this ever, so get it through your head and leave me alone."

He doesn't even want to talk to me anymore? He looks at me as if it's all my fault. What did I do? He kissed me first.

He kissed me first.

FRIDAY FEBRUARY 22, 1985

This has been stressing me out so much. Even "Psychic Mom" was picking something up. At first I told her it was nothing and then I told her about Randy and the bleachers. I didn't tell her it was me. I just said someone was under there with Randy and he wasn't saying who and Steph was getting slack for it because of the note. Mom told me to comfort Steph and talk to Randy.

"You guys are good friends. I'm sure he'll listen to you."

"Yeah mom. He's all ears," I said to myself.

SATURDAY FEBRUARY 23, 1985

Had lunch break with Steph today. She has been the most stressed out of all of us. She's cried at least once a day. Even with Randy and Evelyn telling everybody it wasn't her, the cheerleaders and Michelle's little clique blamed her. I so want to tell her everything, but I can't. I promised.

SUNDAY FEBRUARY 24, 1985

Another open to close Sunday today. Myself and Tommy. Just the two of us the whole day. Tommy started doing the dance from the video for the song "Jungle Love". This was obviously another challenge. We weren't that busy, so I joined him behind the counter. We were dancing along as the customers looked and laughed. We even got some to dance along.

MONDAY FEBRUARY 25, 1985

"I don't know!!"

Evelyn was yelling in the hall outside homeroom. She entered homeroom shaking her head, slamming her books down on the desk. I didn't even have to ask her what was wrong. I pretty much knew. She's been going crazy because she hasn't found out who was under the bleachers with Randy. She prides herself on knowing all the gossip. Everybody has been coming up to her, asking. This is the first big piece of gossip she doesn't have an answer for.

TUESDAY FEBRUARY 26, 1985

This afternoon was the worst for Steph. Evelyn and I were sitting in French class talking, when we heard Steph and Michelle arguing in the hall. We both jumped up and ran out, Evelyn first. One of the cheerleaders had grabbed Steph and Michelle was about to hit her. Evelyn quickly jumped in, throwing cheerleaders everywhere. Michelle took off before Evelyn could get to her.

The cheerleader who was holding Steph was going to have a nice bruise on her face from where Evelyn punched her. Evelyn wasn't taking any shit.

The hallway started clearing. I went over and consoled Steph. Evelyn joined us, but then turned and said "Excuse me."

Randy was coming down the hall. She headed right to him. She wasn't going to be polite. Evelyn grabbed him by the shirt and slammed him into the lockers. She was pissed.

"Look, I know you made out with some cheap slut under the bleachers and are getting off on the fact that you're not mentioning who it is. That's fine (it wasn't), but you're going to talk to that bitch girlfriend of yours and her little cheerleader friends and tell them to leave Steph alone or I'm going to pound the shit out of each and every one of them. Got it?!"

"OK,OK," was all he could say. Evelyn let go of him and he headed into class, giving Steph and I a quick glance.

WEDNESDAY FEBRUARY 27, 1985

Steph wasn't in school today. She's supposed to work tonight. Hopefully she does so we can talk during our lunch break. I hope she's feeling better. I'm really worried about her.

Steph was at work, but she wasn't any better. Just as we sat down, she broke down crying, saying that she can't take much more.

"Why won't he say who it is?" she asked me.

Just before our break was over, I told her to meet me at my car after work.

"Why?"

"Just meet me there," I told her.

After work, she met me at the entrance and we walked out to my car.

"It's freezing," she says, sitting in my car. I started the car and turned on the heat, sitting there thinking how I'm going to tell her.

"What do you want to talk about?" she asked me.

"Um...I want to say how thankful I am that you are keeping my secret. You're a really good friend to me and friends don't let friends get so stressed out...I need you to keep what I am about to tell you a secret from everybody, even Evelyn," I said.

"OK," she said nervously.

"Oh God, I promised Randy I wouldn't say anything."

"Randy told you who he was with?"

"He didn't have to. It was me he was with," I said, shaking my head.

"What? But I thought you said…"

"The night of the dance, while I was looking for you, I found out it was Randy who sent the note and I went to confront him. Based on Evelyn's "story", I was mad at the idea of him taking advantage of you. Seems he just wanted to talk… (Why is she laughing?)…What's so funny?"

"Derek saw the shadows of you and Randy talking and thought the two of you were making out. Why didn't you guys just tell everybody that? It would have made things easier. It's not like you were making out under there," she said, before laughing again. Except I wasn't laughing back. I was staring at her.

"What, you were not making out. You're joking with me, right? Josh, just tell me you're joking…

I turned my head forward and put my hands and head on the steering wheel.

…You're not joking."

I shook my head no.

"But how?" she continued.

"You remember how you said it was like he wanted to tell you something, but seemed afraid to ask."

"Why me?"

"He saw how you were friends with me and kept it a secret. Even though you told him, which you should have told me, he thought he would talk to you about it. He finally had the courage that night, but things went wrong and he got me. He needed to tell somebody. I told him I didn't believe him and it was a joke. I guess his feelings took over. He kissed me, so I kissed him back. We kissed for a little bit and then he thought of something, freaked out and took off...Steph?" She sitting there stunned. I needed her to say something.

"Steph? Say something, please," I beg her. She doesn't. She just got out of the car and left.

THURSDAY FEBRUARY 28, 1985

I couldn't sleep last night and needed to clear my head. I left the house early and headed to school. The senior parking lot was empty when I got there. I picked a spot facing the school. I'm just lying on the hood of my car, looking up at the clouds, wondering what I should say to Steph.

"Hey," this soft voice enters my brain. Where is it coming from?

"Hey," the voice says louder.

Knock knock.

I come out of my daze and turn to see Steph standing there. She's tapping on my car.

"Hi," I say, glad to see her there. She climbs up and joins me on the car.

"I'm sorry about yesterday. I shouldn't have just left like that," she says.

"No, it was my fault. I never should have let you become so stressed out. I should have told you everything sooner," I tell her.

She told me that the harassment and hit-ons would have happened anyway.

"At least now I know why Randy couldn't tell anybody. Have you talked to him?" she asks.

"No. He totally ignores me."

"Maybe I should try talking to him."

"No! I don't want him even thinking somebody else might know."

"I wouldn't tell him I know. It would be just to talk.

"Bad idea, just let him cool off and then I'll talk to him. Once things calm down a little, I'm sure he'll talk. I hope."

FRIDAY MARCH 1, 1985

ATTEMPT # 3

Anytime I would see Randy in the halls, I would approach, but he would always take off or make sure to have the Bitch or Derek with him.

SATURDAY MARCH 2, 1985

Steph's a lot calmer now that she knows the truth. The cheerleaders are still bothering her, but she's not letting it get to her. A few walked by our table while we were taking our lunch break. They said something, but this time Steph just laughed. I'm so glad that she's smiling again.

SUNDAY MARCH 3, 1985

Whereas Steph is calmer, I'm not. I'm trying, but all I think about is the kissing. I need to get it out of my mind, but I just can't. I really need to talk to Randy.

MONDAY MARCH 4, 1985

Evelyn is still going crazy trying to figure everything out. Today I decided to sit out by the bleachers, but I sat in a different spot. I watched Evelyn go over to the far end bleachers. Curious, I walked over to see what she was up to.

"What are you doing?" I asked her.

"Searching for clues," she said, scouring the ground.

I tried my best to hide my laughter.

TUESDAY MARCH 5, 1985

Thank God for my secret space. It's the only time during the day I feel calm. Every time I hear a noise in the auditorium, I hope it's Randy wanting to come up and talk.

WEDNESDAY MARCH 6, 1985

This was weird. Right after French class, Evelyn asked me to join her at the mall after school. When I got there, she wanted to play air hockey.

I instantly knew something was up. She's never played air hockey with any of us. She's either watched or headed out to shop. At first she was quiet, but then as we started playing, she started talking about Steph and how she's calmer. Then she says that she thinks Steph is hiding something from her. She was trying to get the answer out of me. I just played dumb.

"You know what it is, don't you? Tell me," she says.

I wasn't falling for her trick. I put on my calm face.

"Steph and I had a talk about everything and afterwards she felt better. You've been going crazy with everything lately, you're over judging," I said.

I don't know if she bought it, but she did stop prying.

THURSDAY MARCH 7, 1985

Randy's still avoiding me. Even the calm relaxing feeling of music wasn't helping. Tonight he came into Total Eclipse. Well Michelle came in, dragging him with her. They were here for about 20 minutes. He wouldn't look up and if he did, he would just look at the exit. I knew he just wanted to get out of there. Then some bitch cheerleaders came in and started talking to Michelle about something and she handed the cassettes to him, asking him to pay for them while she headed out with the cheerleaders.

The last thing he wanted to do was be near me. He placed the cassettes on the counter, looking in every direction but at me.

"You can't ignore me forever," I told him.

He just threw the money down and left. He didn't even wait for his change.

FRIDAY MARCH 8, 1985

After yesterday's drama with Randy, I wanted nothing more than for him to at least talk to me. When I walked into homeroom, he was already there. As I walked by his desk, I put his receipt and change from yesterday down. Then I sat down and tried talking to him.

"Please talk to me," I asked.

(nothing)

"This is really hurting me and I just want to talk about it," I said quietly, trying again.

"Not now," he finally answered.

"When?"

"Later."

"Later today?"

"Just later later."

"What the fuck does "later later" mean?" I think to myself.

We spent the rest of homeroom in silence.

SATURDAY MARCH 9, 1985

Well "later later" didn't mean yesterday or today. Hopefully it means tomorrow or Monday.

SUNDAY MARCH 10, 1985

Off from work today. Spent the whole day over Steph's house. We hung out, talking, watching MTV and then movie rental night. "Red Dawn" with Patrick Swayze. Steph's big movie star crush. He's cute, although I kinda prefer C. Thomas Howell.

MONDAY MARCH 11, 1985

More ignoring from Randy. I went up to my secret spot for break and didn't come down until Math class and only because we had a quiz. I didn't care. I needed some peace.

TUESDAY MARCH 12, 1985

Well now it's March 12th. Randy said nothing in homeroom, still silent, still ignoring. Today I would make him uncomfortable, hoping to get him to break. I was pissed and he knew it. I was in his face all day. It didn't help him that Michelle was absent.

I didn't say anything to him. I was just there, always staring at him. I want him to open up. He still won't. No luck.

That's it. I've had it.

WEDNESDAY MARCH 13, 1985

"EXPLOSION!!" "BA-BOOM!!"

I hate my life. I hate Randy. I hate everything. I tried talking to him today and what do I have to show for it? A black eye, a swollen lip, some bruised ribs... He called me a fag...

OK, the beginning. He was silent in homeroom. Things would be different in Gym.

"I'm going to talk to him today. I can't take anymore. I'm not giving up and backing away until I'm satisfied. This needs to be settled," I tell Steph as we head out to the track to jog.

"Good luck," she tells me.

Randy jogs alone. He's been doing this for the past few weeks. I pick up the pace and catch up to him. He sees me there and jogs faster.

"Oh no you don't," I say to myself, keeping up with him.

"Go away," he says.

"Not today," I tell him. He speeds up a little more. I keep pace. "You're not going to lose me that easily. I'm not giving up today. We're talking."

"Go away. Not here. Not now."

"No, I'm not accepting that "later" shit anymore."

He stops jogging and starts walking across the field.

"Stop following me," he says .

"No. We're talking."

"Everybody's looking."

"So, let them look."

"I don't want to talk right now," he says, still walking.

"Well I do...and if you don't stop...I'll tell everybody. Steph already knows. I'll just tell Evelyn and that will be it."

That got him to stop. He's pissed. He shoves me.

"I told you not to tell anybody," he quietly yells.

Ms. Annasandy has now come running up, separating us. I looked around and saw everybody staring.

"Everybody in!" Ms. Annasandy tells the class. "Sawyer! Parker! Two more laps!" Randy and I both stop and start jogging. "Opposite directions!"

We both look at each other. I jog in the other direction. He doesn't look at me the two times we pass each other. We finish the laps and head inside. The next period's class is changed and in the gym already, so we are alone. It doesn't matter, I've given up. I splash some water on my face and go change. I just want to change and get out of there. I need my quiet time. I'm outta here.

"Hey," I hear as I get to the door. I turn. Randy is standing about 10 feet from me.

"What?" I ask him.

"Look, I don't know what happened that night, but whatever did, it wasn't supposed to happen," Randy says. His voice is nervous and quivering the whole time he's saying this. "I'm not..."gay," he says, whispering the word gay. "What are you doing?" he asks me.

The whole time he's been talking, I've been looking into his eyes and moving closer and closer.

"Nothing," I say. I'm now face to face with him. He turns his head away, but I don't move. "It's OK," I tell him. I know he's scared and I just want to help. He slowly turns his head back. Our eyes meet. We move to kiss.

All of a sudden the locker room door opens. In walk Derek and Garrett. Randy panics. I have no time to react; he throws me to the ground.

"Stay away from me you fag!" he yells.

The word fag never hurt me worse than it did then.

"You OK man?" Derek says to Randy, running up with Garrett.

"Yeah, I'm fine," Randy says, acting all macho.

I started to say something, but Garrett came right up to me.

"I'm gonna kick your faggot ass," he said. I did a quick backward crawl until I hit into the lockers.

"It's OK. It's over. Let's go," Randy says, stopping Garrett.

Garrett raises his fist as if to punch me. He punches the lockers above me and they all leave.

I don't know what to do. I'm so hurt and confused. I just want to go home. Shit, Spanish test today. Hell, Mrs. Tavares will let me take it tomorrow. I just want to get to my locker, get my jacket and get out of here.

The hall is so quiet. I keep thinking of Randy shoving me to the ground. I'm in such a daze. I turn the corner and don't see them until it's too late. Garrett and Derek were waiting for me. They dragged me into the bathroom.

"Leave me alone!" I say as Garrett grabs me. I break free, but Derek is blocking the door. He grabs me and I try breaking free. I don't see the punch to my stomach that Garrett has just thrown. I double over and he knees me in the head. Derek lets go and I fall to the floor. I try to get up to fight back, but it's so rough. They take turns; one grabs me while the other punches me. If I fall to the floor, they kick me. My pleas for them to stop fall flat. I have no strength to fight back. I crawl into a ball. They kick me a few more times as I lie there.

"Watch your ass, fag!" Garrett says. "Get it, ass fag," he says laughing, turning to Derek. They hi-five, kick me one more time and leave. When they've gone, I crawl into one of the stalls and stay there.

After they beat up Josh, Garrett and Derek will head to their classes. Garrett will walk into English class, late, making up some lame excuse to the teacher, who will wave her hand for him to take his seat. His seat is behind Randy and in front of Evelyn. She will overhear Garrett talking to Randy.

"Where have you been?" Randy asks.

"Derek and I were taking care of your little fag problem," Garrett says.

"What did you do?"

"Don't worry about it. He won't be bothering you again."

Randy will be stunned, not knowing exactly what Garrett means, what to say back or how to react. He'll remain silent, not wanting to know.

After a little bit, I got up and checked myself in the mirror. I started crying again. I try cleaning myself up. There is blood coming from my nose, lips and other parts of my face, or is it just smeared there. Oh I don't know. Why? Why? Shit, someone's coming in. I run back to the stall, but slip and fall.

"Are you OK?"

I look up to see Stuart.

"Oh my God, what happened? Are you ok?" he asks.

"I'm fine. It's nothing. Just a little fight, that's all. I'll be fine."

"A little fight?" he says, turning to look at my face. "C'mon, let's get you to the nurse," he says, grabbing my arm.

"No, I'll be fine," I tell him, getting angrier.

He doesn't give up. He tries pulling me.

"Just leave me alone! I don't need your help!" I snap at him.

"Whatever dude, I'm just trying to help," he says, before leaving.

Once he's gone, I finish cleaning up. I was angry now. I no longer want to go home. I don't care how I look. I'm not going to let them think they won. I'm walking right into that room and taking that test.

After the period ends, Evelyn quickly leaves and heads to the cafeteria. Steph will be sitting at their usual table. Evelyn will ask her if Josh is ok.

"I haven't seen him since gym," Steph says.

Evelyn will fill her in on all the details. They will get up and start to look for Josh. As they leave, they will run into Megan and Stuart. They were coming to the cafeteria to ask Steph's help in finding Josh, so they could get him to the nurse. Stuart fills them in on what happened in the bathroom. Not having any idea where he might be, they'll search everywhere for him, starting with the parking lot. His car will still be there. They know he hasn't left.

"Maybe he went to class?" Steph says.

"Not the way he looked," Stuart answers.

The bell for the end of 4th period rings and I head to this empty classroom. I'll wait until the halls clear before going to class. As I'm waiting, I look out and see Megan and Stuart go into the boy's bathroom, obviously looking for me.

Time for Spanish class. I walk down the empty hall, nervous about what I'm doing.

"They didn't beat me. They didn't beat me," I keep repeating to myself.

I get to Spanish class. I'm trembling as I grab the handle. I take a deep breath and go inside.

All eyes turn up as I enter. Normally they would go back down, but with the way I look, they keep staring. I can feel their eyes on me. Derek and Garrett are laughing and hi-fiving. Mrs. Tavares has this big shocked look on her face. She goes to say something, but looks at the class watching and takes me out in the hall.

"What happened? Who did this to you?" she says. I remain silent, trying not to cry. "You need to go to the nurse."

"I'll go. I just want to take the test first."

"No, the test can wait. You need to get checked out first."

"Please...they can't think they won," I say softly.

I can tell she doesn't want to, but she gives in. "OK, but you go right after."

I nod my head yes and we re-enter the classroom. All eyes were back on me. I took a test off her desk and headed to my seat. "Ass fag," Garrett says softly as I pass.

Every once in a while one of them would make a comment. It was so hard to concentrate. I tried ignoring them, but with everything that's been going on the past few months, it was really pissing me off. I had to quickly finish the test and get out of there. Luckily it was an easy test. I finished it quickly. Now to get out of here. I place the test on Mrs. Tavares' desk. She has a pass already written for me. I head back to my seat to get my backpack.

Garrett makes another smart ass comment as I approach. I can't take anymore. My hand becomes a fist and I punch him straight in the face. He doesn't see it coming. I'm real angry now. I grab his desk and tip it over. It's one of those desk/chair combos and his fat ass is wedged in the seat, so when I tip it over he goes with it. Derek gets up and starts jumping over my desk. I use my foot to push the desk while at the same time swinging my backpack at him. The motion of these two causes him to slip off the desk and tumble to the ground. Garrett is still on the ground trying to unwedge himself as I take off for the door. I see Mrs. Tavares coming up the row to my left. She has left her desk and is trying to stop everything. I just want to get out that door.

"What the hell? Let go!" I yell. Michelle has grabbed my shirt. I can't break free.

"Shit." Derek and Garrett have gotten up.

"I got him. Hurry," she says, turning towards Derek and Garrett.

I have no choice. It's right there. I grab the Bitch's hair. Michelle screams as I do.

"Let go or I pull it out!" I yell.

All of that bleaching has left her hair fragile. She lets go and I take off, a few strands of her hair in my hand.

I'm out the door just in time, slamming it in Derek and Garrett's faces. I start running. They come after me. I have no idea where to run. I just want to get away from them. We run up and down every floor of the school. I'm running out of breath, as I get back to the first floor. I turn a corner and am by the Shop classes. I've never been to this side of the school. It's kind of loud. I get about halfway down the hall and stop. At the end of the hall is Randy. He's over by the water fountain. Derek and Garrett round the corner. They stop when they see I've stopped. They look down and see Randy. He's watching the three of us.

My eyes go back and forth between them and Randy. I'm trying to catch my breath and decide what to do. I choose Randy, hoping he won't do anything. I run towards him, figuring I can just run around him.

"Get him!" Derek calls to Randy as I get closer. He wouldn't listen to him, would he? He would.

"Let go. Please!" I beg Randy. I see Garrett and Derek coming. He won't let go. He's keeping his eyes closed. They're almost here. I get one arm free. He still won't let go. I have no choice. Wham! One quick shot to his manhood. He lets go now. I give him a sad hurtful look while he looks at me and winces in pain. He starts to say something, no time to listen to him, I take off.

They're still a little distance behind me. I head towards the office, even though I don't want to go there. I turn the corner by the locker rooms. I figure I'll duck in there, but at the last minute I get another idea.

Across from the boy's locker room door is a janitor's closet. The door is open. I quickly open the boy's locker room door wide and duck into the janitor's closet. Garrett and Derek turn the corner, see the locker room door closing and go in, falling for my trick. I just stay put in the closet.

When I think the coast is clear, I head out. I'm too stressed to talk to anybody now. I want to leave but I can't risk the chance that they may be my car waiting. I need to clear my head. I go to the auditorium, time for my secret space. I swear, if Randy comes up or tells one of those dumb jocks where I am, I will knock them off the ladder.

Steph and Evelyn are looking for me, along with Megan and Stuart. Stuart must have told them. I was sitting up here for about 20 minutes when I heard Megan and Stuart's voices. They entered the auditorium. They were calling my name. "He's not here. Let's see if Steph and Evelyn found him," Megan said, and then they were off.

During 6th period, Megan and Stuart have to stop looking. They have a big Science test and can't miss it. Evelyn and Steph continue to look. They decide that maybe he'll go to French class, seeing as he usually feels safest there.

They arrive at the classroom, no Josh. They continue to talk outside the door, wondering where he could be, hoping that he will still show. Randy will be coming down the hall, but before he can reach the classroom, Michelle will come running up, asking him if he found Josh. He'll ignore her and a little fight will erupt.

"What's your problem today? Don't you care about what that little faggot did to me?" Michelle says, angrily.

"What do you want from me?" he asks her.

"What do I want? I would think that maybe, you being my boyfriend and all, would defend me and do something!" she says, her voice getting louder. Randy continues walking. "Randy!!" she yells, running after him.

"Look, I just need a little space right now, OK."

"No, it's not OK. You better do something or it's over between us, you hear me," she yells, before storming off in a huff.

Thinking he's in the clear, Randy will enter French class. The class is partially full and Mrs. Rosario hasn't arrived yet. Just as he takes his seat, Evelyn and Steph walk up to him. Evelyn begins to say something, but before she does, not caring who's around, Steph pushes by her.

"What?!" Randy says, angrily.

"How could you do that to him?" Steph says.

Randy will stand up, remembering that she knows his secret. He tries to calm her down. She starts shoving him around.

"Calm down," he says.

"No, I won't calm down. What did he ever do to you, besides try to be your friend?"

Randy is asking her to keep her voice down, but Steph's on a roll. Evelyn just steps back and lets Steph go. Randy grabs her by the hand and leads her outside the classroom, just as the bell rings. He leads her across the hall to the empty classroom. Evelyn follows. He has now managed to calm her down some and get a word in edgewise.

"Now will you listen to me? You've gotta understand that I had nothing to do with Josh getting beat up. Everything happened so fast. I wasn't even there. I didn't know they were going back to get Josh or I would've stopped them."

Steph doesn't totally believe him.

"Look, I was just as surprised as you," he continues.

"We've just spent the last 2 periods looking for him and we can't find him. His car is still here and I doubt he walked home, so he has to be here somewhere. Wherever he is, he's scared. We have to find him before Garrett and Derek do," Evelyn says.

Randy looks at Steph. She is near tears.

"I think I know where he is," he says.

"Where?" Steph asks.

"Josh has a secret place in the auditorium where he goes to get away. It's high above. There's a rope ladder just behind a curtain to the left of the stage. Don't ask me how I know, I just know."

"Let's go," Steph says. Evelyn follows. They stop when they realize that Randy isn't coming. "Come on," Steph says. Randy shakes his head

"I can't...not now...you guys go...make sure he's alright."

They both leave and head to the auditorium. Randy heads into French class, watching them go.

A little after the bell for 7th period rang, they found me. Steph and Evelyn were in the auditorium calling my name. I wouldn't answer them back. I listened as they made their way up the stage steps, across the stage and up the ladder. I quickly turned around. I didn't want them to see me. How did they find me? They were calling my name. Steph was up the ladder first.

"Josh?" she said, still calling my name.

"Josh," she said, relieved as she saw me. "He's here," she called down to Evelyn. She walked across the platform as Evelyn climbed up the ladder.

"Please go away," I said, softly.

They wouldn't. Steph put her arms around me. I really needed a hug.

"Everything is going to be alright," she said as I was turning around.

"No it's not," I said, tears in my eyes. I knew I looked bad, based on the expressions on their faces.

"Oh man," was all Evelyn could say. They saw the black eye, the swollen lip and the bruise marks on my face and arms. They didn't see the bruises on my chest, legs and stomach.

"We've got to get you to the nurse," Steph said, lightly pulling me towards the ladder. I lightly shoved her away. I didn't want to go.

"You're safe now. We'll take you," Evelyn said.

I started crying.

"Why would he do this to me?"

"Because Garrett's a Neanderthal scumbag. He gets off on...," Evelyn was saying before I cut her off.

"Not Garrett!"

Evelyn was looking confused. I heard Steph whisper "Randy" to her.

"In the locker room, after Gym... He threw me to the ground. He called me a fag."

"C'mon, forget about him. He's just a dumb jock protecting his macho image, that's all. Let's get you to the nurse," Steph said.

I didn't move.

"But I thought he really cared, you know. All the times we hung out, talking, studying, video games, air hockey...and then the dance last month."

Evelyn had enough. "What about the dance last month? Will somebody please tell me what the hell is going on?"

I looked at Steph, trying to find a sign that it would be OK to tell. She signaled that it would be OK.

"So are you going to tell me or what?" Evelyn said, looking at both of us. I took a deep breath.

"Well...you know that little piece of gossip you've been going crazy over for the past month."

"Yeah...wait, you know who was kissing Randy under the bleachers? (I nodded my head yes)...and you didn't tell me? I've been losing my mind trying to figure it out. Nobody seemed to know."

"That's because only 3 people know...Randy, Steph and me."

"So it WAS YOU under the bleachers," Evelyn says, turning to Steph.

"No!" Steph snaps back.

"Wait, wait a minute. I'm confused. If it wasn't you kissing him, then who was..."

I slowly raise my hand.

"No, no-ho, no way, no friggin way. You're telling me Randy Sawyer, football jock, Mr. Beautiful, oh so popular is gay?"

Both Steph and I nod our heads.

...but he's dating Michelle," Evelyn continues.

We both shrug our shoulders. Evelyn is totally stunned. I can tell this is not the answer she expected.

"Oh my god. I don't believe it. Wait til I tell...

She stops when she looks at me, realizing she can't tell anybody.

...nobody"

This is going to be tough for her to keep to herself, but I know she doesn't want to see me hurt anymore. She comes over and hugs me.

"You're secret's still safe with me."

"Thank you," I tell her.

"On one condition," she says. I look at her.

"You let us take you to the nurse."

I shake my head and smile as her and Steph help me up and take me to the nurse.

Nurse Welsh was freaked out when we walked in. She started cleaning me up, asking me if Angelino knows about this. We told her we were going after here. We were lying, because all I wanted to do was get out of this building.

As I'm sitting there, I look out the window. She has a clear view of senior parking. I saw Derek and Garrett; sure enough they were standing by my car. Garrett's pick-up truck was parked right next to my car. Then I saw Randy heading towards them. My eyes stayed on him the whole time. He joined them. Then I don't know what he said, but they all got in their cars and left.

"You want to go home?" Steph asked as we left the nurse's office. I didn't want to go home yet.

"We'll do whatever you want," Evelyn said.

"Can we just go for a drive? Maybe get some food?" I asked.

"Sure"

We all got in her car and drove around, stopping at the diner for food and Carvel for some ice cream.

It was a little after 8 o'clock when I got home. It was impossible to hide the damage that was done to my face. I opened the door. Mom was in the kitchen. I didn't see my brother and sister, so I just started heading quietly up the stairs.

As I was halfway up, Alexa came down the steps. "Mom! Josh got hurt!" she yells, big mouth little sister. Taylor came running out of his room

"Whoa, what happened to your face?"

I couldn't get past them. Of course mom came running out of the kitchen. She was screaming all these questions at me.

"What happened? Who did this to you? Are you ok?"

"It was just a little fight. I'm fine," I tell her.

"Why did you fight? Who did you fight with?"

"I'm fine! It's over!" I say, breaking through my brother and sister. I get to my room. I'm about to close the door when she says

"Well I'm gonna call the principal tomorrow and get this straightened out."

I quickly run back down the steps.

"No, you'll just make it worse."

"Look at your face."

"God, don't you get it? I said I'm fine!! Can we just leave it at that? It's over!" I scream at her before storming up the steps and slamming my door. I need music.

I grab my Walkman and put in this new cassette I just bought the other day called "Diamond Life". It's by this new singer called Sade. It's such a relaxing album. The first notes of "Smooth Operator" come on and my breathing returns to normal.

THURSDAY MARCH 14, 1985

"You're not going to school," Steph said to me last night when she dropped me off.

I left 30 minutes early for school, avoiding any conversations with my mother. Steph and Evelyn met me in the senior parking lot.

"So where do you want to go?" they asked.

I wanted something outdoors and something as far away from here as possible. Evelyn said she knew of a perfect place. They got into my car and we went for a drive. We made a pit stop to get some junk food and then we headed out. Two hours later we were at Garden State Park.

We went out and started walking the nature trails. It was so wonderful. The first signs of spring were starting. Everything was great and it was a beautiful day. Boy did I need this. Peace and quiet...until I got home.

I dropped Evelyn and Steph off at the school around 4 and headed home. I instantly knew something was wrong. I entered the house and Taylor flashed me the signal that mom was pissed. I didn't even have a chance to react. She came out of the kitchen.

"Where were you today? Why weren't you in school? I come home and get a message from your principal!"

Shit, I forgot that he would probably call. I tell her that I didn't want to be there today after yesterday.

"Well if you didn't want to be there then something is wrong. I didn't call your principal this morning, but I did talk to him a little while ago. We're going to see him tomorrow. So before school starts, I want you in the principal's office. No if's ands or but's about it."

I didn't get a chance to respond. She turned and went back into the kitchen, not wanting a response. I went up to my room, slamming the door.

FRIDAY MARCH 15, 1985

I told her that this would be a problem, but did she listen? No. Now my whole life is over. Garrett and Derek now know I'm gay and I don't think they're going to keep it a secret. I knew that this would happen. This is all Randy's fault. I saved his closeted ass. Don't ask me why. All he had to do was say one word and because he doesn't, I'm going to be out to the whole school.

Let's start at the beginning, shall we.

I'm sitting in the office with Mom, waiting for principal Angelino to be through with the morning announcements. The office staff is trying their best not to stare, but I see them. I'm just glad that Mom didn't drive into school with me. I'm embarrassed enough as it is. I don't want to be here. She has no idea how bad this is.

I listen as Angelino talks about band practice and school lunch and how Suzie Perkins won the county science award. I'm waiting for him to say "and Joshua Parker is in the office with his mom." He doesn't.

Finishing with the announcements, he approaches me and my mom, shakes her hand and invites us into his office. We sit down and he starts talking to Mom. I stare out into space, looking around the office. I've never been in here before. There are pictures of his wife and kids, some awards, trophies, some obscure item made out of clay, probably something his daughter made in art class.

"Those are some nasty bruises you've got there," he says, breaking me out of my trance. "You want to tell me how you got them?"

I don't know what to say, so I say nothing, sitting there with my arms folded, wishing I could just fall through the floor.

"He won't tell me anything either," mom answers.

Angelino comes out from behind the desk, bends down and gets eye level with me. He's staring. I turn my head.

"Josh. Look at me. We both know who the culprits are, but I can't do anything unless you tell me."

"You know who did this?" mom says to Angelino.

"For the most part. There was a scuffle between Josh and two other boys in his Spanish class. The problem is, Josh had the bruises when he entered class. Both boys said they didn't do anything."

I was so frantic. My fingers were digging into the wood on the chair. I wanted to shout it all, but I knew all the harm that could be done if I did, so I continued staying silent. Mom broke the silence.

"Well, why don't we bring them down here and straighten this out. I'll get them to tell the truth."

"I don't feel it would be appropriate to have them here without a parent if you are going to be here," Angelino said.

"Thank God," I thought to myself.

Angelino goes back to his desk and buzzes Maggie, his secretary to the office.

"Maggie, can you please place a call to Mrs. Olsen and Mrs. Bankman and see if they can come down to the school."

"What?!!...no no no, oh God no," I think. My heart starts to race.

Maggie returns a short time later. "I was able to get them to come in, but Mrs. Bankman can't make it until 1. I have them both on hold right now."

"Can you come back at one?" he asks, turning to mom.

"Sure."

He turns back to Maggie and tells her to have them come in at one. He then thanks my mom and tells her he'll see her at one. She stands and thanks him.

I was still sitting there, trying to process what just happened and what is going to happen. I notice Mom kneel down next to me.

"I know you're scared, but you have to tell what happened, OK?" she says, running her hand through my hair. "I'll be back at one. I love you no matter what, remember."

So now I'm going to have this hanging over my head all day. She leaves and I'm sent to my first period class. Great. English with Michelle.

Class has already started when I enter. My eyes meet with Michelle's. I'm giving her the deepest hated look I can. I take my seat and I can see the eyes all upon me. Rumors have been circling about what happened in Mrs. Tavares' class.

Science class wasn't any better. Luckily the last lab project was finished before all of this occurred. A new project is set to start today. I missed the paperwork for it yesterday. Mr. Jennings hands it to me as I enter class. Derek isn't here yet. Hopefully he's not here today. Damn, here he comes, big shit eating grin on his face.

"We were wondering whether or not you were ever gonna show up again fag. Garrett's got a little surprise for you," he says, upon sitting down.

I ignore him as Mr. Jennings passes out the supplies needed for the next lab project.

"What, nothing to say? Derek continues.

"Let's just start this project," I answer.

"Well enjoy your peace while you can, because when Garrett sees you...."

"Look, not that I should tell you this anyway, but you'll find out soon enough. My mom came and talked to Angelino today."

This pissed him off.

"What?! If you said anything, you're dead."

"As if I wasn't already. I didn't say anything, but because I didn't, Angelino wanted to call you guys into the office, but with my mom there he didn't feel it would be appropriate," I said, turning away and starting the project..."That's why he felt it better to call your mom and Garrett's mom and have them come in."

"You pansy assed faggot!!" he said, grabbing my arm.

"It's not my idea, you think I want this. I said everything was fine," I told him, pulling my arm back.

"Oh ho, you're dead. So dead."

"Well you better make it before one o'clock, because that's when we all meet in Angelino's office."

Who knew there were so many different ways to say "You're dead." All the way to Gym class, Derek kept saying it in various forms, even as we entered the locker room. Garrett wasn't there yet. I don't think I've ever changed clothes faster. I changed and headed right out to the gym floor. Nobody else is here. I'm all alone. I need somebody. Where are Evelyn and Steph? Where is Ms. Annasandy? Oh shit, here come Derek and Garrett. I stand up, awaiting the confrontation.

"No you don't!"

Evelyn and Steph have come running out of the girl's locker room. Evelyn is blocking Garrett.

"Out of my way Evelyn. This fag is gonna get what's coming to him," he tells her.

"It's over!" she shouts.

"No, it's not over. Queer boy had to go and tell his mom-my."

Evelyn is still blocking his path. I then watch as Ms. Annasandy comes out, blowing her whistle. She breaks everyone apart and tells all of us to take our seats.

"This isn't over fag boy!" Garrett yells, before taking his seat.

I told Evelyn and Steph what happened this morning.

"I don't know what I'm going to say. I want to get them in trouble, but I don't want any of the gay stuff coming up," I told them.

"What gay stuff?" Megan says. I didn't notice her and Stuart sit down.

"I don't want to go into all the details now. Let's just say I got beat up because of it."

I didn't want to tell them anything else right now. I looked over and saw Randy leave the locker room and take his seat. Steph comes up and hugs me from behind.

"For some reason they haven't mentioned him," I tell her, glancing at Randy.

"Then you don't mention him either. They won't bring it up. They're just protecting him. Just tell them about the fight in the bathroom. If his name comes up, do what you have to. Everything will be ok."

While Steph is talking to me, I can hear Megan and Stuart pressuring Evelyn for info. She tells them that I'm gay and that's why I got beat up and they have to keep it a secret. Part of me was upset that she told them, but they were my friends and I can use all the support I can get.

"We're all here for you, unlike some other people," Steph said, directing that last part at Randy, who pretends not to hear it.

I looked around at my friends, making eye contact with each one. They smile and nod their heads yes...except one.

"Stu?" I say. He won't make eye contact with me. I really needed his support. I wouldn't get it.

Ms. Annasandy calls for everyone to head out to the track. Stuart gets up and quickly walks out. I get up and run, catching up to him, putting my hand on his shoulder. "Wait up."

He pulled my hand away and took off for the track. I really don't want to jog right now. I really don't want to do anything but crawl into a corner and die.

"It'll be ok. I'll talk to him," Megan says.

Time for Spanish class. My first time back since the fight. As I approach, I see Mrs. Tavares at the door. She takes me aside. She wants to know what happened and if there is going to be a problem today. I apologized for the other day and told her that all the guilty parties are meeting with their moms in Angelino's office at one.

"I moved your seat to the other side of the room. I thought you might want that," she said.

"Yes, thank you." I said, smiling.

"You should have told me sooner that you were having problems with them."

I just nodded my head and took my new seat. As I sat down, I looked up and saw Randy and Michelle. They are just outside the door, hugging and kissing each other. They're talking and laughing about something and my heart breaks a little more. He gives her a quick kiss goodbye and his eyes open and see me staring at him. That smile quickly leaves his face. He kisses Michelle goodbye and gives me another look before taking off. Michelle enters the class with Derek and Garrett. They all look at me. Derek mouths the words "You're dead." I turned my head away.

French class. Eighteen minutes until one o'clock. Evelyn has been trying to calm me down since History class. I have nothing to say. I'm too nervous. We take our seats and my eyes go to the clock. I watch that second hand counting down, circling the clock, making it closer to one. Mrs. Rosario is absent today. The sub has busy work for us.

My eyes turn from the clock as I see Randy enter. He avoids looking at me. I turn from the clock and stare at the back of his head as he takes his seat. I know he can tell that I'm looking at him. My eyes return to the clock. Somewhere in my head I hear Steph. She's saying hello, but it seems too distant.

The minutes tick away and my body can't take much more. I start to sweat. I can feel my whole body shaking. I feel Evelyn's hand touching mine. She's saying something, but I don't care right now. Now it's Steph's turn. I only care about the clock. All of a sudden I hear Randy's voice. He's calling my name. He shakes me. I turn from the clock.

"Hey man, hey…It's gonna be alright," he says.

I turn and stare straight into his eyes. Is he for real? My anger level goes through the roof.

"Look, I'm sorry…" he starts saying. I cut him off.

"GO FUCK YOURSELF!!!" I yell, loud enough for the whole class to hear.

I can't take anymore. I have to get out of here. I grab my books, put them in my backpack and get up. The sub is asking me to sit down. Good luck with that. I stop at Randy's desk. I want to tell him off. I extend my arms to him, looking right at him. I can't. I just stare, put my arms down, heave a heavy sigh and run out of the classroom.

One o'clock

I got to the office just at one. I spent the last few minutes out by the bleachers, not wanting to go to the office. Mom would have killed me if I wasn't there. Everybody else was there. Derek and Garrett gave me these ugly looks.

Angelino felt that his office was going to be a little small for this, so we all left and headed down the hall to an empty classroom. Right as everyone took their seats, you could see that sides were chosen. There was a whole row of desks dividing my mom and I from Garrett, Derek and their moms. Mom was sitting to my left, Garrett was two rows to my right, Derek was sitting behind him and their moms were to their right. Angelino is standing at the front of the classroom, leaning on the teacher's desk. He's looking around at all of us. He doesn't seem to know where to start.

"Tell him what happened. It will be ok," mom says. So I begin telling the story, leaving out specific details. I started the story in the boy's bathroom. I mention them dragging me in there, attacking me, how I became angry when I walked into Spanish class and they started laughing and insulting me. "I just snapped and went after Garrett."

"My son would never do anything like that," Mrs. Olsen says.

"Mine either. He may be big, but he's no bully," Mrs. Bankman says, joining in on the delusion.

"Are you saying my son's a liar? Look at his face, why would he make this up?" Mom snapped.

Angelino started calming everybody down, then he turned to Derek, asking him if what I was saying was true. He denied it. Same question to Garrett. He also denied it. The he turns back to me.

"Why did they do this?"

"I don't know why?" I said, getting angrier. Angelino then turned to Garrett and asked him why.

"I don't know what happened to him. Maybe he fell," Garrett said.

"Fell?! Fell?!" I'm thinking to myself. I had enough.

"Yeah, I fell on your fist a few times, Neanderthal scumbag". The Neanderthal scumbag part set him off. He stands up and starts yelling.

"Screw you fag boy! You got exactly what you deserved!!"

I was smiling now, the dumbass just incriminated himself. Unfortunately my smile didn't last long, because the dumb jock doesn't stop.

"Look, we were only defending Randy."

Derek shot Garrett this evil look.

"What does Randy have to do with all this?" Angelino asks.

Then not realizing that she's doing more harm than good, Mom opens her mouth.

"Randy Sawyer? Josh wouldn't do anything to Randy. They're good friends. He's been over the house for dinner a few times, hanging out with Josh."

Oh my God, the looks on Garrett and Derek's faces after she said that. This causes Angelino to call the office and have Maggie call Randy and Mrs. Sawyer down to the classroom. Patricia Sawyer arrives first. She sees all of us and our moms.

"What's going on?" she asks Angelino.

Angelino thanks her for coming and she takes the seat next to mine. When Randy enters, you can see the scared look on his face. Garrett and Derek were staring at him. Then he notices his mom there and he starts to panic. He takes the seat behind her. The second he does, Angelino asks him to tell what he knows about all of this. Randy of course has no idea what was already said. I think that's what Angelino is counting on.

I'm sitting there hoping he doesn't say the wrong thing. The first thing he mentions is the locker room. I could hear the closet door expanding.

"It was just a misunderstanding between me and Josh that got a little out of hand and maybe Garrett and Derek misinterpreted it and overreacted."

Garrett, still on a roll from before, snapped, "What do you mean misinterpreted? You said you thought he tried to hit on you. You threw him to the ground."

"You tried to hit on him?" Mom whispered to me. I didn't answer, because while she was saying this, it was Mrs. Sawyer's turn to try and help and do more harm than good.

"I don't understand it. There was never a problem before. They always seemed to get along real well whenever Josh came over."

"He was over your house?" Derek asked.

"Oh man, are you gay too?" asked Garrett.

This causes everyone to start talking loudly, except me and Randy. Randy was sitting there with his head down, running his hands through his hair. I knew I needed to get this under control or we were both going to be out. I stood up and started yelling.

"Shut up! Shut up! Everybody just shut up!" (Everybody got quiet). "Thank you. Now before all the gay rumors start, let me say that Randy is not gay. We were over each other's houses because he wanted to talk to me about Steph. I'm sorry Randy, I have to say it. Randy was interested in Stephanie and he wanted my help. Nobody knew about it, because of what you guys thought of me."

"Is this true man?" Derek says. Randy is still looking at me, knowing that he's being saved. He turns to Derek and nods his head yes.

"Dude, you should've come to us," Derek continues.

"Yeah, we could've helped you with that, not this geek." Garrett chimes in. Randy is silent so I step up again.

"Yes, but I'm good friends with her, what she likes, what she doesn't". Crisis averted, now things could go back to normal, except...

"OK enough of that. Let's get back to the matter at hand. Why the fighting? Let's get back to the locker room," Angelino says. Then he turns to Randy, "Did Josh hit on you in the locker room?"

Now it's Randy's turn to save me. All he has to do is say no and everything should be fine. He doesn't answer Angelino. He's still a little frazzled, but now that he's off the hook, he's been talking with his friends, completely forgetting about me. Angelino asks again and he finally answers.

"Yes"

"And you threw him to the ground?"

"Yeah...but..." He finally realizes what he's done, but it's too late. Angelino turns and asks me if I hit on Randy. Everybody sees the look on Randy's face. They know the answer. I don't believe it, but I hear the word coming out of my mouth.

"Yes."

There goes the closet. I was now in the open, completely out.

"Damn, he really is a fag," I hear Garrett saying. Angelino then asks me if I'm gay. I don't answer. I just start crying. Mom comes over and tries to comfort me. I lightly push her away. "Mom, no," I say lightly. She goes and sits back down.

Angelino turns to Garrett and Derek. "So you beat him up for hitting on your friend? True or false?" Neither answers. "True or false?" he asks again, more forcefully.

"True." Derek says.

"What?!" Garrett says, shooting Derek a look.

"Look, it's over. Yeah, we did it," Derek confesses. Garrett shakes his head and folds his arms. Angelino continues.

"And then you insulted him in Spanish class."

Derek nods his head yes and then Angelino turns to me.

"And when they did that, you went after them."

I nod my head yes.

"Alright, now that we have the story, what are we going to do about it? Randy, you can go." He heads out. Mrs. Sawyer gets up. "Thank you Patricia." She comes over and gives me a hug before leaving.

"Based on what was done, you should all be suspended, but this is a tough one. So I'm going to do something I don't normally do. I'm going to forego punishment, because I believe that in this case it won't solve anything, but...you two are going to stop harassing Josh...and Josh, you are going to tell somebody or walk away if anything occurs. One incident from any of you and I can assure you, the punishment will be severe. You guys can go."

He sends us on our way while he stays and talks with our moms for a little bit. I head to Math class, unsure about what just happened.

After class, as I'm heading to my car, I see that Steph and Evelyn are at my car waiting for me.

"So what happened? You're still alive. That's a good sign. Were you suspended? Were they suspended?" Steph asked. Her questions just kept coming. I shook my head no to many of them.

"Nobody got anything," I told her.

I started telling them all about what happened. Then I dreaded having to tell Steph I brought up her name.

"Everybody was yelling, so I needed to do something to throw them off track."

"What did you do?" Evelyn asked.

I grabbed Steph's hands and looked straight at her. "Don't hate me," I said.

"What did you do?" she asked, knowing it wasn't good.

"I may have said that we were over each other's houses because he has a crush on you and wanted my help in getting you."

Evelyn started laughing. Steph let go of my hands.

"Are you nuts? After all the bleachers crap. You guys have to stop putting me in the middle of your gay drama. Now Michelle is going to give me more shit. Her and her bitch cheerleader friends."

"I'm sorry. I didn't know what to say. It just came out."

"It's alright, I guess. I'll survive. I've dealt with Michelle before. I can handle it. At least you're still in the closet."

I lowered my head. They were both in shock.

"Oh my god, you're out? How?" Steph said.

I explained to them what happened and how Randy fucked up.

"But of course his secret is still safe," Evelyn said.

"Oh, Josh," Steph said, coming up and hugging me. "You going to be alright?"

I shrugged my shoulders and asked them if we could go to the arcade.

"Sure. Let's go. My treat," Steph said.

While at the arcade, they tell me that they'll help me through this and that everything will be OK.

When I got home from the mall, Mom wanted to talk to me. We went into the kitchen. She baked a chocolate chip cake, my favorite, and told me to sit down. We sat there and I told her it all. My crush on Randy, the kiss under the bleachers, how he ignored me, the little argument on the track and everything else that happened the other day. She told me that she thought Randy might be gay. She gave me her support and told me everything will be fine.

"You should give your uncle a call and tell him what's going on. See what advice he has."

Luckily my uncle was home. I told him everything. He was excited that I got the quarterback. Then he gave me some pointers on surviving.

"Expect Randy to totally distance himself from you. He's probably going to act real straight for a while, putting on a heavy macho image. Just let him be. If he truly is gay, he will come to you when the time is right. Just don't expect it to be anytime soon."

SATURDAY MARCH 16, 1985

I'm just glad this all happened on a Friday. Two days to clear my head, gather my thoughts and figure out how I'm going to handle this.

This morning I got to see that support my uncle said my mom would be giving. Mom was outside in the front yard doing some gardening, when our neighbor from across the street, Mrs. Bellaski, came over. I heard her and Mom talking. Mrs. B. is a snobby busybody. She tries to get into everyone's business. I was staring out the living room window watching them.

"I'm so sorry," she said to my mom.

"Sorry for what?" Mom asked her.

"Sorry that your son is gay."

"I'm not sorry. I love my children, gay or straight."

That made me so happy to hear that. You would think that upon hearing that, the woman would get the hint. Nope. She actually started quoting the bible, standing there telling my mother that I was going to burn in Hell if I didn't repent.

I couldn't wait for mom's response. I knew it wasn't going to be pretty. Mom went all ballistic, telling the woman off, pretty much saying what everyone on the block has wanted to say to her. Mrs. B. turned five shades of red, before storming off back to her house. Too funny.

It seems that I wasn't the only one who saw and heard Mom and this woman arguing. I headed upstairs. When I got to the top of the steps I took a quick glance into my Mom's bedroom.

Standing, looking out the window was Taylor. Nobody had talked to him about all of this yet.

"Are you going to Hell?" he turned and asked me.

"Come here," I told him.

We sat down on his bed and had a brother to brother talk about homosexuality, what it means, what people think about it, etc., etc. He would ask a question and I would answer. Then he fired one off I didn't really know how to answer.

"Am I going to be gay too?"

He's 12 years old. How do you answer that? I mean, when I was 12 I was pretend kissing with girls. Millie Stark and I would always hang out. We always went to the school dances together, but I never thought of her "that" way. At the time I didn't even know what "that" way was. I didn't know what any way was.

I was raised that boys date, kiss, fall in love with and marry girls. I mean, even now I can look at a girl and say she's attractive, but she does nothing for me physically. It was around the age of 13 that I started thinking about guys. I don't know why. I can't pinpoint a date. It just started. I believe that if you are gay, you are born gay and your environment shapes how you end up acting. So how to answer him.

"I don't know. Maybe, maybe not, but no matter what happens, you've got a big brother to stand up for you."

I also told him that he might start hearing things in school about me. Many of the seniors, Garrett included, have little brothers and sisters in his grade.

"What do I say to them?" he asks.

"Ignore them. If you have to say anything, say "I could care less if he's gay".

He looked a little confused, but I think he understood what I was saying.

SUNDAY MARCH 17, 1985

HAPPY ST. PATRICK'S DAY

I didn't want to leave the house, but I was scheduled to work today. It's St. Patrick's Day. I wasn't in a festive mood, but I did find something green to wear.

Heading into the mall, I stopped and donated a few dollars to the local veterans group raising money. They handed me a green poppy pin.

"Whoa, you run into a wall or something?" Mr. Totino said, laughing as I entered Total Eclipse. This was my first day back since the fight. I explained the whole situation to him. I wanted him to know everything, in case any problems arose. He told me he has a nephew who's gay and offered to set me up. We both laughed.

"Hey, if anybody gives you trouble, I will personally kick them out of the store," he said.

Mr. Totino was true to his word. A short time later, Garrett came in with a few wrestling jocks. He would occasionally yell a gay slur across the store. Now I don't know if I mentioned it before, but whereas Garrett is a chunky slob, Mr. Totino is 285 pounds of muscle. I mean a walking brick wall. Nobody gives him shit. He heard Garrett and came out from the back. I watched, all he did was walk up to Garrett and that was it. He whispered something in his ear. Garrett looked like he was going to pee himself. He quickly left with his jock friends. It's so good to have safety at work.

MONDAY MARCH 18, 1985

I didn't want to get out of bed. The whole school had to know by now. Joshua Parker is gay.

Just like the 1st day of school, heads turned when I entered the parking lot. Except this time they weren't looking at the car, they were looking at the driver. Everybody was staring. I pulled into a space and didn't want to get out. I was hoping I would see Evelyn or Steph there, but all I saw were jocks and cheers. Time to face reality. I walked past them, not making eye contact.

"Faggot!" said a jock.

"Flamer!" yelled a cheerleader.

I quickly headed inside and to my locker. Oh how sweet, someone was nice enough to write the word "Faggot" across my locker in pink nail polish. I grabbed my books and headed to homeroom.

Evelyn was standing outside the homeroom door. She was surrounded by many students wanting info. They all turn when they see me. Evelyn is the only one to give me a smile. I'm about to enter class when I hear...

"He's all man and he's all mine."

Michelle and Randy are coming down the hall. I watch as some students come up, asking him if he's OK. As if getting hit on by a gay guy is a life threatening crisis. I watch as he brushes them off with a slight laugh. I head into homeroom.

How am I going to handle him? Will he want to talk? Despite what my uncle said, I hope he'll want to talk. Here he comes...where's he going? He's sitting down in a seat on the other side of the room. What, now he won't even sit near me? Miss Carter will make him move back. She didn't assign seats, but she did say there would be no seat changes. Why isn't she saying something? She knows that's not his seat.

"How are you?" Evelyn says, kissing me on the cheek.

"OK...so far," I say.

She tells me that it's all over school. Everybody knows I'm gay and that I tried to hit on Randy. I asked her about Randy's seat change. She said she heard that Angelino had a meeting with all my teachers this morning and he told them to do whatever it takes to keep the peace. So I guess that includes seat changes. She saw Mr. Stanton talking to Randy and Derek about it.

"It will be OK. It might be tough for a little bit, but I'm doing what I can to keep things under control. Your only problems really are the jocks and cheerleaders. They still have it out for you, but Angelino's keeping a tight watch. He's not going to let anything happen to you. Plus, you've still got Steph, Megan and, of course, me."

"Stuart still doesn't want to talk to me?" I ask, picking up that she left him out.

"This hit him hard. You gotta give him some time. He and Megan have been arguing about it. She'll get him to come around. Has "he" said anything to you?" she says, looking at Randy.

"No, nothing yet. I don't think he will."

"Cheer up."

Easy for her to say

Science class. Time to deal with Derek. He's not here. I saw him earlier. He'll be late again. Yup, here he comes.

"I'm going to sit over here," he tells Mr. Jennings, pointing to another table, making his way over.

"Take your assigned seat, Mr. Olsen," Jennings says.

"But…"

"The assignment has already started. Take your seat."

"I don't want to sit…"

"You can either take your seat Mr. Olsen or you can leave and take an F."

He decided to take his seat.

"Don't talk to me. Don't look at me and if you even "remotely" touch me, so help me god, I'll kill you…faggot," he says angrily to me, moving his seat as far away from me as possible.

I ignore him and work on my part of the assignment. Of course, the moron can't do his part of the project and God forbid he should ask me for help. I sigh and help him through it. Brainless wonder.

When the bell rang, Derek took off, leaving me to clean up. I didn't care, but now I was running late for Gym.

Stuart...He's standing by the locker room door. I figured he was waiting to talk to me.

"Hey, what's up?" I say, smiling.

He doesn't say anything. He moves to the front of the door, blocking it.

"I'm running late," I say, trying to reach for the handle. He won't move.

"What's this?" I ask.

"Look, I've been asked by some of the guys to have you wait out here until they've changed."

"Why?"

He goes and shrugs his shoulders, moving his head, giving me that "You know" sign. Now I'm angry.

"Out of my way!" I tell him, trying to push him away from the door. He won't budge. "Stuart!!" I yell.

"You're not wanted in here Josh...

I stopped pushing and looked at him.

...Nobody wants you in here. Just stay out," he says, before turning and entering the locker room.

I stood there hurt and stunned. I leaned against the wall and slid down, sitting on the floor, taking in what Stuart said. This would hurt if it was someone else, but it just kills with it being Stuart. Here's a friend, or someone I thought was a friend, not only avoiding me, but standing up for the jocks and helping them keep me out.

A few minutes later I entered the locker room. Many of the guys have already left and the others there are already changed. They all give me these strange, hurtful stares and quickly leave. I'm all alone. I've never felt more alone than I do now. I change and head out to the gym floor.

Of course class has already started. Ms. Annasandy doesn't say anything about me entering late. She continues warm-up exercises. I see that Randy and Derek have changed their seats. They are sitting closer to Michelle and Garrett. I sit down, giving Stuart an angry look. He turns away.

"Are you OK?" Steph asks.

I nod my head yes and begin stretching. Both she and Evelyn are looking at me, not believing me.

"I'll tell you later," I say to them. I just keep looking at Stuart. Megan turns and smiles at me. I smile back. We head out to the track.

Right as we got to the track, I told them what happened.

"He What?!?!" Evelyn said.

"Screw them. You have just as much right in there as they do. You shouldn't have to wait because of them. I can't believe Stuart would do that," Steph says.

"I tried to talk to him," I tell her.

"I'll go talk to him," Evelyn says.

"No, I can..." I start to say, but she's off.

She catches up to Stuart, who of course is jogging with Megan. Steph and I catch up and are a little behind them. We listen in.

"Hey Evelyn. What's up?" Megan says, her usual perky self.

"Just need to ask your boyfriend something...

Stuart is ignoring her.

...How could you do that to him?" Evelyn asks him.

Megan is puzzled, wondering what's going on.

"What did he do? What did you do?" Megan asks. Stuart is still silent.

"Oh, he didn't tell you? Why don't you tell her Stuart? Come on. Tell her how you kept Josh from entering the locker room today, telling him not to go in, blocking the door. Telling him he's not wanted in there and that NOBODY wants him in there."

"Did you do that?!" Megan says angrily.

"Look, they asked me..." Stuart finally speaks, but Megan's not taking it. She cuts him off.

"They who?" He doesn't answer. "They who?!!" she yells.

"Just a few of the guys alright. They don't want to get changed with him there. So they asked me…"

"And you listened to them!?" she yells, cutting him off again.

"I said no at first, but then I had no choice. They were saying that because I was friends with him and wouldn't do it, I must be gay too. So I …"

"So what?! So you sacrificed a friendship and made Josh feel even worse because you can't handle a few names? He needs friends right now. I can't believe you. On Friday you said that you just needed a little time and now you go and do this."

Before Stuart can respond, she jogs away from him. She's disgusted. Stuart stops jogging and stands on the side. Evelyn falls back, joining me and Steph.

After class, Ms. Annasandy talked to me, giving me her support. In Spanish class, Mrs. Tavares asked me if I was alright, telling me I got a 100 on the Spanish test. It felt good to have the support of my teachers.

Well not all of them.

Mr. Stanton is by the door, watching the students enter. He gives me this strange look, but I dismiss it, until Garrett enters. He takes Garrett back out into the hall, giving me that look again. I watch as they go down to the empty classroom next door. Evelyn isn't here yet and the rest of the class is talking, so I get up and sneak down to the other classroom. I can't believe what I'm hearing.

"Heard you had a little problem," Stanton was asking Garrett.

"Nothing I couldn't handle," Garrett answers.

"Not what I heard. I heard you let your guard down, lost to a little queer."

I saw Evelyn approach the classroom. I signaled her over. We both listened in. Mr. Stanton was still berating Garrett.

"You never let your guard down. Jeez Garrett, a fag, a freakin fag. I'm so disappointed in you. I thought you were smarter than that."

I couldn't believe that a teacher was calling me a fag. Evelyn was just as shocked as I was, but neither of us said anything. Garrett stood there, taking the abuse.

"I expected better from you. Go take your seat," Stanton continued.

Evelyn and I quickly took off and got to our seats before they saw us. Garrett entered the classroom looking totally deflated. I should have been glad that the Neanderthal got ripped apart, but for some reason I felt sorry for him. Evelyn and I spent the time walking to French class discussing what Stanton said.

TUESDAY MARCH 19, 1985

Just like my uncle said, Randy was playing macho. He never lets Michelle far from his side. They hug and kiss in front of everybody. Nobody seemed to mention what I said about Steph and Randy. I'm sure Randy told them to make sure they keep their big mouths shut about it.

While their "relationship" seems to be stronger, the same can't be said for Megan and Stuart. They broke up. Well she broke up with him. He's devastated. She can't stand to have an uncaring boyfriend. Who can blame her?

WEDNESDAY MARCH 20, 1985

Angelino has been positioning himself so that he runs into me in the halls at least twice a day. He's always asking me how things are going. I always tell him I'm fine, even though I'm not. I have bruises on my arms from being shoved into the lockers. With the hallways being so crowded, I don't see it coming, so I can't balance myself. By the time I regain composure, the guilty party is long gone.

Taylor got his first taste of the backlash of me being out. We hadn't hung out for a while, so I took him out for a drive to the mall. We met up with Steph and Evelyn at the arcade. Well as usual, Evelyn popped in and out. Of course it was air hockey time for the rest of us.

I was playing against Steph while Taylor watched, when Adam came in with a couple of other kids. I watched as Taylor went over to say hello.

"We don't play with fags," one of Adam's friends said, some dorky looking kid with a mullet.

"I'm not gay," Taylor answered. He's learned from me not to use the word fag.

"Well your brother is, so that means you must be, too," Mullet responded.

Adam wouldn't say anything, quiet just like his brother. I could tell that Adam wanted to hang out with Taylor, but he followed his friends

"Fuck off!" Taylor answered Mullet, before heading back to us.

I hi-fived him, but told him to watch the language. He seemed cool about it, but I know it hurt a little. It did help him play better though. He eventually won a game. I have one tough, smart little brother.

THURSDAY MARCH 21, 1985

Randy came into Total Eclipse today. I watched him walk around the store checking things out. We were a little busy, so I had to help out by going on the other register. Randy got in line. The woman I was helping finished. As she left, I looked up at Randy, but he didn't come over. He let the guy behind him go ahead, while he waited for the other register to be available.

FRIDAY MARCH 22, 1985

"I'm sorry about Stuart," Megan said.

She was apologizing to me once again for Stuart. I told her to stop apologizing, but this time I could tell that she wanted to talk to me about it.

"I don't understand. He was never prejudiced against anybody," she said.

I asked her how she's handling it. She has five classes with him, not to mention student council, honor clubs and newspaper/yearbook staff.

"It's tough. He keeps trying to make up, but whenever I tell him that he needs to apologize to you first, he backs away. I can't have a boyfriend who won't stand up for himself and his friends. I need someone who doesn't give a shit what anybody else thinks."

"So what did Mrs. Brandon think about my ideas for an article on homosexuality for the paper?" I asked her.

She told me that Angelino gave Mrs. Brandon strict orders that nothing concerning my sexuality gets printed in the paper. Nothing. No stories, comments, jokes, nothing good or bad.

This sucks. I can understand not wanting to put anything bad in there, but this idea for an article is positive. I'll have to talk to Mrs. Brandon about it on Monday.

SATURDAY MARCH 23, 1985

Garrett came into Total Eclipse today. I was restocking the top 40 albums while Mr. Totino walked right up to him.

"I know. I know. I came to apologize. I'm sorry about..." Garrett started saying.

"Don't apologize to me. Apologize to Josh," he said, cutting Garrett off.

He walked right over to me and apologized. It was the fakest apology I had ever heard, but I didn't want him in my face any longer than it already was, so I signaled to Mr. Totino that it was OK.

He walked around the store for like ten minutes, bought a few heavy metal cassettes and headed out.

SUNDAY MARCH 24, 1985

I'm still learning to deal with the name calling, even though it's really just the jocks and cheerleaders who say it, at least to my face. Everybody else seems to just ignore me, like I've got some contagious disease. Except Evelyn, Steph and Megan, of course.

We'll see what Tommy has to say tomorrow. He's been gone since the 12th, the day before everything blew up. His grandmother passed away, so he had to fly to Illinois with his family for the funeral and to organize her things. He comes back tonight and, boy oh boy, what he's missed. I hope he understands. I have to not only see him here at school, but also at work and I can't really afford to lose another friend right now.

I went to see Tommy. I couldn't wait until tomorrow. I wanted him to hear everything from me. It didn't go the way I thought it would.

"What happened to you?" he said, opening the door. It's been a week since the fight, but I still look bad.

"You missed a lot," I told him, laughing.

His mom was in the kitchen cooking dinner and his dad was in the living room watching TV, so I asked him to join me outside. We went and stood out by my car.

"OK, I want you to hear about all of this from me before you start hearing it from everybody else. You might not like everything you hear, but regardless of what you think, you have to let me finish," I said.

"OK," he said nervously.

I had spent the whole ride over to his house trying to figure out exactly what to say. I told him the condensed version of what happened, leaving out all the parts about Randy being gay. I used Randy's words about there being a misunderstanding in the locker room and how things escalated, eventually leading me to be out.

Tommy sat there stunned, listening to every word, looking like he couldn't believe what I was saying.

"Now it's your turn," I said when I finished.

"What do you want me to say?" he asked.

"I need to know if you're still my friend."

"Of course I'm still your friend."

I was so glad to hear him say that. His mom then called him in for dinner, so I got in my car. He came up to the window, saying we should hang out tomorrow after school.

"Sure. Cool. Oh and thank you," I said to him.

"No problem...Oh and you're not the only one," he said, putting his finger to his lips, before running inside.

I watched him go in. Did he just say what I thought he said? I drove away, not knowing what to think.

MONDAY MARCH 25, 1985

I'm so glad that Tommy is also gay. It will be nice to actually be able to talk to somebody who's going through the exact same things that I am. This morning, when he passed by me, he didn't say anything, he just smiled and put his finger to his lips. I'm waiting for him right now so we can go hang out. Here he comes. I'll write more later.

So much for Tommy being out

I watched him coming down the hall. He ran into the bathroom. I know he saw me. I've had enough shit this week. No more baby games. I headed right into the bathroom. We were alone.

"What the hell? Why did...? Are you alright?" I started saying angrily, until I saw that he was crying.

"I can't do it. I'm sorry. I think it's great that you're out, but I can't do it," he said.

I think he's been seeing how I'm being treated. Today was a pretty rough day. A lot of shoves and name calling in the halls. He doesn't think he can handle it.

"I understand, but it's not OK to ignore me. Maybe you don't want to hang out, but that doesn't mean we can't be friends. Just come hang out when I'm with Evelyn and Steph," I said, trying to make him calm.

He nodded his head and told me he would think about it. He also told me that his parents are discussing moving back to Illinois at the end of the school year and that he might go. He would have to choose either to go with them or stay here and live with his older sister.

TUESDAY MARCH 26, 1985

I talked to Mrs. Brandon this morning. She liked my idea for an article about homosexuality, but sided with Angelino, saying she didn't feel right putting it in the paper at this time. I was tired of all this. Another win for them. It was time to put a win in my column. All last week, I would change in the bathroom or wait for everybody to leave. Well today would be different.

"FAG ALERT!!"

This was yelled as I entered the locker room. This seems to be their way of announcing my presence. As I made my way to my gym locker, many of them would say it.

Everybody stopped what they were doing and covered up, even Randy. Nobody would change while I was there. They all waited until I changed and left. I of course noticed this and took my sweet ass time.

As I was leaving the locker room, I noticed a few jocks going up to Stuart. This delay of course caused many of them to be late. Stuart came out of the locker room but didn't say anything to me.

After class I went right back into the locker room, much to the disgust of everyone. I expected Stuart to come up and say something, but he didn't. I really wanted a confrontation. Oh well, maybe tomorrow.

WEDNESDAY MARCH 27, 1985

Guess who was standing in front of the locker room door today? This was not going to be a repeat of last time.

"Please don't," was all Stuart could say as I approached.

"Move," I said. He wouldn't.

"Move now!" I said louder. He still wouldn't.

I was too angry at this point. I grabbed him and shoved him away from the door. I reached for the handle and was about to go in, but I had to say something first.

"You are such a cowardly piece of shit. No wonder Megan doesn't want to go out with you anymore. Stand up for yourself for once."

"FAG ALERT!"

Randy came into Total Eclipse alone again tonight. It was the same routine. What is he doing?

THURSDAY MARCH 28, 1985

This "win" was of course causing more shoving and name calling in the halls, but I didn't care.

Today in Science class, Derek decided to make himself spokesman for the guys in the locker room, seeing as Stuart failed them.

"Like I know I'm not supposed to say anything bad to you (He already has), but what's your problem? Can't you see that nobody wants you in the locker room while they're changing?"

"That's their problem. I'm changing in there. If they don't like it, they can come in late or change in the bathroom," I told him.

This pissed him off, because he knew there was nobody he could complain to. Ms. Annasandy wasn't going to listen to him and if he approached Angelino about it, he would get a lecture. Nobody was on their side. Or so I thought.

"Mr. Parker, can I talk to you for a minute?"

Mr. Stanton stopped me as I was walking into class with Evelyn. I gave her a look before heading into the hallway with Stanton.

"I've been getting some complaints from my players (ex-players, football and wrestling seasons are well over), about you being in the locker room," he says.

Does he seriously think that because he's a teacher, I should listen to him? This is the same man who referred to me as a fag. He's a Neanderthal ex-jock.

"I deserve to be there just as much as they do," I responded.

"Just change somewhere else," was all he could say.

I gave him a "whatever" look and walked away from him and headed into class. Evelyn and I were laughing about it on the way to French class.

As we turned the corner by the French room, we heard yelling. A familiar yelling that we hadn't heard in a while. It seems Randy and Michelle are fighting again. Their first fight in weeks. I knew it was only a matter of time. There was only so long they could stand being that close to each other before things erupted. Evelyn and I walked past them. My eyes met with Randy's. I shook my head and did a light laugh.

FRIDAY MARCH 29, 1985

Oh what an interesting day today was. Before school, I kept wondering how Stanton would act. How he did, I never expected.

As I left Science class, I sensed something was up and it wasn't good. On the way to Gym, Derek was behind me. He was staring at me and he had that shit eating grin on his face. I didn't want him behind me, so I moved to the side and let him pass. He smiled at me as he did.

"What's he up to?" I was thinking. As I approached the locker room door, I saw what was up.

"Not you. You wait."

Mr. Stanton was standing at the boy's locker room door, monitoring everybody going in. Of course he refused to let me in.

"Time to go see Angelino," I thought, but as I turned to head to the office, I remembered that he's not here today. He's away at some conference and won't be back until Wednesday. I knew I couldn't just push Stanton out of the way. What to do?

The Gym door. I'll just go in that way. I rounded the corner towards the gym entrance. As I was passing the girl's locker room door, I saw Megan and had another idea. I told her to get me Ms. Annasandy.

"What's the matter?" Ms. Annasandy asked, rushing out of the locker room.

I didn't say anything. I just waved my hand and had her follow me. We turned the corner and I pointed at Mr. Stanton. He was still at the door. She brushed past me and went right over to him.

"What's going on?" she asked him.

"Some of the students asked for my help," he told her.

"Your help with what?"

"Look, he's not wanted in there. He's weirding the guys out. Get him to change somewhere else," he said, pulling her aside.

She told him that I deserve to be in there and that this is her class and that he needs to go and mind his own business and let her handle her class.

"I'm only protecting my players," he snapped.

"From what?"

"From people like him," he said, pointing at me.

"Go back to your class Mr. Stanton and I never want to see you harassing any of my students ever again."

He walked away and I know I heard this and she did too.

"Stupid uppity dyke bitch," he mumbled.

She didn't respond to it. She just signaled me to go inside and change. When I got to the gym floor, she started warm-up exercises. She stood there for a few minutes, and then she blew her whistle.

"Everybody listen up. I do not want to hear any more about who can and cannot change in the locker rooms. The locker rooms are for everybody. If you are not happy about something, you are to bring it up to either myself or Principal Angelino. I do not want to see any teacher telling my students what to do during my class. They can speak to me if they wish, but nobody NOBODY gets mistreated in my class. End of discussion."

"What was that about?" Evelyn said, tapping me on the shoulder. I told her all about it.

It was all over school by History class. I didn't want to walk into class alone. I didn't know what to expect, so I waited for Evelyn before going to class.

When we entered, he was there standing at the door. He didn't say anything. He just looked at me, slammed the door and started class. Occasionally I would catch him giving me these ugly looks. At first I looked away, but as they got more frequent, I wised up. Whenever he would do it, I would smile. I know this pissed him off, but he held his tongue. Stupid ex-jocks.

One more for the "win" column

SATURDAY MARCH 30, 1985

Was supposed to work with Tommy tonight. I was really hoping to talk to him, but I found out that he told Mr. Totino that he had family stuff and was going to need to change his hours. Surprisingly, the days he needed to change were the same ones we work together.

SUNDAY MARCH 31, 1985

I was originally only working a partial day today, but with Tommy's changes, Mr. Totino asked me to work all day. I had no problem with it. I need the money. Everybody was going to be busy doing other stuff, so I would just be sitting around the house anyway.

MONDAY APRIL 1, 1985

I hate April Fool's Day. Pranks are my least favorite form of comedy. There really is nothing funny about them.

Walking through the student parking lot, I passed Garrett. I knew he was going to say something and it was going to be stupid. I was in no mood.

"Hey everybody. Guess what. Parker's straight," he said.

Before he could say "April Fools", I said...

"Yeah, I fucked your mother."

This pissed him off. He started chasing me. His fat ass is so slow, he couldn't catch a turtle. As we're running, just before I got inside I turned my head back and yelled...

"April Fools!"

We had a morning announcement today that wasn't an April Fool's joke. The big song out now is "We are the World" by this whole group of singers (Tina Turner, Cyndi Lauper, Michael Jackson, etc. etc.). It's about the famine that's raging in Africa.

Well right after the song came out, it was in the news about all these high schools across the country that were doing things to raise money to help.

Well here at Whitfield High they've decided to do a charity football game against our crosstown rivals, Central High. The game was going to be this Saturday, but it's right between Good Friday and Easter (Spring Break starts Friday), so it's going to be held a week from Saturday on the 13th.

TUESDAY APRIL 2, 1985

The hallways were real quiet today. No real pushing or shoving. It seems the football jocks are spending part of the day practicing. They will be doing it every day this week.

When football season ended, many jocks got jobs after school, so they needed to practice during school time. This is fine with me. I say let them practice every day for the rest of the year, have a charity game every week.

Ever since I've been out, Randy has been doing everything in school he can to avoid me. Part of me understands. What I don't understand is why, yet again, he's come into Total Eclipse. You'd think he'd go to Crazy Eddie's or something.

WEDNESDAY APRIL 3, 1985

After last night's thing with Randy, I decided to just stop worrying about it and avoid anything having to do with him, even though he's not making it easy.

Today I was in one of the stalls in the boy's bathroom when I heard him come in with Derek. I put my feet up and listened in. They started talking the usual jock bullshit and then the topic turned.

"So you nailed Perrino yet?" Derek asked him.

"No. I'm with Michelle...remember?"

"So"

It sounded like Randy shoved him. They were both laughing.

"What? You afraid the little fag she hangs out with is gonna hit on you again?" Derek continued.

Now I was very curious to hear his response to this. Randy mustn't have answered because Derek continued

"You are, aren't you?...Oh Randy. I love you Randy." The dumb jock was making fun of me.

"Quit it," Randy answered.

"You never did tell me what happened that day in the locker room."

"That's because nothing happened."

"What did you say to him?"

"To who?"

"Fag boy."

"Nothing."

"You had to have said something to make him want to hit on you."

"Let's not talk about it, OK."

"I would've just decked him if he tried that on me."

"You did deck him."

"Yeah, right here too. Whap! Bam-Bam!"

I'm guessing the dumb jock was making fight moves.

"I don't need the play by play. You shouldn't have done it," Randy told him.

"Why not?"

"Just because, that's all... Let's get out of here."

They left and I stayed in the stall for a few minutes, thinking about what Randy just said. He's obviously still thinking about everything that happened.

THURSDAY APRIL 4, 1985

The jocks are so excited about the practices and being able to get out and play another game. As are the cheerleaders. Michelle got to plan her own pep rally. All the seniors were forced to attend. I hate pep rallies. Overly perky cheerleaders. The announcing of the dumb jocks, like they're celebrities or something and our beloved coach, Mr. "Piece of Shit" Stanton. The rally went over well enough, even with Michelle's speech.

"This famine thing is such a bummer, you know. People are starving and like we have so much food and stuff. So let's get out there next week and not only support the Whitfield Woodpeckers, but also make a difference. We are the world. We are the children."

What a speaker she is. At least she's helping a good cause.

Today was also report card day #3. An "A' in every class but History. History was a "C" (on purpose I'm sure).

FRIDAY APRIL 5, 1985

GOOD FRIDAY

Worked the day shift today. Mom has the day off so I gladly picked up the shift.

"Remember, no meat today," Mom says as I'm heading out the door.

We're not a very religious family. We've all been baptized. We went to Sunday school for about...a year, but we don't really go to church. One of the things Mom likes us to maintain is no meat on Good Friday. So every year I know exactly what we're going to be having for dinner that day, "Fish".

SATURDAY APRIL 6, 1985

Spent all day cleaning. Tomorrow is Easter. No grandma and grandpa this time, but Uncle Matt is coming down, so everything has to be spotless. Mom wanted me to check with Steph and make sure she wasn't going to be alone. Steph's mom is off from work, so they are going to church and then out to dinner tomorrow.

SUNDAY APRIL 7, 1985

HAPPY EASTER!

A nice relaxing holiday. Surprisingly, no dramatics. After dessert, Uncle Matt and I went outside to talk about all the Randy drama. He knows just how to calm me down.

He also told me that he heard that I was one of the final twelve and that they should be calling sometime this week to set up an appointment later in the month.

"I'm not supposed to say anything, but I was so excited. I just had to. So just act surprised when they call. They're going to be doing the interviews on Saturdays, because everybody is in school," he said.

SO COOL

MONDAY APRIL 8, 1985

I may be off from school all week, but so are the brother and sister, so that means babysitting duties. Today I just spent all day playing video games with Taylor.

TUESDAY APRIL 9, 1985

Steph stopped over today to keep me company. She told me that Megan was over her house last night and wanted to talk to her and Evelyn about Stuart. Steph said that Megan is so upset. She asked me to try and say something to Stuart. Say what though?

WEDNESDAY APRIL 10, 1985

Got the call for the internship interview today. Yes, I pretended to act as if I didn't already know. My interview is in the City on the 27th.

I called my uncle and left a message telling him. He called me back a few hours later and told me to make a weekend of it.

When I sent the application in, I gave Mr. Totino a heads up. Today, I called him to tell him about getting the interview. He was so excited for me. He's going to rearrange the schedule.

Tonight it was time to take Mom out to dinner for her birthday. We were all asleep when she left for work, but I got with Taylor and Alexa and we performed a really corny version of Happy Birthday right as she walked in the door. She's not the only goofy one in this family.

THURSDAY APRIL 11, 1985

Not really knowing what to say or thinking anything would come of it, I tried calling Stuart today. I left a message on his machine, basically telling him that we should hang out and talk about everything and that Megan really misses him. He never responded.

FRIDAY APRIL 12, 1985

The football game is tomorrow. I'm off from work and my plan was to go and sit far in the back. Well, Mrs. Brandon called me this morning, asking me if I'm off tomorrow. Before I could think what she would want, I said "yes".

She needs me to take photos of the game. I don't want to be that close to the field.

SATURDAY APRIL 13, 1985

Why must my life go from bad to worse? This is so not good. Not good at all. I should have stayed home. Why did I get up today?

I spent the whole morning thinking of ways to get out of this. Couldn't think of one. The whole place is packed. The bleachers on both sides are completely full. There was a $2 admission fee for today's game. I could have just showed my press pass from Mrs. Brandon and gotten in for free, but I wanted to help the cause.

I found a nice spot to take pictures...far back by the bleachers. This was great, until Mrs. Brandon saw me and made me get closer. So off to the sidelines I went. I just wanted to avoid Randy. Thank God the sidelines were a little crowded. Coaches, players, fathers, local media and cheerleaders. They were using both Varsity and Junior varsity cheerleaders. Michelle was pissed.

The only problem I was having at this time was that with all these people, it was hard to get a really good shot. I'd been taking some OK ones, but I needed a really good one or I was going to hear shit from Mrs. Brandon.

There was only 3 minutes of the game left. We were down by 4. We needed to get the ball downfield. I overheard Mr. Stanton discussing the next play. He was having one of the guys go deep. So this would be Randy's chance to throw the winning touchdown.

Hearing this, I figured if Randy threw the winning pass, it would be the perfect shot, getting his reaction after. Even if it was unsuccessful, it could still be a great shot. So I moved myself up field.

It was perfect. I was a little ways away from everybody. There were only a few people around. Where I was I would be parallel to Randy when he faded back. No interference.

The huts are called. Randy calls hike, grabs the ball and steps back to throw. I've got the camera right on him.

"Throw it. Throw it," I'm lightly saying to myself.

What happens next just seemed to happen in slow motion. He's looking for someone to throw to. He turns slightly and sees me on the sidelines. He seems to freeze. I lowered the camera and our eyes met. Then I saw the other team coming. Randy didn't see them until it was too late. He went down. Then there were two sounds. The first one I didn't know. It sounded like something broke. The second sound was Randy screaming in pain. "Oh fuck" was all that I could think.

Everybody quickly came running up. It looked like something happened to his leg. Randy couldn't move. I wanted to run up, but he was now surrounded by Stanton, some other players and the local EMT's. I couldn't see him, but I could still hear him crying out in pain. Michelle was trying to get through the crowd. Bitch!!

Next, I saw them putting him on a stretcher, asking everyone to move out of the way. Michelle had now managed to be on one side. Randy's mom and dad were on the other side. He was holding his mom's hand. They quickly took him to the ambulance and then they were off to the hospital. Everybody seemed to be in shock, myself included.

"What the hell just happened?!?

I broke out of my shock to see Mr. Stanton and a few players standing in the spot where Randy went down. Stanton was yelling at Derek.

"I don't know. He seemed to freeze up," Derek answered.

"What do you mean freeze up?! Stanton continued yelling.

"He seemed distracted by something?"

"Distracted by what?"

"I don't know. Something on the sidelines I guess."

I heard him say that and had no time to get away without being spotted. They all turned and saw me. I quickly got the hell out of there.

SUNDAY APRIL 14, 1985

"I'm not here. No matter who calls. Nobody."

I told this to my mother this morning. I didn't want to talk to anybody. I didn't want to leave the house. I didn't want to talk on the phone. I didn't want to leave my room. I was just hoping that everything would calm down by tomorrow.

MONDAY APRIL 15, 1985

I called Evelyn when I got up this morning. I told her to wait for me in the parking lot. There was no way I was walking into school alone.

There were a lot of empty spaces when I pulled into the senior lot. I spotted her standing by her car. She parked on the far end of the lot. I parked my car and walked over to her. There were a few students around her. I didn't see any jocks or cheerleaders though. They all looked as I approached.

"I'll talk to you all later," she told the group. They all left and Evelyn and I were alone.

"Details!" was all she said. She wanted my side of the story. I told her it all. The rumors were already strong and the jocks weren't even there yet. Believe it or not, the jocks and cheerleaders were given permission to go visit Randy, who's home, thank God, and come to school late today.

"What happened to his leg?" I asked her. She wouldn't look at me.

"What happened to his leg?" I repeated.

"Don't think it's your fault," she said.

"What happened to his leg?"

"I've been told there's some permanent damage."

"What do you mean permanent damage?"

"I don't know all the details yet, but something happened with his leg and back. I was told that eventually he'll be able to walk somewhat normally and it will function OK, but I heard his football career is over."

I started walking back to my car. I couldn't breathe. I needed to get out of here. She came up and grabbed me.

"It's not your fault."

"Yes it is. If I would have just stayed away he'd be OK," I said, starting to cry.

She hugged me, telling me it was OK. Leading me into school.

I spent all day in a panic. Nobody has done anything to me. No shoving, no pushing, no insults. They did still say "Fag Alert", but that was it. That and they just stared at me.

"Mr. Stanton told everybody to leave you alone and that he would handle it," Evelyn tells me as we're taking our seats in History class.

"Mr. Parker, come with me please," Stanton says, entering the room.

I was really panicking now. We went to an empty classroom. He slammed the door and told me to sit down.

"I think I'll stand," I told him. He seemed to have this crazed look in his eyes and I did not want to be in a position where I couldn't move.

"Fine…What the hell's your problem?" he says to me.

"Excuse me?"

"Don't play stupid with me. The football game. Randy's never going to be able to play football again. Career GONE, scholarship GONE, future GONE, all because you can't keep your faggot self away from him. He's a man, not some friggin queer and now his whole life has to change because of you."

I was scared. I told him it wasn't my fault and I was just trying to get a picture for the paper. He parroted what I said in a mocking voice, then called me a "stupid faggot."

That was it. I don't take shit from the jocks or that bitch cheerleader, why was I letting him talk to me like this?

"And I'd appreciate it if you'd stop insulting me when I'm being wrongly accused of something," I snapped back.

"What did you say?"

"You heard me."

"Who do you think you're talking to?"

"If I had to take a guess, I'd say a big washed up homophobic ex-jock."

This pissed him off.

"Oh ho, so now you're all tough? You maybe want a piece of me?... C'mon faggot. Let me tell you something, unlike Garrett, I don't go down that easily," he said, raising his fists.

Is he threatening me? He's totally serious. I just backed away from him.

"Yeah, I thought so, pansy-boy. Go and get your stuff and get out of my class. I can't stand having to see your face today."

I was more than glad to get out of his class, but I was pissed now. I grabbed my stuff. Evelyn gave me this "What's the matter?" look. I couldn't say anything. Stanton was standing at the door, waiting for me to leave. I left and knew exactly where I needed to go. Angelino and I needed to have a long talk.

Maggie is at the desk when I enter. She's so sweet and friendly, asking what she can do for me. I ask her if Angelino is in. I'm so nervous. I'm taking deep breaths, trying to calm myself.

Angelino comes to his office door and invites me in, shaking my hand, asking me to sit down. I start to say something, but it won't come out. I'm breathing too heavily.

"Take your time. Start at the beginning. Is it Garrett and Derek?" he asks.

I shake my head no, take a few deep breaths and tell him everything about Mr. Stanton. I started with what I overheard Stanton saying to Garrett.

"He used the word "fag"?" Angelino asked. I nodded my head.

"Even though it was a teacher, I dismissed it, just like all the other names. Then at the end of last month, he was blocking the locker room door, not letting me in. He got into an argument with Ms. Annasandy about it... (Angelino was surprised that he hadn't heard anything about it)...well you obviously know what happened at the game the other day."

"Yes, I was there. Poor Randy."

"Well I was there taking pictures for the paper. All I wanted to do was get a good shot of Randy, you know, but he froze...staring at me. That's when he got tackled. It was my fault."

"Don't go blaming yourself. It wasn't your fault."

"Tell that to Mr. Stanton."

"Did he tell you it was your fault?"

I went into full detail about what happened today. When I was done, he was just staring at me, looking perplexed. What I was saying sounded so unbelievable. I think with most people, he would have thought they were making it up, but he knew I wouldn't lie. We talked fully about it the whole rest of the period.

When the period ended, he told me he would get to the bottom of it and then he sent me on my way.

All had been quiet for the rest of the day, except for one stupid jock. I said goodbye to Steph and Evelyn after French class and turned the corner for Math class. This Junior Varsity football player grabbed me and shoved me into the lockers, calling me a faggot, telling me I was going to pay for what I did to Randy. Was I scared? No, I would have fought him, except I didn't have to. He looked at me and I looked over his shoulder and smiled.

"What are you smiling for?" he said.

"You might want to turn around."

"I'm not turning around. Do I look stupid?"

"Ahem", came this sound from behind him. He turned around and there was Angelino, standing behind him, arms folded. Three days in school suspension for him. Dumb jocks.

One more for the "win" column

TUESDAY APRIL 16, 1985

I was talking to Evelyn in homeroom when the beep from the office came over the school intercom. It was Maggie. I was asked to go down to the office. I looked at Evelyn and shrugged my shoulders. I had no idea what it could be.

When I get to the main office, Maggie brings me into Angelino's office. I see Angelino and Mr. Stanton. I was worried, unsure about what this was all about, although I had an idea. Angelino asks me to take a seat. As I do, in comes Ms. Annasandy. She saw me, smiled and put her hand on my shoulder, before taking the seat next to me. I didn't feel as worried anymore. Angelino closed the door. Stanton started to speak but Angelino cut him off.

Angelino started talking about me and all the things he's been hearing. Stanton kept trying to speak, but Angelino would always cut him off.

I was then asked to describe what happened with Stanton and Garrett. Stanton didn't know I overheard them. When I was done, he asked me to describe yesterday's incident. After I told him, he asked Ms. Annasandy to describe what she saw that day at the locker room door. She told him everything. Then it was Stanton's turn. He's been standing this whole time, looking angry.

At first he denied everything, but then just like Garrett, that Neanderthal jock mentality took over. He took Angelino into the corner and whispered and I quote, "Who are you going to believe, me, or some gay boy and a dyke teacher?"

Senility must really be hitting him, because he didn't falter in his convictions. Angelino was standing there in shock. Ms. Annasandy was shaking her head, laughing under her breath. Angelino went back behind his desk, wrote out a pass and asked me to go, thanking me for coming down.

In Gym class as I was telling Steph and Evelyn what happened, Ms. Annasandy came over, bent down, patted me on the back and said "Problem solved." I didn't know what she meant until History class.

Once again I waited for Evelyn before entering. We entered class. No Stanton. Behind the desk was a woman. A sub? A permanent sub. Her name is Miss Levino. She said she'd be taking over the class for the rest of the school year. When asked what happened to Mr. Stanton, she said she didn't know.

"Bye bye, Mr. Stanton. Can't say it hasn't been fun, cuz it hasn't".

One big giant victory for the "win" column.

WEDNESDAY APRIL 17, 1985

Michelle was talking about visiting Randy and bringing him flowers. She was saying this to everyone within listening distance in English, Gym and Spanish. I'm sure in all her other classes, too.

Guess who stopped into Total Eclipse tonight.

She wanted the "Vision Quest" soundtrack, so she could have the new Madonna song "Crazy for You" to show Randy how much she loves him. She tells this to me, all syrupy sweet. I'm sure just to piss me off. I just wanted to puke.

THURSDAY APRIL 18, 1985

Found out today from Evelyn that Stanton was let go, well he was asked to retire early. Seems that after I left them Tuesday, the three of them talked some more and then the Teacher's Union rep was called in. Stanton was originally going to retire at the end of the next school year, but they all felt that he needed to retire with a little dignity. They were also worried that Mom would press charges against him and the school for threatening me. So instead of fighting it, he decided to retire now.

FRIDAY APRIL 19, 1985

More Michelle talk about all the things she's been doing for Randy. The only thing she said that made me listen was that Randy might be back to school Monday.

SATURDAY APRIL 20, 1985

Hung out with Steph and Evelyn today after work. I asked Evelyn if she heard anything about Randy. I was kind of hoping that what Michelle said was true. All she heard was that Randy might be back Monday. She hasn't heard anything else.

SUNDAY APRIL 21, 1985

All day at work. During our lunch break, Steph told me that Evelyn heard that Randy will definitely be back at school tomorrow. She asked me why I was caring so much.

"Just curious, that's all."

MONDAY APRIL 22, 1985

RANDY'S BACK! AND BACK IN A NEW WAY.

I was sitting with Evelyn in homeroom, waiting for him to come in. I really wanted to talk to him. I needed to know what he thinks. Does he think it's my fault? Would he even want to talk? Does he think I ruined his entire life?

We watched him come in. He's on crutches. There's a giant cast on his leg. He seems in good spirits. Whether or not he wanted to talk, I was determined to at least say something, but every time I tried to approach he was either with the Bitch or mobbed by people asking him questions.

After gym class I was stressed out. I just needed my quiet space. Even though it's known by three other people, it's still quiet. Evelyn and Steph promised that they wouldn't come up there without letting me know well in advance. They understand all the pressure I'm going through and my need to be alone for part of the day. As I'm heading over, all I see are freshmen heading in the same direction. OK why are all these freshmen walking this way? Noooo, not a stupid freshman assembly. Dammit. Quiet time would have to wait. I headed out to the bleachers.

The bleachers weren't helpful. It was a nice warm day and the bleachers weren't crowded, but as I tried clearing my head, all I kept thinking about was the tackle and the look Randy gave me before it happened.

In Spanish class, Michelle kept babbling about Randy and how this has brought them closer together. It was all so fake. She was just showing off.

So now Spanish class is over, back to try the auditorium. I hoped that whatever assembly was there is cleaned up and gone. I needed to be alone. Empty...yes...quiet time for me.

It's common for people to occasionally come into the auditorium. Most people who enter, come in and sit down. Then I hear them leave. They never see or hear me. I only worry when someone comes on the stage. It's been months and I haven't been discovered. There's no evidence that anybody else has been up here.

I bring this up because someone is now on the stage, but it doesn't sound like a normal footstep. Something is different. I don't want to look over, they might see me.

Shit, they're climbing the ladder.

I go to the far end of the platform and look over. It's Randy. He's almost at the top. He looks and sees me.

"What are you doing?" I ask him.

"Climbing?" he says, the smartass.

"Are you nuts? You're going to fall," I say. He has his crutches under one arm and he's climbing with the other, using his good leg for support.

"I'll be alright. Just give me a hand."

"Yeah, you'll be alright. You fall and break your neck and they'll blame me for that, too," I think to myself. I grab his arm and give him one strong pull onto the platform. He thanks me and then looks at me, smiles and says...

"Hi. How's it going?"

"Hi. How's it going?" He hasn't been friendly to me in months, unless you count that time I told him off in French class. Now it's "Hi. How's it going?" I stared at him.

He tells me he came to talk, but he's sitting there silently. I'm still staring. He finally speaks.

"Uhm…All that time at home gave me a chance to think about some things…I really appreciate what you did for me, with Derek and Garrett at that meeting. Most people would have just said, "Screw you, we made out. He's gay, too."

"I'm not most people…", I countered.

"…plus it would have been better if you didn't say I hit on you. And then you turned, realizing you fucked up. I couldn't defend it," I said.

He apologized for that, saying he panicked. Now we're sitting here in silence. I keep glancing at his leg. I need to know what he thinks. He notices my glance.

"I don't blame you for this. I know you've been getting a lot of shit for it. I'm sorry for that," he said.

"Do you mean that?" I ask.

"Yeah, it was my own stupid fault. You had nothing to do with it. Believe me when I say that. I've heard about what you've been thinking."

"Evelyn," I said, laughing.

"Maybe," he said, laughing with me.

"…Even if I don't show it. I want you to know that I really appreciate all you've done for me," he continues.

"It's ok, you…"

"You have no idea what it's like," he says, cutting me off.

I looked at him, giving him this "What the hell are you talking about?" look.

"No, I know you know what IT'S like, but you don't know what it's like for me. See, you're out and there are some problems…"

"Some?" I think to myself. Oh, I think he should stop. He's digging himself a hole.

"But if I came out I would lose everything, my family, my friends, my scholarship, which is lost anyway, my…"

I don't believe him. Nice guy to douchebag in 60 seconds. I cut him off

"Yeah, it's so much harder on the popular people. They're so much more important."

"I don't mean it like that."

"That's the way you're making it sound. Look, I've been shoved to the ground, beaten up, outed, endured weeks of name calling and abuse, only to sit by and watch you ignore me and make out with Michelle."

"I didn't come up here to argue. I came up here to say I was sorry. I truly am. I hope we can be friends again."

He wants to be friends again? He does know what's been going on the past month.

"What happens when we see each other in the halls?" I ask him.

"I don't know," he says, after two minutes of silence.

"You don't know? You want to be friends again but you don't know."

He seemed lost. We need to get this settled now.

"OK, I need to know right now. What do you think of me?" I asked.

"I...uh"

"What do you think of me?" I said softly, looking into his eyes, moving closer. We move to kiss.

All of a sudden there is a noise below.

The band is coming in to set up for rehearsal. Guess what Randy does? If you guessed shoved me to the ground in a panic, you would be right. If you thought this would be a repeat of last time, you would be wrong. I got back up and shoved him back. He hurt his leg when I did that.

"Good for you. Great, now we're stuck up here. I should just leave you here."

I can sneak back down. I usually have to, but there's no way Randy can do it without my help. Well he can, but it wouldn't be quiet and there's no way I'm losing my secret spot because of him.

"Well you might as well get comfortable. They'll be here for a while," I tell him.

I went back to my lunch and my homework, ignoring him. At first he tried apologizing, but I refused to listen to him.

Forty-five minutes later, band practice finishes. Enough destruction of classical music for today, I guess. Once I'm sure all the band members have gone, we make our way down. I go first. I have to steady him as we descend the ladder.

"My crutches," he says.

"Leave them. I'll climb back up and get them. Use your other hand for support." The climb down is a slow one. We get about a third of the way down when the auditorium doors open.

"Shit, now what?"

I look around the curtain. It's Michelle and a couple of cheerleaders. They're standing by the auditorium doors.

"What are they doing here?" I ask Randy.

"Probably practice for this end of school year thing they want to do," he tells me.

"That's two months away. We have to go back up."

"I can make it down."

"You want to risk it? One of those airheads hear us and it's over. They'll see me with you….and I don't think pushing me down will work this time."

"Haha, very funny. Just help me back up."

I help him back onto the platform. Once again we are stuck. Michelle and her friends have made it to the stage. They turn on the boom box they brought. "Don't you forget about me" by Simple Minds comes pouring out. Michelle and the cheers sit on the stage and talk while waiting for the others to arrive.

Randy and I are lying down, looking over the side, listening in on the conversation.

"So has anybody gotten their prom dress yet?" says cheerleader #1. I don't know their names, nor do I care to know.

"No, my mother took me the other day and everything was so gross. All this retro yuck. I told her it has to be just right. I have to look better than everyone else. I am after all going to be chosen prom queen." Michelle says.

I was making faces and rolling my eyes the whole time, making Randy laugh and fun-smack me.

"You think so?" says cheer #2

"I know so. As long as I'm with Randy I've got it locked. He's going to be named Prom King and as his girlfriend AND one of the most popular girls in school, I'll be chosen queen. "

"Oh my God, she's so full of herself. How do you stand her?" I whispered to Randy.

"I don't know. She really loves me... (I give him this strange look)...she does. She was over every day, taking care of me the whole time I was out of school," he says.

"Speaking of Randy, Where is your king?" says cheer #1.

"Don't know. Don't care." She says lightly laughing. "He's probably out doing some jock thing or having one of his "Quiet times"," she continues.

"Quiet times?" cheer #2 asks.

"Yeah. He says he needs to be alone. He's been like this since the whole gay thing."

"Oh man, can you believe we have a fag in this school?" says cheer #1.

"I'm surprised he even shows his face. They say it was his fault that Randy got hurt. That he was on the sidelines staring at him and Randy freaked," cheer #2 chimes in.

"Yeah, I know. He won't talk about it," Michelle answers.

"I heard that Randy used to hang out with Josh," says Debbie, who's just arrived.

"Not true!!!" Michelle screams…"The only time they hung out was when he went to study at that bitch Perrino's house."

"Not what I heard. I heard they hung out at each other's houses, because Randy wanted info on Stephanie."

Randy and I both looked at each other. He was pissed. He was shaking his head. He mouthed the word "Derek". Debbie and Derek used to go out together in Junior High and have remained friends ever since. Except for the time Debbie was dating Randy, they would occasionally hook up.

"That's a lie! Randy would have told me. That bitch and her little fag friend just better stay away from him…

Debbie shrugs her shoulders and walks away. Michelle continues talking to the other cheerleaders.

…"Randy's mine. At least til prom. I want my crown. I earned it. I deserve it. I have been dating him for a year now. After I get it, who cares."

"Oh yeah, that's love there," I said, laughing.

I turn to Randy. He's gotten up and is heading to the ladder. He's really pissed. I quickly get up and drag him back.

"Are you high? Let it go," I whisper to him.

"That bitch. She's using me. Using me for a fucking crown."

Meanwhile down below, the other cheerleaders have arrived. They stop their conversation and begin working on the routine. Randy is furious. I'm trying to calm him down.

"Ooh, I'm so mad, I could just..."

He stops mid-sentence, grabs me and kisses me. I'm stunned but I don't resist. We part lips. I look into his eyes. This time he smiles at me. No fear. We kiss again. We proceed to make out. He wanted to get it all out and I was more than willing to help. We heavily explored our sexuality this afternoon, doing more things than either of us have ever done before. All with Michelle right below us.

It was already 8th period by the time the cheerleaders were done. We were finally able to climb down. When we got to the bottom, I asked him what he was going to do.

"Are you going to break up with her?" I asked.

"No, not yet. Maybe I'll wait til the day before prom or maybe even the day of prom and embarrass the hell out of her in front of everybody."

I just smiled at him. I could tell in his mind, he was planning something. He turned to me...

"Look, I really like you. I do...It's just..."

"I know. I understand."

"We can still meet here."

"Yeah, I guess."

"Don't worry, I'll figure something out...I just don't know what yet, but I'll figure something. It'll all work out. I promise," he said smiling.

We kissed and then he rubbed noses with me.

"What was that?" I asked, smiling.

"That's my way of showing that I truly care about someone."

"I've never seen you do that with Michelle."

"Exactly."

Then he kissed me again and went on his way. There was no way I could keep this to myself. I skipped Math class and headed to Steph's house.

TUESDAY APRIL 23, 1985

Evelyn and Steph were in total shock when I told them yesterday. In Homeroom, Evelyn asked me for more details. I told her I would tell her more about it later when we study.

Speaking of Randy, I decided to play the safe route and just keep my distance. He would smile at me if our eyes met. We didn't speak to each other, but I'm just happy with the fact that we are on friendly terms again. You could see it in her face that Evelyn wanted to ask him all about what has been happening, but she knew it wasn't possible with people around.

Randy was there when I entered Steph's house. He lives right around the corner and walked over. Well crutches walked over. He was apologizing to Steph about everything and telling her and Evelyn that he hopes they will continue to keep his secret. They said they would. Then Evelyn started prodding him for his side of the story. He told them pretty much the same things I did. Then it was time to study. Back to normal. Kind of.

WEDNESDAY APRIL 24, 1985

Randy once again joined me in my secret spot. It's so funny watching him climb the ladder. He says it's a great and challenging exercise for him and that it's helping build great arm strength.

The second he got to the top, he wanted to make out. Oh my God, it feels so good to be in his arms. It feels so safe and warm. It just sucks that we have to keep up the charade in the halls, but I'm at least happy for what I've got.

We had a newspaper meeting today. Megan asked me if I'd like to do an article on Stanton's departure. I said I would.

"Nothing too evil," she said, laughing.

THURSDAY APRIL 25, 1985

When Randy joined me in my secret spot today, he wanted to talk about getting back at Michelle. We tossed a lot of ideas around, but while many were great, there was no way we could pull any of them off.

Ran into Stuart at the mall tonight. I was in the toy store looking for a new video game for Taylor and I to play. He walked up to the video game display, at first not noticing me. When he did notice, he seemed real tense. He left before anything could be said.

FRIDAY APRIL 26, 1985

Even though nothing was said, I guess seeing each other in the toy store last night sparked something.

I entered the locker room and sat down to change. "Fag Alert" is still said, but I've gotten over it. As I started changing, Stuart came over and sat down near me. He sat there trying to say something, but seemed unable to. Based on the expression on his face, I knew what he wanted to say. I extended my hand and said...

"Friends again?"

He smiled and shook my hand. "Friends again."

As we were leaving, one of the jocks made a comment about the fag having a new boyfriend, but we both ignored him and headed to the gym. We talked all the way to our seats, with everything he's wanted to say to me the past few weeks just pouring out. Lots of apologizing.

Although she never turned around, I knew that Megan was listening to every word.

When we got out to the track, he wanted to jog with me. We were jogging together, joking around. Of course some gay comments came from the jocks. Stuart was starting to get a little upset by them, but he didn't stop jogging with me.

This was all made better when Megan came up, jogging on the other side of Stuart. They looked at each other and without even saying a word, they kissed and made up, right there. I just faded back and jogged with Evelyn and Steph, leaving the lovebirds alone. I'm so glad they're back together.

SATURDAY APRIL 27, 1985

Woke up early and headed to Manhattan. Uncle Matt met me at the train station. Before he could say anything, I told him about what's going on with me and Randy.

"I knew he'd come around. Closet jocks can't stand losing the attention. You just be careful...So are you taking Randy to the prom?" he said. We both laughed at that.

My interview was at three, so after we dropped off my bag and I changed into my suit, we went to lunch. I was starting to get nervous, but he calmed me down.

"Sweetie, just relax. It will be fine. Just be yourself."

My uncle was right. The interview or should I say interviews weren't as bad as I thought they would be. I was interviewed by five different people.

Before the interviews, I was brought into this room. There were four other people there. We were all given a three page test to take. Most of it was translating words and phrases.

Once I was finished, (which I did quickly) I was brought in for the 1st interview. I was basically asked to describe myself, why I wanted the internship, a little about my foreign language knowledge and what my plans for the future were. Each interview lasted about fifteen minutes.

With each interview I felt real comfortable. The 3rd interview was with this guy who's friends with my uncle. I was so relaxed by this time that we spent most of the time talking about my uncle.

Uncle Matt was waiting for me when I left. He wanted all the details. I filled him in while we walked around Central Park. As it got later, he took me out for a celebratory dinner.

SUNDAY APRIL 28, 1985

All day spent just walking around Manhattan with my uncle. He asked me what I wanted to do.

"Walk, eat and shop," I said.

"You are definitely my nephew," he laughed.

"Well I have one more thing for us to do," he said, pulling out two tickets.

He had two tickets to this new musical called "Big River." I love musicals. It had just opened on Broadway. It's based on Mark Twain's "Adventures of Huckleberry Finn." I was so excited. The musical was totally cool.

After the musical, we grabbed something to eat and then it was time for me to head back. I thanked my uncle for everything.

"Well when you get that internship, we can do this some more during the summer," he said, before I headed down the steps to the train. Such a great weekend.

MONDAY APRIL 29, 1985

"Prom? It's over a month away," I said as Steph and Evelyn started talking about it. We were sitting at the pizza place with Megan and Stuart.

"Well, prom tickets go on sale next week," Evelyn said.

I didn't care. I had no intention of going. Then Steph says...

"Would you like to go with me?"

I nearly spit out my pizza. I started laughing. She had to be kidding. She was still looking at me.

"You really want to go to the prom with me?" I said, shocked that she was actually being serious.

"Yes. That's why I asked," she said

"I'd love to," I said smiling, excited that I have a prom date.

"So are we renting a house down the shore for after graduation?" Evelyn asks us, changing the subject.

"I know it's still about two months away, but we really should decide now, because many of the houses will be taken quick, if they haven't been already," Evelyn continues.

"My dad has a friend who lives down there and can probably find us a place," Megan answered.

Everybody else said they were in. It sounded like fun, so I said I was in too. I have a date for the prom and friends to share graduation and post-graduation with. I can't believe it's almost here.

TUESDAY APRIL 30, 1985

Megan's dad's friend found us a place. A big five bedroom, two blocks from the beach. His neighbor rents out his house and has been doing repairs on it, so it hasn't gone up for rent yet. Her dad told her that the repairs will all be done by June. She asked each of us if we were all still in. We all of course said "Yes".

WEDNESDAY MAY 1, 1985

Prom season is upon us. It's May 1st and prom is May 31st, but things are already in full swing. Today is officially the first day for Prom King and Queen promotion. All the wannabe candidates are allowed to pass out flyers, hang up posters, banners or whatever to announce their desire to be chosen king or queen. So all the posters started going up.

Of course Michelle has been hanging the most. Her and the other cheerleaders have put up posters, banners, you name it, everywhere. A couple of other girls are placing up posters, including Sharon Fessman, a member of one of Megan's brainiac groups. I saw Michelle and her clique laugh at her as she placed a few posters around.

THURSDAY MAY 2, 1985

The halls are filled with yet more posters for Prom Queen. Nobody seems to be putting up anything for Prom King, although Michelle did put up a few posters with both her and Randy's names on them. He is most definitely going to be named King. Nobody seems to be running against him.

Michelle has been clinging extra hard to him, waving at everybody in the halls, trying to be friendly. Anything to hawk votes.

FRIDAY MAY 3, 1985

Megan asked me to meet her at the newspaper room after school and to bring any photos I had of Randy.

Heading into the newspaper room, I'm forced to pass a poster of Michelle that has her picture on it. It's right outside the door. It takes all my power to keep from ripping it down...or hurling.

"Next week's paper we endorse Randy for King," Megan tells me as I enter.

"What are we doing about prom Queen?" I ask.

"Not sure yet."

"I say we don't endorse one. That will piss Michelle off more than if we endorse one of the others."

"Hmm," Megan said, laughing at the idea.

Next week's paper is going to be all about preparations for prom. Stuart is spending the whole weekend trying to get sponsors for the next few issues, because a couple of them are going to be larger ones. This, of course, means that they're going to need more from me. Megan wants me to come up with some fun articles about prom to add.

SATURDAY MAY 4, 1985

Today I stopped into the tux shop in the mall to start on the tux rental. I'm getting so excited. So is Steph. We are going to start looking for her prom dress this week. She wanted to go this weekend, but she was working the day shift today and I was working the night shift and tomorrow I'm working an open to close. She hasn't checked any of the stores at Garden Creek. She wants to check them all out, but she wants to start at Center City Mall and Park Bridge Mall first. They're both smaller malls nearby, way smaller than Garden Creek, but she thinks that she might find something special.

SUNDAY MAY 5, 1985

Another full work day. Randy stopped in to say hello. His mom dropped him off at the mall. He was heading over to get things started on his tux rental, but he wanted to stop in and say hello to me first. I can't wait to see what he looks like in a tux.

MONDAY MAY 6, 1985

Today I asked Mr. Totino for some extra shifts. Prom is going to be expensive. He doesn't have any right now, but if someone needs a shift covered, I get first dibs.

TUESDAY MAY 7, 1985

Randy is getting more used to his cast, although he's getting a little crazy. He visited me during lunch and almost fell as he tried to bolt up the ladder. I almost had a heart attack. He slipped, but was lucky enough to hold on. Of course he was laughing about it.

He's been telling Michelle that he still needs his quiet time. She's so busy with prom that she could care less what he does.

As soon as he sat down, he told me that he has a plan for getting back at Michelle.

"Ok, Michelle is building everything on winning prom Queen. We have to keep her from winning. Now, all the populars are probably going to be voting for her, whereas everybody else is going to vote for her, but split some of their votes with the others. What we need to do is get that group to swing their votes for a non-running dark horse. Someone who they like, but the populars don't," Randy says.

"Evelyn," I answer.

"Yes, there is only a small percentage of populars, so we have to figure a way to get a majority of the others to vote for Evelyn, allowing her to win, thus destroying Michelle," he says.

He's so evil. I love it, but...

"Evelyn's not going to run. She hates the idea," I say.

"She doesn't have to. Write in candidate on the ballots."

"But how are we going to do it without her, or God forbid Michelle, finding out?"

"I haven't figured that out yet. My plan is only in the beginning stages. I figured that we could figure something out together."

"Prom is three weeks from Friday," I tell him.

"I know, but you're smart. We'll figure this out."

"You are so evil," I say smiling and shaking my head.

"She's evil. I'm nice," he says, kissing me.

"True," I say, kissing him back.

He also thanked me for the great photo of him in the paper. He also wanted me to thank Megan for the great article and everyone at the newspaper staff for endorsing him. I said I most certainly would, kissing him again.

WEDNESDAY MAY 8, 1985

Right after school, Steph and I started out on her search for a prom dress. We headed to Park Bridge Mall. She wanted to start with the smallest mall and work her way up, if needed.

Park Bridge Mall is on the southern edge of town. It's more like an indoor/outdoor strip mall. It has about fifteen stores outside and there's an indoor mall area with about forty stores.

"I might find something and then we won't have to go to the other malls," she says.

She didn't find anything there, so it was on to Center City Mall. Just like the name says, it's located in the center of Whitfield. It's about halfway between Park Bridge and Garden Creek. It's also about double the size of Park Bridge and less than half the size of Garden Creek.

No luck there either.

At seven, we got to Garden Creek. As we were passing Total Eclipse, Mr. Totino spotted me and called me in. He still didn't have any shifts, but some of the other business owners in the mall owe him favors, so I'm going to get my tux rental for half price and Garden Creek Florals is going to provide the corsage and boutonniere for free. This was so great.

Steph never found a dress, so we are going prom dress shopping around Jersey on Saturday.

THURSDAY MAY 9, 1985

"Are you still OK with Saturday?" Steph asked me on our way to French class. Just as I was about to answer...

"Hi" came this voice to our left.

It was David Bernado, the backup quarterback. He's also on the baseball team. He's one of the populars. He was directing it at Steph. This was weird. Since Randy came back, all the jocks have backed away from Steph. A few weeks ago this wouldn't have bothered me, but today for some reason it seemed peculiar.

David just recently broke up with his girlfriend Angela Marconi. I've seen them making out in the parking lot. She graduated last year and goes to New Jersey University.

Steph was intrigued. We kept walking, with her turning back to look at David, who was still watching her and smiling. I started talking to her about Saturday, breaking her concentration on David. She's determined to have a dress by Saturday night.

FRIDAY MAY 10, 1985

"Why didn't the paper endorse me for prom Queen?" Michelle said, getting in my face in English class.

To calm her down, I told her they were probably going to endorse a queen next week. I forgot that there's a blurb on the cover stating that we will not be endorsing a queen. Oops.

"Bitch bitch bitch..."

I told her to take it up with Mrs. Brandon. The paper came out four days ago. I couldn't figure out why she waited until today to start bitching.

On my way to Science class I saw the reason why. It seems that Debbie has put up posters announcing her wish to become prom queen. She wasn't originally going to run, but I guess she saw that there wasn't enough competition to keep Michelle from winning, so she decided that if Michelle is going to win, it's not going to be a landslide. She wants her to work for it.

During Spanish class, Michelle's tone had changed. All day she has been beefing up her campaign, trying to be nice to everybody, except me.

After Gym class, she came up to me all sweet, asking me to talk to Mrs. Brandon and the rest of the staff at the paper about endorsing her. This from the girl who bitched me out. When I told her I had no control over it, she turned into the evil one.

Even if I did say something it wouldn't have worked. On the way to French class, Steph told me that Michelle tried to start some shit with Megan today.

SATURDAY MAY 11, 1985

Oh my god, how do straight boys handle this? Hours and hours of driving around, looking at prom dresses. It is now nine pm, twelve hours after we first headed out. Did she find a dress? (Yes). In which store did she find it? (The very 1st one we went to). Did she buy it and save us from having to look all day? (No). She saw it. She loved it, but wanted to look at others, the whole time talking about that 1st dress.

At the ten hour mark, I lost it. She said she wanted to check another store. Instead I headed to the 1st shop. She seemed pissed at first, wanting to go to the other shop. When we entered the store, she went right for that dress. She still seemed undecided.

"Look, you saw this dress. You like this dress. This is the dress you want. As your gay friend I'm saying this is the dress for you," I said.

"Yeah, maybe," she says, looking over the dress.

"Aaaaaargh!" I said laughing, because I knew at this point she was playing with me. She laughed back and took the dress.

"But now I need to find shoes and a bag to go with it," she said.

"Take Evelyn," I said.

We laughed all the way home.

SUNDAY MAY 12, 1985

HAPPY MOTHER'S DAY

Took Mom out to breakfast this morning. I bought some flowers, gifts and a card yesterday. I had Taylor and Alexa sign the card and said the gifts were from all of us.

As soon as I got home, I headed over to Steph's house. We were all getting together to finish the French paper that's due tomorrow. I barely had it started.

As we were almost done, the doorbell rang. Seeing as we were all busy, Mrs. Perrino answered it. It was Michelle. She came in all sweet.

"Hi, everybody. Are you about ready to go sweetie?" she says, kissing Randy on the cheek. Randy gets up and gets ready to go.

"Bye everyone. Oh, don't forget to vote for Randy for King and me for Queen," she says, placing down some new prom Queen cards she had printed up. Then they were gone.

"Was that Michelle? She seems so sweet. How come she doesn't study with you guys?" Mrs. Perrino said. We all just stared at her.

MONDAY MAY 13, 1985

Another issue of the paper came out without an endorsement for prom Queen. This time, Michelle went to Angelino. He feels that we should endorse a Queen, seeing as we did endorse a King.

We are having an assembly on Friday. This will be all the candidates chance to tell the senior class why they should be queen. Michelle is pissed that there are so many candidates. I'm guessing that most of the girls figured with Debbie running, the votes would be split between her and Michelle and maybe they would cancel each other out and they could slip in and win with just enough votes.

Michelle feels that this assembly should be a primary and that we knock it down to 3 candidates. I agree with her.

There's no way our plan could be fully destructive with so many candidates. She could actually lose on her own.

So when I overheard Angelino talking to Mrs. Brandon about it, I told them that I agree with Michelle. They were caught off guard. I was actually agreeing with Michelle on something. I told them that this would be good and it would help the paper decide who to endorse. I also mentioned that they keep the write-in candidate section, so that anyone could vote for someone else if they don't agree with the final three. They agreed with me.

A couple of prom articles I submitted were in the paper today. One was the Question of the Week. This is a section where we ask various students a specific question and take their picture and put their response under it. This week's question...

"Are you looking forward to prom?"

I wasn't going to just ask the populars. I even asked a few burnouts, just to get the negative side. I'm nothing if not thorough. I also convinced Megan to have the students choose the prom song this year. Normally the prom committee chooses it.

"Give them five selections to choose from," I told her. We put them in today's paper and at the end of the week the ballots will be passed out in homeroom and collected. The 5 choices are...

"You're the Inspiration"   by Chicago

"I Want to Know What Love Is"   by Foreigner

"Sea of Love"   by The Honeydrippers

"Crazy for You"   by Madonna

"Can't Fight This Feeling"   by REO Speedwagon

Randy was there when I climbed the ladder. He had that look on his face. I knew what it meant. Michelle was pressuring him to ask me.

"Ok. I will make it look like I talked to Mrs. Brandon," I said.

"Thank you," he said. Then he took out the school paper and started complimenting me on how great my articles are.

"I'm going to vote for Foreigner," he tells me.

"Me too. I love all five songs, but Foreigner is my favorite of the five," I said.

TUESDAY MAY 14, 1985

"You got some mail," Mom said as I walked in the door, coming home from school.

She was all excited. It only meant one thing. It was more college stuff. I'm still waiting to be accepted somewhere. I've applied to 15 colleges and 5 language schools. I've heard back from 10 colleges (7 rejections and 3 wait lists) and 2 language schools (2 rejections).

I grabbed the mail. Five letters. OK, here goes nothing. Mom was standing, watching. She wanted to know what each one said. She has me do this ritual whenever I get a letter back from a college or school. I have to tell her which school it is and then say what the response is.

"Envelope 1…Premier Multilingual Language School, London…Rejection"

"Envelope 2…Premier Multilingual Language School, Paris…Wait list."

"Envelope 3…Eastern Connecticut University…Rejection"

"Envelope 4…New Jersey University…Wait list"

"Envelope 5"

I didn't want to open it. I froze when I saw that it was from Garden State University. This was my first choice. This was going to be harder for me to get into. My chances were so slim and based on how the other Universities have responded, I was not optimistic. This is also where Steph, Evelyn and Randy are going.

After the football injury, his scholarship to his big football university was terminated. He actually signed the contract with it saying that if he became injured before playing for them, the scholarship would be null and void. He could still go to school there, but it's far away and even though his parents have the money, it would be a huge burden on them, so he chose Garden State. Unfortunately Derek and Garrett are also going there. Maybe even Michelle, she has to choose between there and beauty school. Decisions, decisions…dumb blond.

I kept looking at the letter.

"You OK honey?" Mom asked.

I nodded my head yes.

"Envelope 5…Garden State University"

I still couldn't open it.

"Would you like me to open it?" Mom said.

I shook my head no. I had to do it. I opened it, looking at that familiar white sheet of paper.

"What does it say? What does it say?" Mom was screaming.

"I've been accepted," I said, smiling.

"What?" she said, running up, looking at the letter. Then she hugged me. "Congratulations honey."

This is going to be so cool. The phone rang, so while Mom went to get it, I reread the letter. I couldn't believe it.

"Josh," Mom said, extending the phone in my direction. Mom grabbed the letter from my hand while I grabbed the phone.

"Hello?...Uncle Matt...How are you?" I said.

He congratulated me on Garden State and then he told me the reason he was calling. I got the internship. I'll be working in NYC this summer. I can't believe it. I couldn't wait to tell Steph. We were going to be hanging out tonight.

When I was in the shower getting ready for tonight, Steph called. Mom told me that she said she had to cancel tonight. She said that something came up.

"Yo goofus, you want to go to the mall?" I said to Taylor, not wanting to stay home.

Of course he said yes. We headed to the mall. On our way to the arcade, we passed the pizza place. Inside I saw Steph at a booth, talking with David Bernado and another jock who I didn't know. They didn't see us. Steph and I will talk tomorrow.

WEDNESDAY MAY 15, 1985

Randy didn't come to my secret spot. Michelle enlisted him to help her. All the old posters came down (the ones that weren't already torn down) and all new ones were put up.

Steph had been quiet to me all day about David. I didn't want to bring it up. I was hoping she would. In French class it came up. When I entered French class, I saw Steph and Evelyn talking. Evelyn looked at me and then Steph.

"Oh my God, I forgot I promised Josh," I heard Steph say.

"Promised Josh what?" I asked.

Steph was silent, not knowing what to say. So Evelyn answered for her...

"David Bernado just asked her to the prom."

I let out three "Ohs". The first "Oh" was excitedly. Then the second "Oh" came when I realized what this all meant. The third "Oh" was fake acceptance.

"Hey, that's great. Good for you. He's cute," I said, not angrily. I didn't want to upset Steph. She was obviously caught up in David's eyes and forgot about me entirely.

"I promised to go with you. I'll just tell him no," she said.

I said "No (really wanting to say "yes"), you go. Don't worry about me. I'll be fine. I don't have to go."

This really upset her. Evelyn told me to still come. She's co-dj that night and she's going solo. So to make Steph happy, I said I'd go. I paid for the tickets already. Why waste money? Although I don't trust David Bernado. Something just isn't right, but I won't say anything to Steph. I don't want to make her feel guilty or ruin her chances at a prom with a cute guy.

THURSDAY MAY 16, 1985

Steph came into Total Eclipse today, asking me again whether or not I'm OK with her going with David. My thoughts on it have been all over the place. I told her once again that it's fine.

"We would still get to hang out...but I do have one request...you have to dance with me at least twice. One fast song and one slow song," I said.

"Deal," she said, smiling.

FRIDAY MAY 17, 1985

The final chance to register for prom queen was at the end of the day yesterday. Prom is two weeks from today. There must have been a run on nominations, because there are twelve girls running for prom queen, five more than I knew about. Many didn't know that this assembly would be a primary until

Angelino announced it at the start. The twelve girls ran the gamut of school cliques. They were:

1.   Michelle Danielson (cheerleader)

2.   Debbie Paletto (cheerleader)

3.   Sharon Fessman (brainiac)

4.   Tina Tronka (populars)

5.   Patty Seamorten (burnout)

6.   Tracey Parnett (jockette)

7.   Mya Recont (brainiac)

8.   Stacey Palmer (burnout)

9.   Sally Costello (jockette)

10.   Amanda LaChapette (exchange student)

11.   Paulette Sellman (populars)

12.   Alison Jackson (jockette)

What an eclectic group of girls. Patty came on stage in punk regalia, all leather. The anti-prom queen. It was great.

Each of the candidates came up and got two minutes to tell everybody why they should be queen. The judges were Mr. Angelino, Mrs. Brandon, Mr. Taylor (science head), Mrs. Carter (head of the prom committee) and Mrs. Stratham (P.E. head).

The final three would not be announced until Monday, but the newspaper head (Megan) would know after school, thus to help decide who to endorse and have it in the paper on Monday.

The final three are Sharon, Debbie and Michelle. I met with Megan and Stuart after school. We have to get the paper ready for Monday. My story on the assembly is going on the front page. Now, who to nominate.

We were against nominating Michelle, (for obvious reasons). We couldn't nominate Sharon, (it might seem like favoritism, although Megan isn't that great of friends with her) and we couldn't nominate Debbie, (she seemed to be looking for revenge).

Angelino stopped in with Mrs. Brandon, asking our decision. We told them we couldn't decide.

"Do what you feel is best. I'll be back in a little bit," he told Mrs. Brandon, so that's what she told us, so back to deciding.

"I have an idea. How about we say that we don't endorse anybody...BUT, what we do is give each girl their own page. Each girl will have a page dedicated to them. Their campaign slogan, some photos, anything to give them print," I told the group.

"I like it," Megan said.

Mrs. Brandon liked the idea, too. Now to convince Angelino.

"I like it, but we should probably go with just half a page each to save on costs," Angelino told us.

We have the extra funds and it wouldn't be a problem, but I had an answer for him.

"OK, which one gets her own page while the others share a page?"

He backed off. Each gets their own page. We're spending all day tomorrow setting this up.

SATURDAY MAY 18, 1985

Spent all day with Megan and the rest of the newspaper staff getting the paper set up. The assembly article is still on the front page with a great photo of all twelve girls. I was also in charge of Debbie's page. She's on page two. Michelle has page three and Sharon page four. The rest is sports and small school news.

SUNDAY MAY 19, 1985

Today when I woke up I was so tired. I wanted to stay in bed, but I had to work all day. At least Evelyn stopped in to say hello.

"Thank God it's a calm day," I told her.

"You sure?" she said, pointing to the front.

"Oh hell. Here comes the Bitch."

Evelyn goes and walks around the store while I get to see what Michelle wants, although I should have known. She walked right up to me.

"Hi...So...Am I one of the final three?" she asks all perky and nice.

"You'll have to wait until tomorrow to find out," I answered.

"Pretty please," she said, starting to play sickeningly sweet.

I glanced over at Evelyn and saw that she was lightly laughing at all this. I wasn't laughing. I thought I was gonna hurl, so I acted all syrupy sweet right back.

"No-o-o-o-o-o"

She stormed off in a huff.

"Fag!"

MONDAY MAY 20, 1985

The issue was sold in Homeroom. Michelle said nothing to me. She did go up and thank Megan during Gym. I get all the shit and none of the praise. Whatever. The other girls loved it, even the ones who didn't make the final three. Debbie and Sharon were flattered at the pages dedicated to them.

Debbie joined me during my lunch break today, which I took out by the bleachers. We had a good talk about her, Randy, her hatred of Michelle and how, oddly enough, she doesn't want to be prom queen. She just doesn't want Michelle to win.

"I hope it's Sharon who wins," she says.

Without telling her what Randy and I have planned, I say...

"I don't think Michelle will win...nor you...nor Sharon."

"What's up?" she asks, smiling.

"You'll have to wait til prom to find out...oh and keep it a secret or it might not happen," I said.

This brought a big smile to her face. She said she wouldn't tell. She wouldn't do anything to ruin an opportunity against Michelle.

Even though she helped spread the rumor that led to me being outed and Steph being harassed for a while, I find her fascinating.

TUESDAY MAY 21, 1985

Randy told me that Michelle was so excited about the newspaper. I just rolled my eyes. He laughed and grabbed me, kissing me on the lips.

"Thank you," he said.

WEDNESDAY MAY 22, 1985

Steph was going on and on today about David. I don't know. This is just weird. I mean, he talks to her at school and on the phone and they sometimes hang out at the mall, but they don't seem to be dating. It doesn't seem normal, you know. They only occasionally hold hands. I've yet to see them kiss. Steph says he's taking it slow, seeing as he just broke up with Angela. Too slow if you ask me. He's up to something. Evelyn thinks I'm crazy and jealous.

THURSDAY MAY 23, 1985

I have been so busy with everything; I haven't really seen or talked to Tommy. He usually avoids me if we pass in the halls. I didn't need any more crap than I already had, so I just let him go and do what he wants.

Well today he stopped me in the hall and said "Hello". Nothing else, just "Hello" and then he was off. This caught me completely off guard. I didn't see him the whole rest of the day. Then he came into Total Eclipse. He said he needed help with French. So like all the others who have come in and out of my life, I let him back in. It was late and I was tired, but I told him to come over to the house.

He's fallen completely in French. So he needed a lot of help. We didn't finish studying until midnight.

"Do you think I can stay over?" he asked.

Mom was asleep, but I knew she wouldn't mind. He called his house. His dad gets home from work around midnight, so he was up when he called.

So he's staying over. There he is, lying in a sleeping bag on my floor, with my Walkman, listening to the new Bon Jovi cassette I just bought (and haven't listened to yet).

"Juniors"

FRIDAY MAY 24, 1985

"What is Tommy doing in my bed?"

I woke up at seven o'clock. When I opened my eyes, I knew that I wasn't alone in bed. Tommy was lying in the bed next to me. He had his arm around me. Why wasn't he in the sleeping bag? This was not good. He was asleep, so I tried to move his arm off me. As I did, he woke up. He looked right in my eyes and smiled. Then he did what he shouldn't have done. He kissed me.

"No, no no no no," I said, jumping out of the bed.

"Why?" he said, looking hurt.

"It has nothing to do with you...It's just..."

I wanted to tell him about Randy, but I just couldn't. He was pissed. He got dressed, not saying a word and left.

"Shit."

SATURDAY MAY 25, 1985

Worked the day shift today. I was hoping that Tommy would come in. He didn't, but David did. He was all friendly. I don't know whether he thought of this on his own or Steph said something. I do not trust jocks, just take a look at Derek. I'm sorry, no matter how nice he seems, I just don't trust him. He seems fake.

SUNDAY MAY 26, 1985

"Oh my God, you're not going to believe it," Tommy said, all excited, coming into Total Eclipse. I guess he's talking to me again.

"I have a boyfriend," he continued.

"Details," I said.

"I went to Masquerade yesterday and met this guy. His name's Michael Turner. He's a junior at Central High. We hung out and talked for a while and then headed to his house. Michael's not out either, so we have to keep everything quiet."

He's so excited. I'm so happy for him.

"Are you OK with this?" he asked me.

"Why wouldn't I be?" I answered him. As if he's the only other gay boy in school.

"I'm going to let you in on a little secret. The reason I pushed you away the other day was because there's somebody at school I'm seeing," I told him.

"Who?" he said, getting real curious.

"I can't say right now."

"Aww, c'mon."

"No...and I thought you were moving to Illinois," I said, trying to change the subject.

"I might not be after all and now that I have Michael, I don't want to."

My God, it's been only one day and already he's glued. I'm glad we're talking again.

MONDAY MAY 27, 1985

MEMORIAL DAY

Another day off from school. Mom was off, too. Thank God. Another shift I was able to pick up at work. Tommy came in today with Michael. He wanted to introduce us to each other. Michael is cute. Not really my type, but he and Tommy make a cute couple.

TUESDAY MAY 28, 1985

Mom picked up a double today, so it was babysitting duties. Steph and Evelyn came over. We nuked some popcorn and watched "Bachelor Party" with Tom Hanks. We were laughing so much. A fun night.

WEDNESDAY MAY 29, 1985

TWO DAYS TIL PROM

Stopped over Steph's house to study for a little bit. Her prom dress came back from being altered. She wouldn't let me see it though.

"You'll have to wait."

After studying, I left and headed to the mall. I had to pick up my tux. I stopped into Total Eclipse to say hello to Tommy first.

Michael was there. Tommy was just finishing up his shift and they were getting ready to head over to the arcade. They asked me to join them, but I needed to pick up the tux.

They look like they are having so much fun. I wish I could hang out with Randy like that. Our relationship, (if that's what you want to call it) is good, but still very secretive. Oh well, on to the tux place.

Randy was there picking up his tux too, but he was with Derek and the Bitch, so I couldn't talk to him. He did signal to me that his cast is coming off soon.

My tux...

This is the first time I'll ever be wearing one. I headed home and put it on. Looking in the mirror, I like the way it looks, but then I broke down. I started having a conversation with my reflection.

"You look great."

"Yeah, but I'm going alone."

"You'll still have fun. Your friends will be there."

"Yeah, but it will seem like just another dance, not the prom. The prom is supposed to be special, my special day. I have no date, male or female."

I left my reflection and laid down on the bed, just staring at the ceiling.

"Are you OK?" Mom said from the doorway.

I nodded my head yes. She knew better. We had a mother/son talk. She was telling me all about her prom. It made me laugh and I felt better.

"Now get up. You're wrinkling the tux," she said laughing. She left and I got up and looked at myself in the mirror again.

"You look great. You're going to be the best looking one there. Randy's going to wish he asked you instead of that bitch."

THURSDAY MAY 30, 1985

ONE DAY TIL PROM

There was a meeting tonight at Megan's house. Randy had told Megan about his plan and we were meeting to discuss how we were going to do it. It was me, Randy, Megan, Stuart and a few members of the brainiac group.

Randy and I came up with the idea of having a few small cards made up. They will be attached to clipboards. Stuart and a couple of the brainiacs will stand in different places outside and call select people over as they enter. These people would then tell others. The cards were great. They basically said...

"Do you really want Michelle to be prom queen?"

"Do you think she deserves it?"

"Has she been nice to you ALL YEAR?"

If you answered no to any of these questions, we ask that you vote for someone who deserves it. Under the write-in portion on the ballot, write

Evelyn Ramirez

A true queen

Pass it on, but keep it a secret. We want it to be a surprise.

If all goes well we will have the right prom queen tomorrow.

FRIDAY MAY 31, 1985

PROM

Only a half day for seniors today. Our day was Homeroom, period 1, then another assembly (a final chance for the three finalists to make speeches declaring their desire to be chosen prom queen.) Then we went to periods 3 and 4 and that was it, time for everyone to go home and get ready for prom. Except the prom committee, they had to head to the catering hall to get things ready.

The Lady Victoria Manor is about a mile from the school. I didn't want to sit around all day waiting for the prom to begin, so I drove home, grabbed my tux and headed over to help Megan and Stuart.

"You're the Inspiration" by Chicago won prom song, so that's the theme. It looks like a whole bunch of neon ribbons, banners and balloons. I guess that's inspiring. It was amazing how quickly everyone worked. There were only about eight of us. Tommy was one of them.

"Shouldn't you be decorating the Junior Prom?" I said, laughing as I entered. The Junior Prom is being held in the gym tonight.

"Nah, I volunteered to take pictures of the Senior Prom. It's going to be more fun over here than in the stuffy gym. So I decided to come early and help you guys out."

At around 5:30, they seemed to have almost everything under control, so I went and changed into my tux. When I came back out, Evelyn had just arrived and was setting up her equipment. She was with Marcia Walker, a junior who's also a DJ. She'll be taking over Evelyn's spot as school DJ next year. Marcia will be acting as Evelyn's assistant tonight, so that Evelyn can get out every once in a while and enjoy herself. Everybody complimented me on how great I looked. I hung out with Evelyn, keeping her company while she set up.

Prom starts at 7 and it was about 6:45 when the first guests started to arrive. Megan and Stuart were still running around, trying to make sure everything was ready. Evelyn and I were telling them that everything was fine and that they needed to go change. Then I turned to Evelyn, "You too." She still hadn't changed either. She cued up "Everybody Wants to Rule the World", the new song by Tears for Fears and then headed to get changed.

Stuart came out first, looking great in his tux. Then came Evelyn. Oh my God, Evelyn was wearing a prom dress, well if that's what you want to call it, this was Evelyn, so you knew it wasn't going to be like everyone else's. It looked like it came from Stevie Nicks' closet. Lots and lots of flowing lace. She looked fabulous.

As I was complimenting her, in came Randy and Michelle, along with Derek and Debbie and Garrett and some other cheerleader. Michelle was standing there hawking votes.

Meanwhile, Stuart went outside and joined our plants just outside the front doors, pulling people aside. Megan finally came out from the back and she looked amazing.

"Where are your glasses?" I asked.

"Contacts, I just got them the other day. Decided tonight would be my first time wearing them," she said.

It was hard to even recognize her. Evelyn and I couldn't stop complimenting her. Then my eyes went to the front doors. I did not believe what I was seeing. I quickly tapped Evelyn to turn and see. David Bernado just entered arm in arm...with Angela Marconi. They went over to Michelle, (I didn't know where Randy went). They all turned, saw us looking and flashed us evil smiles, lightly laughing. Evelyn wanted to kill all of them.

"That Bitch...I have to go find Steph," I told Evelyn.

I wanted to go right up and tell David and Michelle off, but I was too worried about Steph to deal with them. I quickly raced out of there and headed to Steph's house. Luckily she doesn't live too far from the hall.

"Hi Josh," Mrs. Perrino said. She was standing on the front porch as I approached.

"Hi Mrs. Perrino. Is Steph here?"

"Yeah, she's locked herself in her room. David is just a little late and she's upset. She won't talk to me."

I brushed past her, went inside and knocked on Steph's bedroom door.

"Hey Steph, it's me. Open up."

She opened the door and I went and joined her on her bed.

"He didn't show. He said he would pick me up at 6, so that we could be there early and say hello to everybody," she told me, wiping tears from her eyes.

I told her the bad news. She couldn't understand why he would do it, until I mentioned Michelle.

"Oh my God...and I fell for it all. I'm such an idiot. I'm so embarrassed. I can't go now."

"Sure you can. You just need to go with someone special."

"You have somebody in mind?"

"As a matter of fact, I do."

She was still a little hesitant.

"Look, I did not spend twelve hours on a Saturday, driving all around Jersey looking at prom dresses to have it lay there on your bed," I continued.

She laughed and got up, looking at herself in the mirror. Her makeup had run, causing streaks on her face.

"I need to fix myself up. I look a mess," she said, running into the bathroom.

While she was doing this, I decided to head into the living room and talk to her mom. She overheard our whole conversation. She started thanking me for being such a good friend to Steph, wishing I was straight, because she thinks we make a great couple. Fixing my tux the whole time. We watched Steph run out of the bathroom and into her room to put on the dress.

"I'll be out in a minute," she said in passing. Her mom and I just laughed.

"Wow, you look beautiful," I told her, as she walked out of her bedroom.

The dress that looked fabulous already, looked even more so now.

"Thank you," she replied as we started to head out.

"Wait, wait," her mom said, stopping us. She wanted pictures. A few shots and we were off to the prom.

It was only a little after 8 when we arrived, not too bad. The prom goes to 11. Plenty of time left. Evelyn, Stuart and Megan came running up to make sure everything was alright.

"I'm fine. I'm with a much better date now," she told them.

I noticed Randy standing by the punchbowl, so I excused myself and headed over.

"Did you see what Michelle did?" I said, talking softly out of the side of my mouth, so it looked like I wasn't talking to him. He did.

"Is Steph OK?" he asked.

I said she was and then he apologized for not knowing what Michelle was up to.

"Don't worry, if all works out well, Michelle will get hers," he said.

I laughed at that, crossing my fingers. I left him and went back to Steph, who wanted to dance. Of course I said yes. They were playing this cool new song by the Mary Jane Girls called "In my House". It was great seeing Steph smile.

As the night went on, we would dance a lot. I got my fast song and my slow song, many times over. It was getting late and I still hadn't danced with Evelyn yet. I haven't seen her in about 20 minutes. It's almost 10 o'clock.

"Where were you?" I ask, watching her approach.

She had this wicked smile on her face.

"Just taking care of some business."

"What did you do?" I asked, dying to know. I knew it had to do with David and Angela. She wouldn't say. I looked around and didn't see David or Angela. As a matter of fact, I hadn't seen them in a while. I spent most of the early part of the prom keeping Steph away from him. Evelyn had been giving Angela evil looks the whole evening. You could tell that Angela was scared.

"What did you do to David and Angela?" I said, laughing.

"I didn't do anything...to David," she said laughing. "Angela must have slipped and her head landed in the toilet bowl."

I cracked up. I love Evelyn.

"OK everyone, can I have your attention please? It's now time to crown your prom King and Queen," Angelino announced to the crowd.

Megan had two thrones made up for the occasion. They were brought up to the main platform. Evelyn stepped out from behind the DJ booth as everyone got quiet and gathered around. She's going to announce the prom King. Derek stepped through the crowd and made his way to the platform. He's going to announce the Queen. Evelyn's first. Mr. Angelino passes her the microphone.

"Your Whitfield High School Senior Prom King for 1985 is...Randy Sawyer," she announces.

Everybody was applauding as Randy made his way up to the stage. Evelyn placed the crown on his head. Now the moment of truth, would our plan work? I crossed my fingers. Derek made his way to the microphone. As I was watching, Megan came up and told me that many people have been coming up to her and Stuart saying that they voted for Evelyn.

"Alright, your Whitfield High School Senior Prom Queen for 1985 is...Oh my God...Joshua Parker."

The dumbass decided to be funny. Of course he got a big laugh out of it. I wasn't laughing. Angelino started to approach.

"OK OK, seriously now. Your Whitfield High School Senior Prom Queen for 1985 is …..

As he's reading my eyes met with Randy's.

…Misshh…(shit she still won)…Evelyn Ramirez," he said slowly. Haha, he was saying Michelle, thinking she won. Michelle and her clique were polling people yesterday. She figured she had it locked.

Our plan worked. All the populars were in shock, but everyone else was applauding. Evelyn was completely caught off guard. She slowly walked over to Derek who awkwardly put the crown on her head.

"Something's wrong!! She wasn't on the ballot!! There's a fix!!" Michelle was screaming.

Randy and Evelyn took their seats. Michelle was still screaming. Angelino's going over to her now.

"Calm down Miss Danielson"

"It's a fix!"

"I watched the box myself."

He did, nobody was getting near it.

It was so great watching her have this breakdown. I looked over and saw Debbie watching Michelle from the other direction. Our eyes met. She was laughing. She clapped her hands at me and mouthed the words, "Thank you".

"But she wasn't even one of the nominees," Michelle continued.

"It doesn't matter. Write in ballots count," he said, before leaving her and going back up to the platform.

"Ladies and gentlemen, I present to you, your Whitfield High School Senior Prom King and Queen for 1985, Mr. Randy Sawyer and Miss Evelyn Ramirez."

They both stood up as everyone applauded.

"Now if we can have everyone clear a path, we will have our king and queen commence with a dance," Angelino continued.

He turned to Marcia, signaling her to play the prom theme song. "You're the Inspiration" started.

"Randy! Don't dance with her!" Michelle was screaming.

He was ignoring her. This was his time and he wasn't going to let her ruin it. Michelle stormed off, taking a few cheerleaders with her.

They looked so beautiful dancing together. "You're the Inspiration" ended and Marcia played another slow song for everyone to dance to, "Open Arms" by Journey. I started looking around for Steph, but then Evelyn came up, grabbing my arm.

"Dance with me," she said, forcefully.

"Sure," I said laughing.

"Randy told me what you guys did. Thank you for this."

"My pleasure, you deserve it way more than she does."

"So are you guys going to tell me your secret?"

"What secret?"

"How you and Randy seem to be able to keep me from finding things out."

"I'll never tell," I said, laughing. She laughed too.

"I'm sorry about Derek's joke up there."

"It's OK. He's a douchebag. There was no way for you to know or to stop it if you did. I wish it could have been true though."

"I bet you do."

We finished the dance and went over and congratulated Randy, who was being mobbed by people congratulating him. I made my way back through the crowd, finding Megan and Stuart, who were super excited our plan worked.

Now it's about 10 minutes to 11. Prom is almost over...what does Evelyn want? She's waving me up to the DJ booth.

"What's up?" I ask.

"We've got a surprise for you," she says, pointing. I look and see Steph on the side, standing by a closet, waving me over. I head over.

"Go inside," she tells me.

"What for?" I ask.

"Just go, it's a surprise."

I headed inside. It was dark, but I knew I wasn't alone. The light clicked on and it was Randy. I was about to say something, when he put his finger to his lips and softly said "shhh". Then he pointed outside. Evelyn was starting to speak.

"Ok everyone, this will be the last dance of the evening, so grab your dates. I want to thank you all for coming and to those of you who voted for me, thank you for making me prom queen. I am truly honored. This last dance is also a very special one and I want to dedicate it to two very good friends of mine. I can't say who, but you know who you are. This one's for you. Enjoy the dance."

The music started. It was "Through the Fire" by Chaka Khan, one of my favorite songs. I was looking at Randy, who was smiling. He had something behind his back. It was Evelyn's crown.

"Can I have this dance?" he said, placing the crown on my head.

"I wanted to have at least one dance at the prom with someone special," he continued.

"Don't let Evelyn hear you say that," I said, laughing.

"Shut up and dance with me," he said, laughing with me.

"What if someone comes in?"

"Don't worry. Steph's standing guard."

We started to dance and I held him so tight. I didn't want to let go. It felt better than any other time that I held him. This was our moment and even though we had to share it in the closet, it was still special, because we were with a large group of people yet we were still alone together. I'll never forget this night.

SATURDAY JUNE 1, 1985

As soon as I got up today, (around noon), I called Tommy. I wanted to see the pictures he took. He has a darkroom in his house. He had the pictures developed and told me to come over. He was spending the day with Michael.

The pictures were phenomenal

"I can ask Angelino to see if we can get the next issue of the paper larger this week and add some of these. The next issue isn't going to be ready until Wednesday anyway," I said, looking at the pictures again.

"Are you going to show him the "other" pictures?" Michael said.

"Oh yeah," Tommy answered, going into the other room. I watched as he returned. He had this big smile on his face.

"Well, as the prom was finishing up, I was taking pictures of people leaving. I looked over and saw Steph and took her picture…and then I saw somebody come out of the closet," he said, holding up a picture of me coming out of the closet and then one of me hugging Steph. I knew where this was heading.

"I thought it was kind of odd that you would be leaving the closet, so I watched you guys walk away and then I waited to see if anyone else came out. Wouldn't you know it, a few minutes later…". He was holding up a photo of Randy.

"Explain!" he said.

"Randy's the guy at school I'm seeing."

"Duh, I figured that. Wow, you and Randy Sawyer. I didn't want to ask, but I really wanted to know."

I filled him in on all the details, but told him it was a secret. He understood. He was so happy for me.

"You have someone special, just like me," he said, kissing Michael.

They started getting all kissy kissy, so that was my cue to head out. I was heading over to Steph's, so I asked to borrow the ones of the main group of us.

"No problem," he said and then I was off to Steph's.

It was only Steph and I hanging out today. Evelyn went to Great Adventure with Megan, Stuart and a bunch of others. Great Adventure is this theme park in Jersey. I'm not into thrill rides and neither is Steph, so we both passed and are spending the day together. I started showing her the photos when the phone rang.

"It's for you," she said.

It was Randy. He's been home all day cleaning his room. He's been looking for me. His whole family is away and he wondered if I wanted to come over tomorrow and hang out. Of course I said yes. He then asked me to bring Steph too. She agreed.

"What's going on with Michelle?" I asked him.

"She's over her aunt's house in Connecticut. She's been leaving messages on my machine all day. I don't want to talk to her.

SUNDAY JUNE 2, 1985

What a magical day, hanging out with Randy and Steph. He was already in his bathing suit, getting the pool ready when we arrived.

We spent the whole day together, having a little bbq, swimming in the pool, listening to music and then after Steph left, playing video games in his room. This time I sat on the bed. Randy asked me to stay over.

MONDAY JUNE 3, 1985

BACK TO SCHOOL. BACK TO REALITY

I didn't have a change of clothes, so I had to sprint out of Randy's house at six o'clock this morning, head home, take a quick shower and then head to school.

{Michelle and a few of the cheerleaders are standing in front of the school before classes begin. The discussion is focused on the prom. Michelle is still furious at not being named queen.

"So have you talked to him?", one of the cheerleaders asks her.

"No, he wouldn't answer the phone. I left dozens of messages. He was probably just out all weekend. We'll talk today," Michelle says. As she does, Debbie approaches the group.

"He wasn't out, at least not on Sunday...and he wasn't alone either," Debbie says.

"What are you talking about?" Michelle asks.

"I got home early on Sunday and I saw your so-called boyfriend having a little pool party with Joshua Parker...and Stephanie Perrino."

"You lying little bitch!"

"Why would I lie? Here comes Josh now. Why don't you just ask him?"

Josh is pulling into the parking lot. Debbie continues...

"Oh and in case you're curious, Steph left around eight, but Josh was there all night. Hmm, I wonder what they were talking about."}

There was plenty of time left as I pulled into the parking lot and parked. My school books were thrown all over the backseat though. I was searching for my backpack. Just as I found it I heard this voice behind me.

"Ahem!"

"Yes," I said, turning to see the Bitch. A group of cheerleaders were standing a short distance behind her.

"I'm going to ask you this just once gay boy and I want a straight answer. What were you and that slut bitch doing over my boyfriend's house yesterday?!" she barked.

The crowd has now grown and gotten closer. My time of sitting back and taking her shit is over. I let her have it.

"First off, I don't think he's your boyfriend anymore. Second, if anyone's a bitch, it's you and third, he invited us over, so if you've got a problem with that you take it up with him."

The whole crowd couldn't believe it. Then I saw Garrett and Derek coming thru the crowd, Garrett ready to fight me. I was ready to fight him. I wasn't taking his shit anymore either, but I didn't have to. Randy and Steph came through the crowd from the other side. Randy stopped Garrett.

"Leave him alone!" he said.

"Did you just hear what he said?" Garrett countered.

"I heard it."

"And you're not going to do anything?"

"No, because it's all true."

A big gasp came from the crowd.

"Can we just go somewhere and talk about this?" Michelle said softly, grabbing Randy's arm.

She doesn't seem to want to lose him, even though it's the end of the school year. I'm guessing that since she lost the crown, she's trying to salvage what's left of her popularity and reputation.

"There's nothing to talk about 'Shel. I mean, getting David to help you trick Steph and try to ruin her prom. For what? Steph and I are just friends and you couldn't see it... What are you worried about? Prom's over. You were going to break up with me anyway, right?" Randy says.

"No, I don't want to break up."

"Then you didn't say, Randy's mine, at least until the prom. I want my crown. I earned it. I deserve it. After that who cares?"

All the cheerleaders started looking at each other, trying to figure out who told. All eyes go to Debbie.

"Don't look at me. I didn't tell him. I didn't even know."

Randy started to leave. Michelle was still holding on to his arm.

"Hey wait…I didn't mean it. I love you."

Randy keeps walking, dragging Michelle along. The whole crowd was still watching, slowly following behind. She kept holding on, until they got to the front doors and then she let go. Randy entered school. She stood there for a few seconds. Then she turned and saw everyone staring. She started crying and then hurried inside. The crowd dispersed, all heading inside and going their separate ways. Evelyn, Steph and I followed slowly behind, laughing as we entered school.

Evelyn and I entered homeroom. Randy was already there. We saw that he had a big smile on his face.

"You OK?" I asked

"Totally fine," he said.

I patted him on the back. He's so glad to finally be rid of her.

Michelle was quiet in English class and Derek didn't say anything in Science. Gym class would be different.

I entered the locker room and a strange thing happened, nobody said "Fag Alert." A few guys turned and were about to say it, but everyone seemed more interested in listening in on something else. I moved through the crowd of people and I could tell by the voices that they were listening to Derek and Garrett. They were talking to Randy.

"I can't believe you dumped her like that. Trashing her in the parking lot in front of everybody. Especially after she lost the crown," Garrett said.

"She's really hurting man," Derek said.

"Let her hurt. She brought it all on herself," Randy said. He wasn't taking it. He was over her.

"You should go talk to her...," Derek started saying, Randy cut him off.

"I said it's over. I've got nothing to say to her."

"Still dude, she may have done some things but she still loves you. If you need to break up, it should be done a little bit more privately," Derek said, calmly.

"Just talk to her...I mean even the fag knew before she did," Garrett said as I turned the corner.

Randy didn't respond. He just finishes changing and heads out. Derek and Garrett follow. Everybody else goes back to whatever they were doing. Most are already changed. The locker room empties out. I started changing. Stuart came up to me.

"So did you know about this?" he asks me.

"Yeah, it was obvious."

"So is he seeing Steph?"

"No, I don't think he wants another girlfriend right now," I say with a light laugh. I finish changing and we head out.

Randy has moved himself back to his original spot on the gym floor. It's so great having him back here. As we head out to the track, we ask Randy to jog with us. He laughs, knowing we are joking. With his leg still healing, he has to take it easy. He can't jog, he either has to sit on the bleachers or walk around the track.

As we were jogging, I filled Evelyn and Steph in on what happened in the locker room.

"I'm glad he's broken up with her," Steph tells me.

"Yeah, now he's all yours," Evelyn chimes in, laughing.

"Damn shoelaces," I say.

My shoelaces have come untied. I tell Steph and Evelyn that I will catch up. I step to the side. I quickly tie them and try to catch up to them. They are about a half a track length ahead.

"Now what?" I say to myself. Michelle is jogging next to me.

"What do you want Michelle?"

"I want my boyfriend back."

"I don't think it's gonna happen."

"I know you had something to do with this."

"Nope, it was all you."

"This isn't over."

As she says this, I notice Derek has come up on the other side of me. I turn and see that Garrett is right behind me. I jog faster, but they keep up the pace. Garrett pushes me. As I'm stumbling, Derek sticks out his foot. I fall right to the ground. I can hear them laughing. Derek kicks me. I put up my arms to block the kicks.

"Where the hell is Ms. Annasandy?" I think to myself.

I'm about to yell, but then I look up and see Randy barreling up. He plows right into Derek, knocking him over. Then he shoves Michelle and Garrett away from me.

"Knock it off!" he tells them.

"What the fuck?! You're protecting the fag boy now?! That's twice today," Garrett yells.

Derek has gotten back up. Randy helps me up and then he defends me.

"His name is Josh, not fag boy, queer, homo, flamer, faggot or any other stupid name you want to come up with…and he's a friend of mine, so if I tell you to leave him alone, you leave him alone!"

"I don't believe this. What the hell's gotten into you?" Derek yells.

Ms. Annasandy finally comes running up, blowing her whistle.

"You, go to the nurse (pointing to me)...The rest of you, inside," she says.

The whole rest of the class were either standing nearby or already heading in. Steph and Evelyn were there to make sure I was alright. We all started to head in. I turned back and saw Derek and Randy still standing there.

"I'll see you in a little bit," I said to Steph and Evelyn. I made my way around the back of the bleachers and snuck up and listened in on Randy and Derek's conversation. They were arguing.

"What's up with you? You've changed dude. You've been acting weird all year. Now you go and break up with Michelle and what the hell was this all about. I thought we were friends," Derek says .

"I am your friend. We've been friends since 3rd grade, remember. I haven't changed, you have. Ever since I started dating Michelle, you've become just like her. You never used to push people around or treat them like shit, like they were beneath you. So why don't you take a step back and look at yourself, because I'm still the same person I've always been, now a little smarter, but you're not."

Randy walked away from Derek and headed in. Derek just stood there. I left and headed to the nurse, smiling at how Randy stood up for me.

"How's the leg?" Steph says to me as I enter French class.

"It's just a scrape. I'll be fine," I tell her.

"I think somebody really likes you," Evelyn says all sing songy.

"Behave," I tell her as Randy enters.

"Here's your prince now," Evelyn says.

He takes his seat. I ask him if he's doing OK. He nods his head yes, but I can tell that he's visibly depressed. The breakup with Michelle he was able to handle. His love for her is gone. Derek is his best friend. He doesn't want to lose that friendship.

TUESDAY JUNE 4, 1985

Randy wasn't at school today. I guess he needed some time off. I tried calling him, but he wasn't there or just didn't want to answer. I've been trying for a while now. I'm worried. I think I should take a drive over there.

As a precaution, I parked my car a few houses away from Randy's. I didn't see Derek's, Garrett's, or the Bitch's car anywhere. Randy's jeep was in the driveway.

"Come on in Josh. Randy's in the garage," Mrs. Sawyer says, inviting me in.

"Josh, do you happen to know what's going on?" she continued.

I told her that he got into a fight with Derek yesterday.

"There has to be something else. They've fought lots of times before, but he's never acted like this. They've always quickly made up. What was the fight about?"

"I think it was about me," I told her. I didn't want to go into details. Randy then came out of the garage.

"We need to talk," I said.

"I'm not in the mood to talk. Just go."

"I'm staying," I told him.

"Fine, you stay. I'm leaving," he said, storming out the front door.

I was about to leave, when Mrs. Sawyer asked me to stay. We went into the kitchen and sat down. She started asking me questions.

"Are you and Randy...together?" she said the last word so hesitantly as if she didn't know what word to put there.

I didn't say anything. What could I say? This was his mom. My silence was enough. I'm guessing she had an idea. Now she knows.

"A mother always knows," I heard my uncle's voice say in my head.

"Was that what the fight was about?" she asked.

This time I said "No". I told her about the fight. We talked for about an hour about Randy, me, Steph, Michelle and Derek. Then Randy came back. He came into the kitchen, grabbed some food, sat down and asked me what I was still doing there.

"We've just been talking," Mrs. Sawyer says, putting her hand over his hand.

Randy looked at his mom and then he turned to me and lost it.

"What did you say to her?! You bastard!! I'll kill you!!" he said angrily. He was pissed. I started to get up. He grabbed me and slammed me into the refrigerator.

"Randy!!!" Mrs. Sawyer screamed, trying to pull him off me.

"I only talked about it because I love you and..." I said crying. I shoved him off me and ran out the door. I ran all the way to my car. He was running after me. I wish I had parked closer. I got in and he came up, knocking on the window. I started the car, ignoring him.

"I'm sorry," he was saying, but I started to pull out. He moved to the front of the car, trying to block me from leaving. I moved the car a little forward and he jumped on the hood.

"You leave, you're taking me with you," he said.

I reparked the car and got out. It was now my turn to yell.

"I'm sick of all your outbursts and poor treatment of me. It's bad enough that everything is secret, but I'm tired of it."

"I'm sorry."

"Sorry's not good enough"

We get back to his house and enter the garage. I'm still yelling at him. The second we get inside, what does he do? He kisses me. I'm yelling and he kisses me. I kissed him back.

"Uhm, uhm," came this voice behind us.

We were so caught up in each other, we didn't notice his mom standing a few feet from us, watching. She turned and headed into the kitchen.

We followed her inside. She just started cleaning. Randy tried to say something, but she didn't respond. He was upset. He ran into his room. I followed. He was on his bed crying. He never wanted to upset his mom.

"I don't know what to do. What am I going to do?" he asked me.

I knew what to do. I grabbed his phone. Fifteen minutes later, she was at the door.

"Eileen is watching Taylor and Alexa until you get there. Go watch them while we talk," Mom said.

Mom to the rescue.

We left and let Mom handle it...and she did. An hour later she was back home. We headed back to Randy's house. When we got there, Mrs. Sawyer came up and hugged Randy, telling him how much she loves him. Then she hugged me. Her and mom are going out to dinner tomorrow night to talk some more.

WEDNESDAY JUNE 5, 1985

Randy came back to school today. The jocks and cheerleaders have been avoiding him. After the events of the other day, many don't want to talk to him. Except one...

Randy and I were heading towards the auditorium when Debbie approached, asking to join us. So instead of going to our secret spot, we headed out to the bleachers.

At first I thought she was there to spy or to try and get Randy back, but no, she genuinely wanted to talk. Randy seemed glad that she was there.

She still has feelings for him, I can tell. But like Evelyn said, it seems more like as a friend than anything sexual or romantic.

"I really missed talking to you," she said to him. She hasn't been able to hang out or talk with him since he started dating Michelle, but with no more Michelle, she wants to be friends again.

The prom issue of the paper came out today. The picture Tommy took of the group of us was on the front page, as was one of Evelyn and Randy. There were many other pictures that Tommy took in this issue. He was so excited to see them in print. He knew that some would be in this issue. What he didn't know was that he was chosen "Student of the Week". I was asked to write a small article on him and his love of photography.

Megan wanted to be the one to write the big prom story. It took up three pages (along with all the photos). She was able to capture all the fun and excitement of the evening.

THURSDAY JUNE 6, 1985

I was walking into school with Randy today when Michelle decided to make a nasty comment.

"Faggot"

She was with a bunch of cheerleaders. I didn't care. I turned back around to say something, but Randy pulled me away, telling me to just leave her alone.

FRIDAY JUNE 7, 1985

Switched shifts with Tommy today. I'm working tonight and he's working my day shift tomorrow.

Tomorrow is the Madonna concert. The instant I heard there was going to be a concert, I handed mom my "Two Tickets to Concert of His Choice" card from Christmas and said "This is what I want."

The day they went on sale she was lucky enough to get two tickets. The concert sold out so fast. They're not the best seats, but I don't care.

"It's Madonna!!!!"

I was just going to head to the concert right after work. It's in Manhattan and only a 45 minute train ride away. I'm taking Steph.

She felt it best that we don't rush, so I switched shifts so that Steph and I can spend the whole day in the City. Uncle Matt was jealous when we got the tickets. He missed out, but he got to see her in Philly and he said the show is awesome.

SATURDAY JUNE 8, 1985

MADONNA!!!!!!

Got dressed this morning for the concert. Steph and I were both going to be wearing the shirts we got each other for Christmas. I threw on a vest and attached all the Madonna buttons I had.

The seats we got weren't really that bad. They weren't close, but still not so far away that she was a tiny dot. She sang all the hits "Borderline", "Like a Virgin", "Material Girl" etc. etc. There were so many girls dressed like her. They were singing along with Madonna, as was almost everybody else, including Steph and myself. It was such an awesome concert.

SUNDAY JUNE 9, 1985

Back to work. I worked all day with Tommy. He wanted to know all about the concert.

"Did she sing "Holiday?" he asked. It's his favorite Madonna song.

"Yes"

"Was there a lot of dancing?"

"Yes"

"Did she sing in a wedding dress?"

"Yes, for Like a Virgin."

He was so jealous. He said that the next time she comes around he wants to go with me to see her.

MONDAY JUNE 10, 1985

Today, the final newspaper of the school year came out. It was a very small issue, seeing as the last one came out Wednesday. It was mostly a goodbye/thank you for everything issue. All the senior writers were asked to write a goodbye/thank you article. I wrote a small one, thanking Megan, Stuart and the rest of the newspaper staff for including me on the staff.

TUESDAY JUNE 11, 1985

Everything is showing signs of winding down. Graduation is in 9 days. Today was the last day of regular classes. Everybody cheered in Gym class as Ms. Annasandy blew her whistle, signaling no more jogging. Finals start tomorrow.

Today was also yearbook day. Megan, Stuart and I were excused from our 5th period class, (no Spanish with the terrible 3, thank god) to help Mrs. Brandon pass out the yearbooks. Everybody came down during their lunch period to pick them up. The yearbook came out better than expected.

Being the main photographer, it was my job to help choose what photos got in. I wanted to make sure that every senior was featured in at least one candid shot. A true challenge, but I had my list of seniors and with Evelyn's help, I got everybody. No students were singled out with multitudes of candid shots. If they were in groups or clubs or on a sports team, then of course there would be more.

The other thing I did was make sure the photos were mostly seniors. No multiple pictures of underclassmen, some for memory, but this yearbook was for the seniors. My feeling was, let the underclassmen have their pictures when they become seniors.

It was the perfect collage of the many different types of seniors. For safety, we ordered extra copies. Good thing we did, many students who weren't going to buy it, saw that the populars weren't singled out and there were actually many pictures of them and their friends in there, too.

This, of course, didn't go over well with Michelle and her clique. They should be lucky, my first impulse was to put unflattering pictures of them in there to teach them a lesson, but then I thought it wouldn't be right and I put in some really flattering pictures of them. Everybody else loved it. That's all that matters to me.

During 5a lunch, Steph and Evelyn came in. The instant I handed them their yearbooks, they started signing them. As the period wore down and everyone had their yearbook, they came back and we signed each other's.

5c lunch was when most of the jocks and cheerleaders came in. Michelle, Garrett and Derek came and grabbed theirs. Debbie came in a little later. She actually asked me to sign hers, so I had her sign mine. I wrote...

"You're not bad for a cheerleader and even though you were partially responsible in my being outed, I'm thankful for it now. Thank you for your unintentional help. Here's hoping we'll become friends at Garden State."

Yes, Debbie's going there too.

Randy came in at almost the very end of the period. I went to go sign his yearbook, when he asked me not to.

"Not yet. Let me get everybody else to sign it first. I want you to be able to write what's in your heart. I'll save a space for you."

I understood and asked him to wait to sign mine.

We're going to be getting together every day this week to study for finals. So tonight, we decided to all meet at the mall and get some fun in before all this studying. Pizza place first. It was me, Steph, Evelyn, Randy, Megan, Stuart, Tommy and Michael. Then it was time for a little air hockey, where we were joined by Taylor, Adam and believe it or not, Mom.

"Play your mother," Mom said.

Everybody thought it was funny, her trying to beat me in air hockey...OK she beat me, so what, who do you think taught me to play? We all had fun playing for a little bit and then we headed to my house to study. Mom started to cook for everybody, so nobody had to go home and eat. We all congregated around the dining room table and studied, helping each other out.

WEDNESDAY JUNE 12, 1985

Today was the first two finals. English and Science. The last time working with Derek. At least he studied.

Tonight was study time at Steph's house. Mrs. Perrino's chance to cook for everybody.

THURSDAY JUNE 13, 1985

I was originally supposed to have the day off because it was finals for periods 3 and 4 today. Those being Gym and my free period. Well Angelino and Superintendent Marshall decided that we should use finals time as a way to improve the school's Presidential Physical Fitness scores.

Tonight was study time at Evelyn's house. Mrs. Ramirez was so excited. She loves to cook, so it was a giant buffet of Puerto Rican dishes.

FRIDAY JUNE 14, 1985

Spanish and History finals today. Spanish was a piece of cake. I finished it in 25 minutes and headed out, thanking Mrs. Tavares. Michelle made a comment under her breath making fun of me. I just softly whispered...

"Bye Bitch," to her, smiling as I left.

History was a little tougher, but yesterday Evelyn and I were quizzing each other. We both had it under control. What a tiring week. My brain is fried and I still have two more finals to go on Monday.

SATURDAY JUNE 15, 1985

Today was my final day at the record store. I worked a double. Mr. Totino told me to bring in my cassettes and play whatever I wanted. He was so upset to see me go. He'd like me to stay on for the summer, but understands my need to do the internship. More fun times coming to an end. New fun times to begin soon.

It was a great day. It seemed like everybody wanted to stop in and see me. Steph was first. She stopped in to say hello on her way to work. Tommy came in with Michael, arcade time for them. Taylor came in with Adam.

"How did you get here?" I asked him.

"Mom," he said.

I asked him "What's up?" knowing full well what he wanted. I handed him a five and told him to get lost. Mom stopped in to see her son on his last day of work. Total embarrassment. Stuart and Megan came in looking for some classical relaxation tapes. Derek came in and bought a couple of cassettes, not saying anything.

Finally, Randy came in just as we were about to close. He was with Taylor and Adam. It seems they were all playing arcade games together. Now he wants to come over and play video games. He had already talked to my mom and was bringing Taylor home. I told them I would see them there when I got out.

I got home and of course they're there in front of the TV. Mom too. Adam had to be dropped off at home. His bedtime is 10. So is Taylor's, but mom let him stay up a little longer. We played for a while. Randy's staying over. He's sitting on the floor of my room going thru my cassettes, critiquing each one, playing some. I just smile. What an interesting, semi sort of boyfriend I think I have.

SUNDAY JUNE 16, 1985

Another arcade/mall day to blow off some steam before we all went over Randy's to study. Mrs. Sawyer's chance to cook for everybody. This study time was totally focused on French. Good thing I already studied for the math final.

MONDAY JUNE 17, 1985

Finals are over. All that's left is graduation. Finished the French final quickly. I had to wait for the Math final and didn't want to sit around, so I headed out to the bleachers. I walked around a little and then sat down. I was joined by Ms. Annasandy. I didn't see her come up.

She commended me on sticking it out and not taking all the crap. Now I pretty much knew she was a lesbian, but I also knew she couldn't just come out and say it. Today she felt she could. I was trustworthy and it was the end of the school year.

She told me what she went through in high school and college. Telling me how she met her girlfriend in college and that they've been together for 15 years now. I thanked her for all her help and advice this year. We talked for a few minutes and then it was time for the Math final.

TUESDAY JUNE 18, 1985

Today was celebration day. Everybody came out for the day. Evelyn, Steph, Randy, Megan, Stuart, Tommy and Michael. It was arcade time and then bowling and then out to the movies. We went to see "View to a Kill", the new James Bond film. Grace Jones is so cool.

WEDNESDAY JUNE 19, 1985

Today was only a report to Homeroom day. We were given our report cards (All A's this time), our caps and gowns and our tickets for graduation. The weather seemed unpredictable, so they didn't know whether the ceremony would be inside or outside.

The weather seemed to be agreeing with us, so we each got six tickets to hand out to family and friends. I didn't need that many, so I gave Evelyn two of mine. She has a big family. I only needed three, one for Mom, one for Taylor and one for Alexa. I kept the other one just in case Mom had someone else she wanted to invite.

We also had rehearsal for tomorrow. They showed us where we were going to sit. We had to march out and pretend it was graduation day.

THURSDAY JUNE 20, 1985

GRADUATION DAY

"What about breakfast?" Mom yelled as I started heading out the door. I showed her the pack of pop tarts in my hand. I had too many things to do before graduation tonight.

The other day, I went to the store and bought a whole bunch of decorations. It was time to turn the Mustang red and gold for the day. Also carefully taping "Class of 85" peel off emblems everywhere. Steph came over and helped me just as I was finishing up. I had some decorations left over, so we touched up her car a little.

"They look great," I heard over my shoulder.

"Uncle Matt!" I said, hugging my uncle.

He came down to see my graduation. Luckily I saved that extra ticket.

We all headed inside.

"Oh yeah, I also wanted to get a look at this quarterback boyfriend of yours," he said. I ran upstairs to get the photos from prom while he said hello to Mom and the siblings.

"Damn, he's gorgeous. You lucky little bastard," he said laughing, as I showed him the photos from prom. I'm so glad my uncle is here.

Graduation starts at 6, but we were told to report to homeroom at 5. We all got in the car at 4:15. I wanted to drive around a little, showing off the car before heading to school. Mom is going to drive the car home. We rented a limo to take us down the shore.

We got to school at about a quarter to five. Steph drove in with her mom at the same time we did. Mom and Mrs. Perrino started gabbing, so Steph and I headed in. We got to my homeroom, said our goodbyes and she was off.

Evelyn was already there when I entered. She arrived earlier to help set up a small DJ stand outside. They're going to have music playing for everyone as they come in. Originally, they wanted to have the band perform, but too many were seniors and it would complicate things come diploma time. Marcia was manning the booth. Evelyn and I took this time to put on our caps and gowns.

"Oh my God, I can't believe graduation is already here," Evelyn said to me.

"I know…You look great," I told her.

"Thanks. So do you."

I gave her a big hug. As we were hugging, Randy came in. He still seemed a little depressed about the "Derek incident". They still haven't talked since that day in gym. Randy was still going down the shore with them though. The jocks and cheerleaders rented two houses down the shore, next to each other in the same town we're going to. Their houses are on the complete opposite side of town, thank God.

"So did you talk to Derek?" I asked him.

"No. Garrett came up and asked me if I was still going. When I said yes, he acted disgusted."

Evelyn and I did our best to try and cheer him up.

At 6 we were asked to line up and march single file outside, just like rehearsal. The field was a little more decorated than it was yesterday. Because our graduating class was small, they were using the smaller field. There was a giant platform in the front with a giant banner "Congratulations Class of 85". A few chairs were on the platform. Angelino was seated there with a few department heads. A podium was set up in the middle and there were steps on both sides. On the field, there were rows of chairs, divided into two sections with a giant red and gold carpet running down the middle.

"Pomp and Circumstance" was playing as we marched to our homeroom's assigned section outside. Our homeroom was one of the last to arrive, so we were towards the back. I looked over and saw all the families on the bleachers. A few made their way off the bleachers to get a closer look. Mom and the others were sitting on the bleachers. I found her. I can spot my mom's cowboy hat from a mile away. I watched Angelino move to the podium. We stood and waited for the last homeroom to fall into place.

"Hello Whitfield High School graduating class of 1985!!" he said to applause and loud cheers. "I would like to thank everyone for coming. Let's start the evening off with the Pledge of Allegiance," he continued.

We all spoke the pledge and then Angelino cued Marcia to play the school song. Many students started singing. I had no idea what the words were, so I pretended to sing along. When the song was over, we were finally able to sit down.

Angelino then proceeded to make a speech. Probably the same speech he gives the students every year, with maybe one or two differences, but overall the same speech about growing up and going out into the world and to remember your time here at Whitfield High.

Then it was time for speeches from the freshman, sophomore and junior class presidents. Many of us weren't listening. I just talked to Evelyn the whole time. We were seated in alphabetical order. Thank God there wasn't anybody alphabetically between us. When the junior class president was finished we stopped, because we wanted to hear who was up next.

"Normally we would have the senior class president speak, followed by the class valedictorian. Well this year they happen to be one and the same. Ladies and gentlemen, your Whitfield High School senior class president and 1985 class valedictorian, Miss Megan Lewis," Angelino announced.

Evelyn and I were watching. Megan had spent all week on this speech.

"Thank you Principal Angelino...fellow students of Whitfield High..."

She stopped and turned. Mr. Stanton was walking quietly onto the platform. He took his seat and she started again.

"Fellow students of Whitfield High, the future is staring us..."

She stopped again. I'm guessing Stanton said something, because she turned in his direction and gave him an ugly look. Now she's just standing there. What is she doing? She crumpled up her speech.

"You know what, I had this speech written, but standing up here looking out at everybody, I want to take a few moments to say some other things instead. When we entered Whitfield High in September of 1981, we were all required to go to an assembly acquainting us with the school. The main thing we were told was to be proud of Whitfield High and all it has to offer. During my first three years here, I would look at everything happening around me, but back then I mostly looked at the good, steering clear of the bad. This year though, I've gotten to see some of the bad up close. You see, I've had the privilege this year of becoming friends with a very sweet guy...and I've seen the disgusting treatment he's received at the hands of some of you, both students and teachers alike. The taunts, teases, name calling and physical abuse he's had to endure and all that proudness I had for this school disappeared. I couldn't see anything proud about that kind of behavior."

"But then I stopped and looked again and I saw the goodness of others here, once again students and teachers alike. Those who remained his friend, stuck by him, supported and defended him. That helped reassure my faith that there is something to be proud of here and that I shouldn't let a few ignorant people tarnish my respect for this fine school. Through all of this, he's survived and his courage to fight back is inspiring to me. I hope he has made others see how special and just like you and I he really is. I'm glad I've gotten to meet him and I'm glad to call him my friend. Thank you Joshua for making my senior year a very special and enlightening one."

Then she blew me a kiss and left the podium. Evelyn and I were the first to stand up and start applauding. Many others followed. Then Angelino approached the podium, thanking Megan for her speech and announcing that the handing out of diplomas was next. I watched as everyone in the bleachers stood. Seeing as our homeroom was in the back, we were going to be one of the last ones getting our diplomas. My heart started racing as they got to our homeroom. I held Evelyn's hand as the letters of the alphabet got closer.

"Maria Maples...Antony Natura...Patrick O'Brien...Joshua Parker"

Off I went. I walked up those steps, of course giving Stanton one more smile, before I grabbed the diploma and shook Angelino's hand. Then I headed back to my spot.

On the way back, I saw my uncle on the sidelines taking pictures. I stopped and waited for Evelyn so he could take a photo of both of us. We got back to our spot and waited for the last senior to get their diploma and return to their seat.

"Ladies and gentlemen, I present to you...The Whitfield High School class of 85," Angelino said, turning to Marcia who started playing "Celebrate Youth" by Rick Springfield. All hats went into the air and we all started cheering. Evelyn and I hugged each other.

We were joined by Randy, then Steph and then Megan and Stuart. Big hugs and handshakes all around. We were dancing around to the music, caught up in the moment.

As I was hugging Megan, thanking her for the wonderful speech, I saw Mom in the bleachers. She was heading off with Taylor but something didn't seem right. I didn't see Alexa. Mom was scouring the crowd. I looked around and saw Alexa. She was at the bottom of the bleachers, making her way through the crowd. Where was she going? Mom kept looking in my direction, but she wasn't signaling me. I know she saw Alexa, but why was she still looking around?

"I'll be right back," I said to everyone. I needed to see what was wrong. I took two steps and a hand touched my shoulder. I turned, expecting it to be my uncle.

"Congratulations," he said, giving me a hug. It wasn't my uncle. I was face to face with my father. I couldn't hug him back. I was just so confused. The others were watching.

"So aren't you going to introduce me to your friends?" he continued.

"What are you doing here?" I said.

"I came to see my son graduate."

Everybody now understood. I had told them all about my father this year.

"We'll catch you in a little bit," Steph said, as everyone left and headed over to their families.

"What, I'm not allowed to see you graduate?"

My anger level was rising. I didn't want him here.

"Why? You didn't come to see me any other time. You walked out. No calls. No letters. Nothing"

I looked and saw Alexa running up. She had obviously spotted dad earlier and ran away from Mom to catch up to him. Mom was right behind her with Taylor. She caught up.

"Wait with Taylor while mommy talks to daddy," mom said to Alexa.

Mom stood by, but I wasn't stopping. All my anger came roaring out. There was no stopping it.

"You chose that skanky little whore over us and now you come here and expect me to be oh so happy. Oh hi dad. Great to see ya, welcome back...well FUCK YOU!! I've gone through a very tough year and a half without you. I needed you, Mom needed you, Alexa and Taylor needed you, instead you chose yourself..."

Mom has moved a little closer. We both noticed her but I still continued.

"...you didn't even try. So just do me a favor and go back to wherever you were. Leave us alone. We're fine without you."

"Are you through? You will not talk to me like that. No matter what's happened, I'm still your father. Don't you forget that," he said, angrily.

"No you're not. I don't have a father anymore," I snapped back.

Then he slapped me. Mom came running up. I just stared at my father. He moved in closer, getting in my face.

"What, you gonna cry now? Don't think I don't know what's been going on since I left. That's a nice car you're driving. Looks kinda familiar."

"Leave him alone," mom said.

"Oh, good job you've been doing. I leave and he becomes a goddamn faggot," he said, turning and snapping at mom. Then he got back in my face.

"One big sissy queer, just like his uncle."

Uncle Matt is now just a short distance away on my other side. Mom has now come up. She tries to hug me, but I push her away. I want to finish this.

"Yeah, just like my uncle and he's more of a man than you'll ever be. You walked out of my life a year and a half ago, now allow me to walk out of yours."

I grabbed Mom's hand and looked at her, signaling that I was alright. Then I looked at my dad.

"Waste of life," I said, and then I turned and hi-fived my uncle. I needed to get out of there. I took off and headed for the bleachers by the football field.

Nick prepares to say something to Sara, but before he can, Alexa comes running up.

"Daddy!" she says.

"Hi baby. How's my little girl? You're getting so big?" he says, picking her up.

"I missed you daddy. When are you coming home?"

"I don't know sweetheart. Give me a few minutes to talk to your mommy."

He puts her down. Taylor has now approached.

"Hey sport," Nick says. Taylor won't go near him. Nick turns to Sara

"Another one turned against me? He gay too?

Sara will not get drawn into a fight. She's happy with her life now without him. She picks up Alexa.

"Say goodbye sweetie. Daddy's gotta go now."

"Why?"

"Say goodbye."

"Bye daddy."

"Bye sweetheart."

Sara puts her down. She goes and joins Taylor. Nick turns to say something to Sara. She cuts him off entirely.

"Goodbye Nick."

Nick leaves, first stopping at the Mustang. He looks at it, taking out his keys, the only thing he has left as a memento of the car. He opens the door and sits down. He intends to drive away. He puts the key in the ignition, but just before he can start the car, the sun comes out from behind a cloud, sending bright sunlight into the car. He pulls down the visor. When he does, he sees the three pictures Josh has there. One of Josh at a young age in the car, one of Josh in the car with his dad and a family photo.

He realizes he can't take the car. He can't do this to Josh. He gets out, takes one last look at the car and walks away.}

I got to the bleachers and took my favorite spot, all the way on the top and in the corner. I stared out at the track and field, remembering all the things that happened around this tiny area of the school. Good and bad.

"You OK?" Steph said, breaking me out of my trance.

"Yeah, just sitting here thinking," I said, smiling.

"The limo will be here soon. You about ready to go?"

I nodded my head yes and we slowly made our way down the bleachers, taking off our caps and gowns as we did. When we got to the track, I stopped and did an impersonation of Ms. Annasandy

"Four laps...That's one mile folks...let's get going...Hey, hey no stopping"

Steph started laughing.

"I don't know if I've said it enough, but I really want to thank you for everything. I couldn't have made it through all of this without you. I'm glad you were there for me, "I told her.

"Aww, c'mon. You're getting me all misty," she said.

As we were standing there, I turned and looked at the track and then I turned back to Steph, a big smile on my face.

"What?" she asked, curious as to my smile.

"One more lap?" I said, putting my cap and gown on the fence.

"Are you nuts?"

I then started singing

"Don't put me off, cuz I'm on fire…"

"I'm doing this barefoot you know," she said, taking off her shoes. I just kept singing.

"And I can't quench my desire. Don't you know that, I'm burning up for your love…"

We started jogging around the track. She joined me in singing the song as I jogged and danced around her. We finished the lap (and the song) and were completely out of breath.

"No more…Medic!" Steph said, laughing. Then we were both laughing. Then we heard applause. We looked up and saw Evelyn, Megan and Stuart. They had watched us jog around.

Evelyn turned and saw the limo arrived. They ran for the limo while Steph and I grabbed our stuff. As we were heading off the track, I passed by Angelino. He had seen us jog, too. He shook my hand and thanked me for my courage this year and wished me the best. I then thanked him for his support.

Steph had already gone ahead, so I left Angelino and headed towards the limo. Almost everybody from the graduation ceremony was gone. I waved goodbye to Uncle Matt, who was taking the munchkins to the car. Then I had one last stop, Mom.

She was standing, waiting for me. She was bag watcher for everybody. I didn't want her to say anything about dad, so I went right up and hugged her.

"I love you, Mom."

She started tearing up

"My little boy, all grown up. You go and join your friends. Have a good time."

Another hug and kiss and I headed to the limo.

As I approached, two more limos pulled into the lot. These were the ones taking the jocks and cheerleaders. They were all congregated to the side, except Randy and Debbie, who were standing a little ways away from the others, talking. They saw me and I saluted him goodbye and waved to Debbie. He saluted me back and Debbie blew me a kiss. Randy looked so sad.

I threw my bag into the trunk of the limo, slammed it down and got in.

"OK Marco, everybody's here. We can go," Evelyn said to the driver.

We started going, then...

"Wait!" a voice came from outside.

Marco stopped. Someone knocked on the door. Seeing as I was closest, I opened it. It was Randy.

"Hi...you got room for one more?" he asked.

"I thought you were going with them?" I asked him.

"Nah, I think I'd be happier here."

I scanned the group for approval. They all of course signaled yes. Randy threw his bag at me and got in. Then as we're all sitting there in silence, Randy turns, looks at me and goes...

"Oh screw it."

Right out of the blue, he kisses me. In front of everybody in the limo. I gladly kissed him back. Everyone was in shock. Evelyn and Steph knew about the relationship, but never saw us kiss. Megan and Stuart's mouths were wide open. Not only the shock of the kiss but the fact that Randy is gay. Then they were a little pissed that they weren't told.

"Details!" Megan screamed.

"I'll tell you later," I said laughing.

Evelyn told Marco we could head out. Another knock on the door. Once again the limo stopped. Randy opened the door. It was Derek.

"Hey," he said to the group. Then he turned to Randy.

"So you're not going with us?"

Randy shook his head no. Derek was upset at this. You could see it in his face.

"Well if you're not going with them, then I don't want to go with them," Derek said.

I watched as he looked around, as if to ask if he could come with us. Nobody knew what to think about this one. After a few seconds of silence, Evelyn spoke up for the group.

"It's alright with us, if it's alright with you guys."

I didn't know what to think. All these thoughts were running thru my head. The fights, the insults, all the bullshit is Science class. I didn't want him to come with us. Then Randy looked at me. I saw in his face that he wanted Derek there, so I threw the ball into his court.

"It's up to you," I said.

Then Randy did something I didn't expect, as if the kiss wasn't surprising enough. He turns to Derek.

"You can come, but you have to know something first."

And not even skipping a beat, Derek says...

"You're gay."

Not in a negative or questioning way, but straight forward as if he was answering a simple question.

"You know?" Randy said, surprised.

"I didn't totally know, but I had a feeling."

"And?"

"We've been friends for a long time, been through a lot together. And what you said to me on the track that day was true. I never used to be like that and if you're gay, I just have to accept it. I don't like it. I don't know if I'll ever get used to it, but I'll try. Friends are friends and I don't want to lose you as a friend."

They both hugged.

"You don't think of me that way, do you?" Derek continued.

"No, you're too ugly," Randy said, punching him. Derek punches him back as everyone in the limo laughed, even Marco.

"OK Marco, let's try this again," Evelyn said.

This time we were finally able to head out. We drove out of the lot and turned right, passing the front of the school. I turned, looking out the back window, getting my last glimpse as a student of Whitfield High.

It's been one giant roller coaster of a ride, but I wouldn't change it for the world. Well, maybe one or two little things, but I have some great friends, a guy who loves me and a life I never thought I would ever have. Here's hoping this summer is a great one and that college brings many new and exciting adventures.

What a year

Acknowledgments

- Everyone who has been with me along this long and fun journey to see this book in print. You all know who you are and I love each and every one of you for your support, feedback and input.

- The state of New Jersey for inspiration. I may not live there right now, but it will always be my home.

- All those wonderful coffee shops where I would spend hours just sitting there reading, writing and thinking.

- And of course, my Mom, Beverly English for always being a wonderful and caring mother. I love you Mom.

Made in the USA
Middletown, DE
29 August 2018